## Date Due

M                                                                    R

| JUN 0 1 2016 | | |
| AUG 0 3 2016 | | |
| MAR 3 1 2017 | | |
| | | |
| | | |
| | | |
| | | |
| | | |
| | | |
| | | |
| | | |
| | | |
| | | |

## ALSO BY MICHAEL PRESCOTT

*Kane*
*Shadow Dance*
*Shiver*
*Shudder*
*Shatter*
*Deadly Pursuit*
*Blind Pursuit*
*Mortal Pursuit*
*Comes the Dark*
*Stealing Faces*
*The Shadow Hunter*
*Last Breath*
*Next Victim*
*In Dark Places*
*Dangerous Games*
*Mortal Faults*
*Final Sins*
*Riptide*
*Grave of Angels*
*Cold Around the Heart*
*Steel Trap and Other Stories*
*Chasing Omega*
*Blood in the Water*

# MANSTOPPER

## MICHAEL PRESCOTT

*Manstopper*, by Michael Prescott
Revised edition copyright © 2012 by Douglas Borton
Originally published as *Manstopper*, by Douglas Borton (Onyx Books, 1988)

ISBN-13: 978-1502966186
ISBN-10: 1502966182

*For my parents*

ATTACK DOG.

An animal trained from birth to kill. Its every aggressive instinct systematically rewarded. Its every gentler impulse punished. So that gradually, by imperceptible degrees, a tail-wagging puppy is remade into a snarling beast of prey.

Though it may resemble a German shepherd or Rottweiler or Doberman, it is not a dog except in form. It is a killing machine, conditioned to lash out at any human being on sight, to leap into action without hesitation, and to slash and tear and go on slashing until its victim is dead.

It cannot be reasoned with or bribed or befriended or outwitted or evaded. Only its handler can control it, and even then its obedience is never assured. It must be segregated from people, kept in isolation, until deployed to patrol a secure facility requiring maximum protection against intruders—military base, research lab, storage depot—any place with barbed-wire perimeter fencing and concrete-block walls and motion-activated floodlights and signs warning: DANGER—KEEP OUT.

It is the simplest imaginable security system and the most perfect, more reliable and tamper-proof than any network of surveillance cameras, alarms, and electrified fences.

It does not come cheap. A single attack dog may be valued at more than two thousand dollars. And it does not come without risks. It comes armed and dangerous—armed with fangs, claws, cobra quickness, and a purpose. A purpose summed up in one word, the word chosen by its creators to describe their handiwork:

*Manstopper.*

# PROLOGUE

RAZOR RESTED his head between his paws, hugging the cold wooden floor of his cage.

A low sound—part whimper, part growl—rose in his throat. He could not tell what made him nervous tonight—whether it was the cold, or the restless stirring of his three companions, or the darkness, or the truck's irregular bouncing on ruts in the road. He was leaving home, he was sure of that, and in some dim way he knew that he would not ever go back; but that thought did not disturb him. Home was only the whistle that hurt his ears, and the leather-gloved hand that smacked his snout, and the dry cotton taste of foam padding as his fangs dug into one of the Bad Men and ripped the hated enemy apart.

These memories, vague and disorderly as a dream, only increased his anxiousness. He jerked his head up, laid his ears back, and flared his nostrils, using all his senses to probe the darkness of the rear of the truck.

In the cage next to his, Cleopatra scratched herself in her sleep, digging with her hind paw at her neck. She was having bad dreams again. She let out a yip of distress and scratched harder, till her chain-link collar jangled noisily, like the dinner bell. Cleo was always nervous and on edge, dozing restlessly throughout the day and night. Razor could not have fathomed what phantoms haunted her sleep. None had ever haunted his own.

From the roof of Razor's cage came a low, steady, maddening *thump thump thump*. That was Bigfoot. The odor of his drool, warm and foul, crowded Razor's cage. It was an odor that always accompanied Bigfoot, like his cloud of fleas, impervious to any flea bath. Razor disliked Bigfoot. He sensed somehow that Bigfoot was different from him and Cleo and Mr. Dobbs. Their bodies were black and sleek and rich with taut, quivering, corded muscle. Bigfoot was slow and clumsy and stupid. He was always slobbering, his tongue lolling, his brown head cocked, his eyes dull and witless. And he would not lie still. He paced restlessly in his cage stacked on top of Razor's, *thump thump thump.*

In the cage on the other side of Razor's own, Mr. Dobbs awoke from a soundless sleep, got up, and flung himself to the opposite corner. He opened his mouth wide and yawned with a whining sound, then lowered his head and was instantly asleep once more. It was a pattern that Razor had seen repeated through the night, as Mr. Dobbs drifted uneasily from sleep to wakefulness and back to sleep again.

Something was wrong. Something had all four of them spooked.

Certainly Razor could feel it, had felt it ever since they had been locked in the cages and loaded onto the truck by the Bad Men. And then the endless rocking motion, the rush of air speeding past, the bewildering variety of smells penetrating the rear of the truck ...

Razor made another low sound, all growl this time. He curled his lips. His yellow fangs glinted.

Above, Bigfoot stopped his pacing and growled in sympathy. Razor smelled the dog's hot breath and the sweat-matted stink of his fur. Mr. Dobbs rolled to his feet and pressed his muzzle to the eight-gauge steel-wire mesh. Cleo, roused from sleep, lay tensed and motionless in her cage, her muscles rigid under her jet-black coat.

Razor sensed their tension. It reinforced and justified his own. He volleyed a staccato series of barks, like the rat-tat-tat of a machine gun, and the others joined him, pawing at their cages, balancing on hind legs, baring their fangs at unseen enemies.

- — -

Mike Tuttle didn't mind his job too much, most of the time, but tonight was different. Tonight gave him the creeps.

He turned the radio up louder. It was the only decent station he had found in this godforsaken stretch of Jersey Turnpike, the only station that didn't seem addicted to the local boy, Springsteen, whose latest album, *Tunnel of Love*, released just weeks ago, was riding high on the charts. He leaned back and let Rachmaninoff's Second Piano Concerto waft over him like a summer breeze.

No use. Even at top volume, or as near to it as he could go without disintegrating the rich chords into blasts of ghetto static, the music could not drown out the cacophony from the rear of the truck.

Mike snapped the radio off in disgust and banged a fist against the wooden partition at his back.

"Hold it down in there, for Christ's sake! Shut up!"

Ten minutes and fifteen miles of empty highway later, the awful barking and howling finally subsided. The howling was the worst of it, Mike thought. It made a man's hair stand on end. What were they howling about, anyway? He was glad they were in cages. He was glad he was only an hour outside Manhattan, an hour and fifteen, tops, if he hit traffic on the bridge. He was glad this lousy job was nearly over.

His big mistake was that he had looked at them. Curiosity, he supposed, but curiosity of the masochistic kind. Mike Tuttle didn't like dogs. He had never owned a dog and never wanted to. And he shouldn't have looked at these dogs tonight. But he had.

Oh, he had let Masterson's guys load the cages onto the automatic lift, one at a time, then shove the cages to the rear of the truck, stack them, and rope them down. But just before they slid down the GMC Van-dura's rear door, cranked the handle clockwise to lock it, and secured the lift vertically against the rear door with the safety chain, Mike had decided that one little look couldn't hurt. He stuck his head in, peering inside.

And there they were. Four sets of red eyes, unblinking in the darkness. Four low, menacing growls that seemed to emanate from the floor and walls and ceiling, from everywhere at once. The stink of canine sweat, musky and oppressive as the smell of death.

"They always growl like that?"

"Attack dogs, Mr. Tuttle. We don't sell 'em for companionship."

*Shit,* Mike said to himself in the cab of the truck, *if I had my way, I'd sell them for medical experiments.*

A sudden sharp bark made him jump. Could the damn things read his mind?

He noticed the windshield fogging up and thumbed the button on the dash to send warm air jetting out of the front vents. Outside it must have been forty degrees, but the cab was comfortable. The Van-dura's rear wasn't heated and the dogs would be cold. Good. He hoped they froze their fucking tails off.

This was what you got for working freelance. No, man, this was what you got for not earning your degree. Well, if he could save up enough money he would go back and get his nine credits and his BA. He chuckled. At thirty-six, he'd be a college grad. But what the hell. That wasn't too old to start over. Was it?

His headlights filled in the outline of a figure on the side of the road. Mike sped past, catching a glimpse of scruffy uncombed hair, baggy jeans and backpack, and a frail, shivering body with arms folded, hugging the chest, and one thumb jutting out in pathetic hopefulness. *Hitchhiking's illegal in this state, kid,* he thought. But tonight ...

Maybe it was the thought that it was cold out tonight, colder than usual for October, or maybe it was the image that flashed in his mind, more vivid than the headlight-smeared pavement streaked with white parallel lines, the image of those four sets of red eyes at the back of the truck, suspended in the dark like fireflies on black velvet, staring ...

He hit the brake and pulled onto the shoulder. The dogs barked again, briefly. He waited.

The hitchhiker approached. Mike could hear the faint crunching of his boots on gravel. Closer ... closer ...

For one disoriented moment Mike had the impulse to gun the engine, shift into gear, and go.

*Mom told me never to do this.*

Then he remembered the dogs and the way they howled.

He waited.

The hitchhiker's face filled the mirror on the passenger side. The door swung open. The kid stood there silently.

"Where you going?" Mike asked.

"City."

"Come on in!" said Mike, trying to sound big and gruff and friendly, the way truck drivers were supposed to sound.

The kid climbed into his seat. Mike saw a pale triangular face, with cheeks red from the night wind, and a blondish fuzz of beard. His blond hair was long and stringy. His eyes looked empty.

Mike waited for a Z-28 to shoot past, then pulled back onto the road.

- — -

Razor lay very still. The premonition of danger was stronger now. Maybe it had to do with the way the truck had stopped and sat, engine idling, till it shifted on its shocks under the weight of a new rider. Maybe it had to do with the silence from the front of the truck. He had detected a man's voice before, and the banging of a fist, and other sounds Razor could not identify—the sounds of music on the radio. Now there was nothing. That silence disturbed Razor. He did not growl this time. He waited.

Vaguely he knew the others waited also. Cleo had not moved in a long time except to worry at her paw. Mr. Dobbs had retreated to the rear of his cage, where he stood swaying slowly with the motion of the truck. Upstairs, Bigfoot had resumed his pacing. *Thump thump thump* reverberated through the wooden floor of Bigfoot's cage and the wooden roof of his own.

Razor's haunches were as tight as coiled springs, tensed for a leap. The fact that he was caged and could not get out did not occur to him. He had been trained to leap and bark and slash, whether his enemy was within reach or behind a fence or a brick wall. Cages and walls had no reality for him. The only reality was the throbbing sense of danger and the quiet, maniacal urge to destroy.

He knew his companions felt likewise. He waited.

- — -

His watch said 3:10. Twenty-five minutes since he had picked up Mr. Mouth over there. Mike Tuttle licked his lips, feeling uneasy. It wasn't normal, the way the kid just sat and stared at his own face, illuminated by the lights on the dash and reflected in the dark windshield.

Mike had made a stab at conversation, but the kid had only grunted without turning his head. Mike studied him out of the corner of his eye and saw his Adam's apple bob up and down at rare intervals with a sudden nervous swallow. What did he have to be nervous about? Too many answers suggested themselves, none good.

The kid had said he was going to the city. *Okay, I'll let him off at the city limits, just the other side of the bridge.* Mike looked up at an overhead sign flaring in the windshield: SHORE POINTS. The chrome letters, sparkling like neon in the orange vapor of the arc-sodium lights, slid up the windshield, misting over at the part of the glass beyond the reach of the wipers, and disappeared.

He knew that exit. It meant he was halfway through Jersey. Still in the nice part of the state, he thought randomly. Not yet at the oil-refinery maze around Newark, Manhattan's poor relation. No, this was the part of Jersey that still lived up to the Garden State's nickname. Farmland and pine barrens; dirt roads with signs that said CAUTION—DEER CROSSING and meant it; shiny new gas stations and old brick buildings that had housed troops during the Revolutionary War; and farther east, at the tip of the state and the continent, the summer resorts— Beach Haven and Seaside and Belmar—little towns with big boardwalks that stood empty now, their swimming-pool pavilions and amusement arcades locked away with the first frost.

"You from around here?" he asked his silent passenger with a kind of stubborn optimism.

The kid turned to look at him this time, but Mike wished he hadn't. The kid's eyes were not just empty, they were dead, like the sightless eye sockets of a skull.

Why didn't he grin, then? Skulls grinned, didn't they?

Mike shook his head imperceptibly to clear his thoughts.

"No," said the kid slowly. "I'm not from here."

Oh, hallelujah, they'd established communication. In that instant Mike felt profoundly foolish at having been afraid. The kid had been cold and tired. He wasn't in the mood to talk, that's all. Now he had warmed up a bit, sure. And the eyes ... Hell, anybody's face looked spooky when it was lit by the dash. He was just jumpy tonight. It was those dogs, those frigging dogs.

"Me neither," said Mike happily. "I'm from Springfield. Springfield, Mass. You ever been up that way?"

"What kind of stuff are you carrying?" asked the kid, in a voice that was low and almost without intonation.

"Huh? Oh ... I'm not sure you want to know."

"I've heard," said the kid slowly, so slowly, each syllable dripping like molasses from a spoon, "that sometimes you guys got to haul stuff one way, then drive back empty."

"Union guys. I'm freelance."

"Yeah?"

"Yeah, see, this job is only temporary. I'm thinking of—"

"So what are you carrying?"

Something in the way the kid said it made Mike's hands go numb, strangest thing, just go numb on the steering wheel. He felt this cold, dropping sensation in his stomach, and suddenly the truck cab and the kid and his own body seemed distant and unreal.

It was a perfectly natural question. No need to get all worked up. Except it wasn't natural to say it like that, like a threat.

"Well," said Mike, wondering why his mouth was dry and the cab was too warm, "as a matter of fact ..."

Mike had seen a magic act on the *Tonight* show last month. The camera had gotten a good tight close-up on the magician's hands. Yet even though Mike watched the twelve-inch black-and-white screen of the Sylvania portable in his kitchen from a foot away, and even stopped munching on the cold pepperoni pizza he hadn't bothered to reheat, he could not for the life of him see where the bouquet of roses or the live turtledove or the red polka-dot handkerchief had come from. They just popped into the magician's hands, out of thin air, like ... like magic. It was remarkable, really remarkable how somebody could do that, and Mike had watched in detached fascination, just the way he now watched the knife.

One second the kid was sitting beside him, hands empty and harmless, and the next second the kid was twisted in his seat, leaning in close to Mike, his breath hot and foul in Mike's nostrils, and *voila,* there was the knife, held in one hand an inch from Mike's face.

Mike saw six inches of rusty steel with a deep nick in the blade, and a cracked handle, and the kid's fingers gripping it so hard his nails were squeezed white.

Then the knife was out of his field of vision, gone, vanished, and *presto,* it was at his throat. He could feel the knifepoint needling the soft skin in the hollow spot south of his larynx.

"Turn off at the next exit."

Mike tried to talk. His voice was hoarse with fear and with the effort of trying not to move his head. "I'm not hauling anything you want. It's—"

"Just drive this fucking truck off the road at the next fucking exit!"

There was an exit just ahead. FREEHOLD, ROUTE 33, the sign said as it glided over the windshield into the mist.

Mike took the exit, pumping the brake gently, terrified that a sudden lurch might knock the kid backward and drive the knife through his neck. Up ahead a toll plaza glittered. It was empty of cars and only one booth was open, with one forlorn figure huddled inside, barely visible through the frosted glass.

"Got to pay to get off," said Mike stupidly.

The pain in his side hit him before he could grasp its source. Then he realized that the knife had done another magic trick, like the glass of ice water with the little umbrella in it that had started out in the magician's hand and wound up in Johnny Carson's vest pocket; it was now pointed at his side, the cruel tip testing the skin between his ribs.

"Pay it. Don't say a fucking word. You make a sound,

I'll kill you." The kid snorted in a way that might have been laughter. "You got it, scum?"

"Got it," said Mike, his voice very normal except for the way the last syllable just cut out, like a bad edit in a movie soundtrack when the last millisecond of an utterance was clipped off.

He kept pumping the brake and shifting down, as gently as he could. He wondered in clammy fear if the dogs would start barking when the truck stopped. If so, would the kid panic—drive the knife home—six inches of steel drilling into his rib cage to deflate his right lung and flood his chest cavity with blood ...?

Then it occurred to him that here he was, being held at knifepoint, and there were four attack dogs roughly a foot away, four dogs trained to rip thugs like this one limb from limb, and they were no good to him at all, and wasn't that ironic?

He almost laughed out loud, then thought better of it.

The dogs were silent as the Van-dura pulled up to the tollbooth. Mike cranked down his window and fumbled in his coat pocket for his ticket.

He handed it to a woman in a blue jacket. Her little booth looked warm and safe and inviting. She had a portable radio on, playing the Pointer Sisters, and a cup of coffee, steam rising from it, which sat on the white counter near the cash register. Mike marveled at these details. He wondered how anybody could ever want more out of life.

The woman, identified by the tag on her uniform as Patti, glanced at the ticket. "One sixty-five," she said without interest.

Mike's fingers dug in his pants pocket and found two bills, which he assumed were singles. He thrust them, trembling, at the woman.

He sat waiting as the cash register clanged open and one quarter and one dime were plucked out and dropped in his open palm. The moment the change was in his hand and the gate lifted to let him pass, he felt a wave of sheer terror, born of the realization that he had to drive away and leave the booth and the bright lights and this woman who suddenly, unaccountably meant so much to him.

He met the woman's eyes. They were brown and un-intelligent and ringed with dark circles. Inside himself he heard a voice crying—not shouting, but really honest-to-God crying like a baby—*Help me, please help me, please please please ...*

"You want a receipt or something?" she asked indif-ferently.

The knife eased in deeper, almost breaking the skin. He shook his head and drove through.

He kept his eyes on the side-view mirror until the lit-tle island of light that was the toll plaza had shrunk to a pinpoint and was gone. He felt a burning sensation and a pressure in his eyes, and realized it was tears. He blinked his eyes wide and tried to keep his head together.

"Get off this road. Take a back road."

"I don't know the back roads."

The knife, *abracadabra,* was at his throat again. "I don't give a fuck what you know!"

Mike took an exit marked ENGLISHTOWN. He drove down a narrow two-lane country road that ran parallel to Route 33, heading east. A few houses glided by, their shapes dim and half-concealed in the pine trees. There were no lights. The road was rough and the truck rattled.

At some point during the endless span of time that followed, Mike Tuttle came to a realization. He could not have said just when the thought had crystallized in his mind. But it had, and try as he might, he could not shake it.

He tried to find some spit to moisten his mouth, and failed.

"You're going to kill me," he said tonelessly.

The kid didn't answer.

- — -

Death was in the air. By some sixth sense Razor felt its presence.

The truck had been rumbling slowly down this new road for a long time. The cages creaked and the wire mesh trembled like the screen of a storm door that had just been slammed shut. The cage on top of Razor's had slid a few inches to the left after one particularly bad jolt, and the ropes had groaned but held, so far, and the cage had not fallen.

None of the dogs made any sound except their slow, regular panting and the infrequent mutter of Cleo's stomach.

The state of high tension had run its course and passed, and now there was only patience, a great, inhuman patience, the kind that cannot be taught.

Through microscopic cracks in the truck's walls and roof, the smell of pine forests reached Razor's nostrils. He sniffed warily. There was another smell, too, a faint salt-air smell. Razor had never been to the ocean. He could not recognize the scent.

These were not danger smells, and the rattling of the truck on the cracked macadam was not a danger signal, and neither was the silence from the front nor the darkness in the rear. All these irritants had faded out, retreated to the periphery of Razor's awareness. Now, occupying the center of his consciousness, there was only a sense, heavy and suffocating like the truck's stale air—a feeling, a premonition of death. Razor could not have traced it to its source. It was there, just there, final, immutable, like the certainty of a dog howling at the moon that that particular night was, yes indeed, a moon-howling night. This, Razor knew, was a danger night. A death night.

He needed only to be patient and death would come.

His teeth felt hard and cool, like icicles, against his panting tongue.

- — -

Mike could not look at his watch without removing his hand from the steering wheel to peel back the sleeve of his coat, so he didn't know what time it was or how much time had passed, and he had no idea when he had come up with the plan.

*Plan.* To call it that was perhaps to dignify it too much. *Resolve* might be closer. The quiet, fierce resolve that he would not go without a fight.

It was only a knife, for Christ's sake. He could snatch it away. Or knock it out of the kid's hand. Without the knife he was just a scrawny runt, quick work for Michael "the Masher" Tuttle, who was, let's not forget it, three times wrestling champ of Harry S Truman Public High School. Even if, in the struggle, he did get cut ... wounded ... even seriously, once the knife was inside him, the kid was effectively disarmed. And if the Masher still had the moves and the strength, he would pin the bastard down and batter him unconscious, then drive to a hospital or a police station or a phone ...

He was still going over the possibilities in his mind, imagining different versions of the struggle, all with the same outcome—triumph of good over evil—when the kid said, very quietly, "Pull over."

"Here?"

"Where the fuck do you think?"

Mike swept his eyes over the road and saw no lights, no black rectangles of mailboxes, no driveways manned by iron statuettes with lanterns raised in welcome, no sign of habitation. There was only the pine forest, rising like a wall of blue-green shadows over the deserted road on the left. On the right ran an unpaved shoulder edging a steep drop to the woods below.

Mike pulled onto the shoulder, and the kid slashed his face and gouged his eyes and buried the knife, finally, in his heart and dumped his dead body out the driver's-side door, to roll over the edge of the shoulder and down the slope into the woods, and the truck pulled away with a scream of tires and the triumphant barking of the god-damned dogs.

No. That didn't happen, except in Mike Tuttle's mind, in the split second before he tensed to take action and finish this episode on his own terms.

He pressed his tongue hard against the back of his teeth and drew a sharp breath through his nostrils. His eardrums were tight with sudden pressure, the way they felt in an airplane in a sudden descent. He felt the pounding rush of adrenaline in his chest, in time with the beat of furious indignation that said one kid with a carving knife wasn't going to waste *him.*

He spun the wheel to the right and slammed on the brakes. The truck skidded. The kid was thrown backward in the passenger seat. Mike ignored the blur of the road in the windshield. He grabbed the kid's knife hand and fought to loosen his grip on the blade. The kid kicked out and caught Mike hard in the stomach with the toe of his boot. Mike tasted vomit. In the back of the truck, the dogs were barking.

The kid kicked Mike again and with his free hand clawed Mike's face, sinking his fingers into the soft flesh of his cheek. The truck spun around and careened backward onto the shoulder. Mike took the calculated risk of removing one hand from the kid's knife arm to sock him in the mouth. His knuckles stung. He punched again. The kid's nostrils squirted blood.

- — -

The truck rolled to almost a dead stop with three tires on the shoulder and the left rear tire hanging over the edge into space.

- — -

The kid, still gripping Mike's face, rammed the heel of his boot into Mike's gut and pressed, digging in deep, squeezing up bile in Mike's throat, forcing him back. Mike blinked and saw rainbow sparkles. His head hummed. The heel twisted in deeper, squashing his stomach flat, flat as it had been in high school when he was a wrestling champ, a long fucking time ago, and this punk might be scrawny but he was half Mike's age, dammit, and he was winning this match.

- — -

The truck began to roll back. It tilted slowly as the right front tire left the ground and the left rear tire dropped onto the rocky soil of the forty-five-degree incline that bordered the road.

- — -

Mike looked at the kid through a haze of white light and the roar of a crowd and somewhere a dog's distant barking, and he saw the kid's lips curl back over yellow teeth. He saw the slow smile that said, more eloquently than words, *I'll kill you.*

- — -

The truck's right rear tire was poised at the edge of the shoulder, prevented from rolling off only by a rock wedged under it, blocking its progress.

- — -

Mike's hand was shaking. His grip on the kid's arm weakened. The kid slowly drew his arm forward while the heavy leather boot ground deeper and deeper inside Mike's gut, till Mike knew he had to let go and draw back or he would vomit and black out and die.

- — -

The small contest between tire and rock, almost irresistible force and nearly immovable object, ended when the weight of the truck forced the rock back, over the edge. It fell, skipping down the slope like a pebble flicked across a pond, hit the ground forty feet below with a soft thud, and cracked neatly in half.

The truck, groaning under the strain, prepared to follow.

- — -

Mike let go of the kid, jerked back in his seat, and retched. The knife flashed, arcing up, then sank into Mike's abdomen and stayed there, jutting out at an angle. Blood spurted from between the flaps of his coat, staining his shirt dark red. He heard a hysterical wheezing, like the bleat of a panicky animal, then realized he was making the sound himself. *Oh Jesus I've been stabbed, he cut me he cut me he cut me.* The kid twisted the knife counterclockwise, like a screwdriver, and Mike pictured his guts turning over like spaghetti around a fork. He lashed out blindly, knocked the kid back, and fumbled for the knife with a desperate, mindless impulse to pull it out, not caring if it unplugged the wound, just needing to get that thing out of his body—his body, oh Christ, his body—but before he could, the truck lurched back and its two passengers spilled sideways.

- — -

Both front tires were off the shoulder and suspended in air. The two rear tires dug into the naked earth of the hill at the edge of the road. The truck hesitated, teetering at an angle, frozen and waiting, as if poised for takeoff, its headlights shooting twin beams at the starry sky.

- — -

Mike and the kid were sprawled across both seats in a tangle of limbs and hatreds.

- — -

The Van-dura moaned and plunged backward. It hit the slope with all four wheels and flipped over and skidded down on its passenger side for a good twenty feet, sending up clouds of dust and pebbles, then slammed into the gnarled trunk of a tree that had somehow taken root in the rocky soil. The tree trunk shattered. The impact blasted the truck onto its back, and then it went cartwheeling the rest of the way down the slope, turning over and over, its one living headlight tracing spirals in the darkness. All four tires blew out in rapid succession, *pop-pop-pop-pop,* like the last four kernels of popcorn in the frying pan. The rear axle, bent out of shape by one jolt, cracked with the next one and split in two on the third try; on the fourth impact the two rear tires skittered out from under the truck in opposite directions and whirled away. The driver's-side door caved in. The door on the passenger side bulged tumorously, then was whacked off and launched into space, a misdirected satellite, to crash in the branches of a pine tree and plummet to earth in pieces.

The truck cab twirled like the cage of a Ferris wheel. Mike never wore a seat belt. It made his shoulder sore, and to hell with their stupid laws. So there was nothing to restrain him as his seat somersaulted and pitched him onto the roof, hammering his skull, then slammed him against the door with a lance of agony through his arm, then dropped him back into his seat, then tossed him in the screaming kid's lap. He kept shutting his eyes and opening them as the dashboard jerked up and down, side to side, a toy on a rubber band. The windshield had disintegrated instantly; now it was only an open frame laced with glass shards that fell like tinkling raindrops with each new blow. Nothing was framed there but a whirling darkness and flashes of dust clouds and rocks caught in the headlight's beam, making kaleidoscope patterns, till that light shattered like its twin. A sapling thrust itself through the opening, into the cab, and Mike screamed at the bramble-prickly fingers scratching his face. Then it was gone and the truck completed its descent and hit the ground.

It landed on its back with the thud of a felled dinosaur. The lock on the rear door snapped. The door, designed to slide down to a closed position when the Vandura was upright, slid open a few inches.

- — -

Mike Tuttle came to with his knees on the steering wheel and the knife still lodged in his gut and his head resting on the roof. His head was at a strange angle—the cab looked sideways, not upside down—and for a second he was sure his neck was broken. But with a painful effort he found he could move his arms and legs. He even wiggled his toes in his shoes. It reminded him of Saturday mornings in wintertime, lying under three cotton blankets and feeling how warm his feet were. He wished he were in bed right now.

He looked to his right and saw that the passenger seat was empty. Where the door used to be, there was now a gaping hole looking out on a vacant, motionless night. The kid was gone. He must have fled. Thank God.

Mike fumbled for the door handle on the driver's side, found it, and pushed. The door was stuck. That side of the truck had been crushed like a beer can. Well, he would just have to go out the other way.

Cautiously he began to inch out of his seat. He became aware of the intense pain in his abdomen, a pain that shot sparks up his chest with any sudden movement. How much damage had the knife done? The hell with it. He gritted his teeth and ignored the pain.

Untold seconds later he was lying flat on his back on the roof of the cab. With a spasm of agony that brought him to the brink of unconsciousness again, he rolled over on his side. He pressed his palms flat against the roof, feeling the cold metal bite his skin, and dragged himself toward the open doorway. His stomach was a giant wound, leaking blood, numbing the lower portion of his body. He still wanted the knife out, but he now realized it might do more harm than good. He could visualize his entrails spilling out like a bucket of eels. The thought made him feel sick. He did not touch the knife. He crawled on.

He reached the doorway. He pulled himself out. The ground outside was as cold and stiff and featureless as a sheet of ice. He slid onto it like some great snake wriggling out of its cave, moaning a little, then lay spread-eagled on his back, a yard from the truck, breathing hard, fighting nausea. He couldn't walk. He knew that. The pain was too great, and the stickiness of his shirt and pants told him he had lost too much blood. Goddammit. How the hell was he supposed to climb that ridge, get back to the road? How was he supposed to get help?

A sound interrupted his thoughts.

The sound of dogs barking.

- — -

The ropes had snapped immediately and the cages had shattered moments later as the truck spun and crashed. Razor was on his back amid a pile of wood splinters and wire-mesh panels. He jerked to his feet. The darkness was broken by a shaft of light filtering in where the sliding door had opened a crack. Razor padded toward it, feeling the ache of a bruise on his right leg and the trickle of blood down the side of his head.

He was dimly aware of his companions, recognizing them more by scent and sound than by sight. Cleo's stomach was rumbling like a distant thunderstorm as she whimpered, chewing her injured paws. The odor of Bigfoot's drool mixed with the sickly sweetness of flowing blood as the dog, too stunned to move from the wreckage of his cage, panted in a corner. Mr. Dobbs was scratching at the wooden partition at the front of the truck, as if seeking help from the Men whose low voices had been audible before the crash.

Razor ignored them all. His mind was fixed on a single objective. To get out.

He reached the door. With the truck upside down, the bottom of the sliding door was now the top; the opening was five feet up. Razor teetered on hind legs, ignoring the protest of his bruised shank, and planted his front paws on the door. His head just reached the opening. Beyond it loomed the three-by-four-feet metal plate that was the automatic lift, still secured vertically to the back of the Van-dura.

Razor shoved his snout through the opening. His nostrils twitched and snorted, drawing in the cold night air. He smelled trees, that salty scent he could not identify, and another scent.

Blood. Human blood.

A Man was out there.

Razor jammed his long angular muzzle farther into the crack. His front paws scrabbled at the door, then grasped hold of the top. He hung on, his back feet off the floor, hind legs flailing, rear end wiggling comically as his clipped tail jerked.

There was no way for him to squeeze through the four-inch opening. Razor tried anyway. He did not know it was impossible. He had never learned fear or doubt. He knew only anger.

He barked in fury at the obstacle to his escape. Cleo and Bigfoot barked briefly in reply, and Mr. Dobbs let out a long banshee wail that reverberated through the truck like the tormented cry of a ghost.

It was these sounds that Mike Tuttle heard as he lay a yard from the Van-dura, unable to move, stuck on his back like an upturned tortoise and losing blood, so much blood, the blood that now burned strong and sweet and close in Razor's nostrils and crowded his mind with images of fangs slicing arteries.

Razor clung to the door, pressing down on it with his full weight, eighty pounds of lean muscle and milk-fed bone, and that weight forced the sliding door down, an inch, three inches, a half foot, more. Each time, the Doberman squeezed farther through the opening, wriggling sideways out of necessity, since the lift still barred forward progress, so that finally he was draped across the top of the door, pawing and scratching and panting furiously. Until with a sudden grating noise, like the scrape of fenders in a parking lot, the door surrendered altogether and rolled down the rest of the way. Razor spilled out in a heap, his head narrowly missing the lift. He hit the ground on all fours, skidded, but kept his balance.

He was free.

Behind him, the others padded in pursuit.

Ahead lay the motionless figure of a Man. Razor sniffed and smelled the fresh blood, intoxicatingly strong. He took a step forward and tensed his haunches, preparing to pounce. He hesitated. He was not trained to attack an enemy who did not move. Still, the Man might move. Eventually.

He peered at the Man and waited, while his mind played an endless loop of images of death and his paws tingled.

- — -

Mike lay very still. He was conscious of nothing but the sharp pain in his gut that flared up with each breath, and the icy ground under his back, freezing his buttocks and shoulder blades through the thin cloth of his pants and coat, and the dog. It was not even a dog, really, just two red eyes at the corner of his vision that swayed hypnotically, eyes fixed on him from six feet away.

The dog was not the danger. The danger was this insane impulse rising in his gourd like a wave of nausea, the impulse to get up and run, run away, run like hell.

He could not get up. He knew that. The pain and the blood loss were too severe. With each heartbeat—how fast was his heart beating, anyway, pretty damn fast, *keep it together, Mikey, keep it cool*—his strength was ebbing, draining away. It was an effort merely to hold back the spiraling dizziness that threatened to drag his mind down into the black well of unconsciousness once more.

Still, he wanted to run. Needed to run. Had to get away.

He fought back panic. To move could be fatal. Trained to kill. These fuckers were trained to kill. Not just guard dogs. Attack dogs. Masterson had tried, casually, with a professional sort of interest, to explain the difference. Mike hadn't listened. The conversation had made him nervous and he had endured it, feigning interest while thinking of colleges to apply to and how nice it would be to cash the check for this job.

But he had gathered enough from Masterson's words to know that the dogs were trained to strike at the first sign of movement, that only by standing or lying dead still, utterly immobile, or by using the special command words they were taught to obey, did a man have a chance to escape attack.

Mike didn't know the command words. He hadn't thought to ask. So he lay still, wincing with each slow breath that tugged at the knife in his belly. He was aware of the steady rising and falling of his stomach and of the sting of cold air on the roof of his mouth. The wind stirred his hair, and he felt he could detect the motion of each individual hair shifting on his scalp, just as he could feel each short hair on his arms prickling.

The dog was growling.

No, not a growl, exactly. A low purring sound, deep in the throat, the sound a dog makes as the prelude to a growl.

Mike wondered if he dared to turn his head, just an inch to the side, so he could see the dog better. Out of the corner of his left eye he still saw the two red eyes, staring. But that was all he could see. He needed to know more. What kind of dog was it? Was it injured? Was it showing its fangs? He would require only the tiniest turn of his head to the left to see the animal clearly. He wondered if that would matter. Such a little thing. Surely the dog would not attack over such a little thing as that. Just to turn his head an inch to the left and see, the most innocent thing in the world, nothing threatening about that ...

No.

*Don't move. Don't move an inch. Don't fucking breathe. Do you need it spelled out for you? The goddamn thing is just looking for an excuse, any excuse, and it will pounce. Pounce and kill. Play dead, asshole. Play dead or* be *dead.*

The two red eyes hovered there, at the edge of his vision.

He rolled his eyes to the right, slowly, as if fearful even of the noise that their rotation in their sockets might make, till he was looking away from the dog. Now he couldn't see it at all. Out of sight, out of mind. He gazed up at the night sky. It was brimming with stars, bright and cold, like diamonds.

He looked at the sky for what seemed like a long time, until gradually he became aware that the pain in his stomach was gone. In fact, there was little sensation of any kind anywhere below his waist. Even when he took a deep, slow breath and let his belly inflate like a balloon, then deflate slowly, he felt only a tickle where the knife was. But he did feel a warm, thick, viscid pool forming under his buttocks, at the point where his undershorts met the skin of his back. His shirt there was heavy with blood, soaked through, dripping. He could picture the shirt sagging like a damp towel. The blood was leaking out and settling there and leaving the lower portion of his body limp and numb.

He seemed to be getting drowsy. He understood, with peculiar clarity, that this was because he had lost too much blood. His heart, slowing down, was drawing in the reserves from his extremities—his legs, arms, head—giving him that tingly sensation in his appendages and the lightness in his head. Well, that was all right. He would just lie here and look up at the stars, which seemed dimmer now, and drift off to sleep, dreamless sleep, and later, when he woke up ...

He would not wake up.

The realization shocked his eyes open wide. He was dying. That simple. He could not lie still much longer or he would die. He would lose too much blood and die. That one word—*die*—kept coming back. He repeated it in his mind, *die die die,* till it lost all meaning, like the sound of his own name repeated too often. He blinked his eyes rapidly to clear his head.

He had to get help. Yes. That was the answer. But he couldn't climb the ridge back to the road. Impossible. Then a thought occurred to him, preposterous in its simplicity. He could honk the horn. The horn in the truck. A good loud horn. If it still worked. It *must* still work. He would crawl back to the truck cab, collapse on the steering wheel, and let the horn blare endlessly, till the battery gave out or he did or somebody came. Why had he ever left the truck? Stupid, so stupid. But no time for recriminations. He had to get back, crawl back, now.

He had almost started to move, before remembering the dog.

If he moved, the dog would kill him.

Now, wait. He marshaled his thoughts. The dog might not kill him. Might not. Probably would. But maybe not. Or maybe, even better ...

Oh, God, did he dare to hope?

There was no sound from where the animal had been.

Maybe the dog was gone.

Who knew how much time had passed. A minute? An

hour? A dog could lose patience too, just like a man. Maybe it had wandered off into the dark. Maybe it had been badly injured and had slinked off to *die die die* in the bushes. Maybe it had never been there at all.

There was only one way to know. He would have to look. Cautiously he rolled his eyes in their sockets to the left again. He saw nothing. No red eyes. Just darkness. The dog was gone.

Hallelujah.

But wait.

The dog might have moved a few feet out of range of his peripheral vision. To be sure it was gone, really sure, he would have to ... turn his head ... and see.

If the dog was there, he was dead.

If it was gone, he had a chance.

So this was what it came down to, thirty-six years of life—one turn of his head and the answer to a single question.

He did it slowly, with consummate care. The back of his head was resting on the ice-cold ground. He rolled his head an inch toward his left, then stopped. He waited for several heartbeats. He breathed in and out, once. He still could not see the dog. He moved his head another inch to the left. He stopped. He probed the darkness out of the corner of his eye. Nothing so far. But he couldn't tell. The dog might be crouching down. He turned another inch. The hairs at the back of his head, glued to the ground by frozen sweat, came loose with small jerks, as painful as pulling whiskers. Still he could see nothing. If the red eyes were there, he would see them by now, wouldn't he? Even if the dog were lying flat? He didn't know. He turned his head the rest of the way and let his left cheek rest on the dirt and stared.

Two red eyes stared back.

The dog growled, softly.

Not a purr, not a warning. A low, guttural, grinding

sound, like the idling of an engine, an engine of destruction about to rev up to full throttle and tear forward.

Mike lay paralyzed, ignoring the bite of the frigid earth against his cheek. He stared at the dog.

He could see it clearly now. It had moved a little to one side, that was all. Two steps, perhaps. Two soundless steps. It was not lying down. It stood as it had before.

It was a Doberman. Its black and rust-colored fur, so closely cropped as to resemble velvet skin, rippled with the electric tension of its muscles. Its legs and body were lean, almost streamlined, an anatomy lesson in bone and muscle structure. The rib cage made a serrated pattern along its right side, the only side visible to him. The dog stood with its body positioned at a forty-five-degree angle to Mike's own, its head tilted to look at him, its eyes bright and pitiless. Mike thought of the hellhound Cerberus that guarded the gates of Hades. He thought of werewolves loping through a ground cover of mist in Baltic forests. He thought of real wolves, gray shadows with moonbeam eyes, padding across the Arctic snowdrifts. But none of these images quite fit. The dog was all of them and none of them.

Then he had it.

A panther. Yes, that was it. The black jungle cat engineered by nature for the single job of killing.

Mike felt the shame of tears stinging his eyes.

He could not crawl back to the Van-dura and honk the horn. The dog would kill him. He could not lie still. He would bleed to death. He could not do anything except *die die die.*

He didn't want to die. He was afraid of the dark, and he felt darkness swallowing him. He remembered crying for his mommy when he was four because a floorboard had creaked somewhere in the sleeping house, as floorboards do, and he had been sure it was the Wicked Witch creeping to his bed to wrap him in her black cloak and steal him away. He remembered sinking to the bottom of a swimming pool at the age of two and a half and staring at the concrete floor in paralyzed terror, swallowing water and choking without sound, till his daddy had fished him out and pumped his lungs dry and forced air into his mouth.

*You're losing it, Tuttle.*

*Just get hold of yourself. You can handle this. You can handle anything, man. Just keep it together, that's all. Keep* it ... keep ...

Oh, no.

Oh, Christ, no.

Four pairs of eyes glowered at him, forming a tight circle around his motionless body.

They had surrounded him silently while his sight and his terror were focused on the Doberman.

Without moving his head even a fraction of an inch, he again rotated his eyeballs, slowly, and made out the faint outline of a second Doberman by his feet, a German shepherd by his right arm, and a third Doberman on the other side of his head.

All three were panting softly, raggedly.

He closed his eyes. He heard the low panting and the first Doberman's growl becoming louder, drawing near.

Something wet spattered his hand.

Drool?

Blood?

*Don't look. Don't look.*

He looked.

The Doberman was standing over him, dripping gobs of saliva, the skin of its mouth pulled tight over red gums and yellow fangs.

Mike stared in fascination. It was the little details that held him. The mole sprouting a single hair on the underside of the dog's jaw. The chain-link collar with the square metal tag. The deep gash in the side of the dog's head, below its clipped ear, releasing a molasses-slow stream that threaded its way through a forest of short hairs, down the thick, muscular neck.

He felt something rub against the inside of his thigh, something warm and living that reminded him of a woman's hand, caressing him, and he looked out of the corner of his eye and saw the second Doberman standing between his legs, sniffing the blood that had pasted his trouser leg to his knee.

He shut his eyes again, not to see the dog there, not to imagine what it would be like if the animal's fangs sank into his knee or his thigh or his ... groin.

*Go away. Go away. Please make them go away. Please, please, I'll do anything, make them go away.*

Mike kept his eyes shut and kept repeating the silent plea until he realized with a dull sense of astonishment that he was praying.

- — -

Razor had almost, but not quite, lost interest in the Man.

The Man was alive—there was no doubt about that—but lying still, he posed no threat. Bad Men moved. Razor knew that. He remembered the enemies in padded costumes who challenged him, taunted him, and tried to fight or run, till Razor's teeth sank into the foam pads and his claws shredded the rubber chest mats and sometimes, the best times, he drew blood, hot sweet-smelling blood, and the Man screamed until other Men pulled Razor away. He fed well after such occasions and listened to the appreciative murmuring of the trainers and slept with a comfortable though mildly unsatisfied feeling, a feeling that everything would have been perfect if only they hadn't pulled him away.

- — -

The buzzing in Mike's head was the hum of a jet engine. He was flying first class. There was a cool drink in

28

his hand and a magazine in his lap, and a pretty steward-ess was smiling at him. He would be landing soon. He would phone Karl Masterson from the airport and tell him that the delivery of his dogs had been delayed. Mas-terson would understand. Everything would be all right.

Then the buzzing faded and Mike was back on the cold ground with the four dogs watching him.

The third Doberman, the one on his right, lowered its head and sniffed at his ear. Mike heard loud, damp, snuffling noises. They filled his brain. He shut his eyes and wished he were on the plane again. The snuffling went on and on as the dog's wet snout probed his ear, pressing in deeper, till each snort of breath was like a small explosion.

The dog withdrew its snout and began sniffing his neck, his hair, the side of his face. Mike's eyes were closed tight. Red sparks danced before his eyelids. Every muscle of his body was rigid. He did not know if he was breath-ing anymore.

His right arm moved.

Odd. He hadn't moved it. Unless it had jerked invol-untarily, a muscle spasm ...

No. There it was again. His arm rose an inch and dropped. Rose and dropped. Rose. Dropped.

He slid his eyelids open, peering past the Doberman sniffing his face, and saw the German shepherd with its teeth in the sleeve of his coat, tugging at his arm.

*To see if I'm dead. It's checking to see if I'm dead.*

The second Doberman was still nosing at Mike's crotch. The third, sniffing the nape of his neck.

They couldn't decide They couldn't make up their minds which part of him to go for first.

Then, mercifully, the buzzing in his head came back and he was floating over an ocean dotted with white sails.

- — -

Razor had never smelled so much blood. The need to

bite was almost overpowering. His mouth foamed with saliva. His tongue was hot, burning.

He took a step closer.

- — -

Mike returned to reality reluctantly, leaving the ocean and the crisp white sails behind.

The first Doberman was even nearer than before.

Mike shut his eyes and made a mental vow not to open them again. Not again. He knew he could not stand it if he looked again.

He kept on fighting panic as the Doberman lowered its head till it hung an inch from Mike's face and he could smell the musty canine smell and feel the droplets of saliva beading like dew on his cheek.

This dog scared him worst of all. He did not know why. There seemed to be no rational reason for it. But in this dog he saw the bottom of the swimming pool; he saw the Wicked Witch's cloak; he saw Death.

Insanely, suicidally, he felt the need to scream.

The first intimation of that need was a choking sound, quite involuntary, which made his head jerk slightly and his closed mouth twitch.

The Doberman barked.

The other dogs were growling now.

*Oh, God.*

Mike heard a sob, his own, strangled in his throat. He had not known his heart could beat this fast. He felt the throbbing pulse in his head, so rapid there was almost no break between beats.

The dog leaned in closer. Mike felt the short hairs under its chin tickle his neck as the animal probed his face. Its rancid breath was hot on his skin.

His chest sagged a little and he grunted in pain and surprise as the Doberman brought one paw to rest on his collarbone.

*It's ... on ... top ... of ... me ...*

He kept his eyes closed. That was his last hope, not to see.

A drumroll of terror pounded at his temples. One dog at his crotch, nosing his balls; one at his arm, worrying it like a bone; one by his head, sniffing; and one, the worst one of all, balanced on his chest like a lion on its kill, its snout inches from his face.

If he looked up, would the dog be looking down at him?

*Don't.*

But would it?

*Don't, for Christ's sake, don't don't don't.*

He opened his eyes—*don't*—and saw the Doberman's face filling his field of vision—*don't*—its eyes more brown than red at this close range—*please stop*—its nostrils dilated—*look away*—its lips curled wide in a saliva-streaked grin—*it's smiling, smiling at me.*

The dog growled again, a puma's blast of hot breath and guttural rage. Mike saw the fang-studded mouth swing wide and he knew, just knew, just *knew* the dog would rip open his throat in the next second.

Mike Tuttle screamed.

- — -

Razor knew. This was a Bad Man. There was no doubt about it now. Razor would taste blood after all.

- — -

Mike Tuttle kept on screaming as the first Doberman tore off the side of his face and the second Doberman sank its fangs into his thigh and the third Doberman clawed at his head, slicing off an ear, and the German shepherd bit deep into his arm.

He was still screaming as the shepherd gnawed his hand to a bloody stump. He was screaming as the second Doberman bit into the meat of his thigh again and again, cutting out red chunks of flesh till its fangs struck bone. He was screaming as the third Doberman raked its claws across his face and scissored his forehead to ribbons, drowning his eyes in blood. But he stopped screaming once the first Doberman slashed his throat with its razor fangs, severing the jugular and the windpipe. Then he could only wheeze like a stuck pig and geyser up blood and struggle weakly to the end.

In his mind the screams and the helpless gasping were coming from someplace far away, someplace where he wasn't, because he was at the bottom of the swimming pool with the black folds of a witch's cloak enveloping him, and he was surprised and mildly pleased to discover that the cloak was not frightening at all, but warm and comforting, like the blankets that kept his toes warm on cold winter mornings, and he didn't even mind going with the witch. He had only one regret, a silly thing, maybe, but he heard it pursuing him as a forlorn voice, his own voice, as he drifted away into the dark.

*You know, I never even got my degree.*

Then he was gone and only his body was left, to twitch like a puppet on broken strings for many minutes longer, as the dogs finished their work.

- — -

When the killing was done, Razor stood over the gored carcass and inhaled the steaming pungence of its entrails. This time no Men had come to pull him away and he had slashed and bitten and gnawed until his bloodlust was, for the moment, sated.

Cleo, Bigfoot, and Mr. Dobbs ringed the corpse, the clouds of their breath turning to frost in the air. Their muzzles and paws were streaked with red, bright against the Dobermans' fur, dark as chocolate stains on Bigfoot's tan coat. Cleo was again worrying her paws in forlorn desperation. Mr. Dobbs was still growling, as if daring the Bad Man to rise from the dead. Bigfoot slobbered brainlessly on what had been Mike Tuttle's right hand.

The sudden stillness unnerved Razor. He raised his

head and sniffed the night air, but the smells of blood and canine sweat were too overpowering to admit any other odors. He pricked up his ears and listened.

The trees—pines and sycamores and oaks—whispered in the breeze, and the branches of the oaks, nearly bare, scraped and creaked and sighed.

Razor did not like these sounds. He did not like the sense of vulnerability, of being alone in a clearing under an open sky. He did not even like the blood smell anymore. He had tasted and breathed in enough blood for this night. Instinct told him that now it was time to run, to hide in the shadowy dark of the woods where the other wild things prowled and took cover, and to lick his wounds and rest.

He trotted toward the woods. Halfway there he stopped, looking back.

The others were watching him, as if making up their minds.

Cleo was the first to pad after him. Bigfoot followed, his tongue lolling stupidly. Mr. Dobbs did not move.

Razor continued into the woods. He did not look back again. He did not care whether any of them joined him or not. But in his wordless way he had known that they would, just as he knew that Mr. Dobbs would follow, as well.

The trio were disappearing into the trees when Mr. Dobbs broke into a run and caught up.

Then all four were gone, four shadows lost in a maze of shadows known to the locals as Denham's Wood, on the outskirts of Sea Cove, New Jersey.

It was the morning of Tuesday, the 21st of October, 1987, and though Sea Cove didn't know it yet, Halloween was coming early this year.

# FIRST DAY

TAYLOR

# 1

POTTERS ROAD began in back of the Andersons' farm, a good old-fashioned farm where Owen and Maggie Anderson raised chickens and planted tomatoes and barely got by. You had to head out past Route 35—past the housing development, the retirement community, the K-Mart, the Burger King, and the new A&P still under construction— four miles inland, to the very edge of Sea Cove, where forest and farmland took over. Then you got to Potters Road.

It was a narrow, dusty, winding road, more of a dirt path, really, barely wide enough for one vehicle at a time, but then, few vehicles traveled here nowadays. The road had been built before the turn of the century, in the days when Sea Cove was all woods, marsh, and empty beaches, and only farmers and fishermen and a few other determined recluses lived here. It meandered lazily through Denham's Wood, circling around Morrison Lake, a medium-size and only slightly stagnant body of water invisible from the road itself but making its presence known by the explosions of black mallards that periodically shot up from its surface to assume triangular formations in the sky.

Pine trees rose on both sides of the road like green walls, bristling with needles. Insects chirruped and toads croaked and choruses of birds greeted the sun. Through gaps in the canopy of pine branches overhanging the road, patches of sky were visible. The sky was a pale, cheerless gray, the color of October, but warming imperceptibly to blue as the sun climbed higher. It was a cool morning, following a frigid night, but the breeze rustling the pine needles promised a milder day, perhaps as warm as the sixties, pleasant weather for this time of year.

After the Andersons' there were no more houses, at least none that were occupied, for a good two miles. But at rare intervals, as you walked along, you could spot the remains of an abandoned shack, overgrown with laurel bushes and dying weeds, a relic out of somebody's past, like the abandoned hulks of cars you sometimes saw littering the sides of roadways.

The next farm along the road was the Bennett place, and not far past that came the Cobbs' and the Whittakers'. You could walk there, if you were so inclined. Or, if you were really energetic, you could just keep walking, traveling the winding road, till about five hours later you would find yourself right back at the Andersons', where you started. It was that sort of a road.

The young man named Alex Driscoll had no such grandiose ambitions this morning.

He was not the sort for ambitions, grand or otherwise. In fact, he had been thinking of turning back, having completed one-half of his daily thirty-minute walk. He would retrace his steps to the Andersons' farm, where he had left his Pinto parked, then head home to fix breakfast. He was still thinking about it when he saw the thing on the road.

It was perhaps twenty yards ahead, in the shadow of a pine, a dark, crumpled, motionless thing. Alex could not tell exactly what it was, not from this distance, not with his eyesight. He was only twenty-nine, but his eyes had been lousy since grammar school. Without glasses he saw objects as clots of colored fog, and even with his heavy, shatterproof-plastic lenses his vision was not quite twenty-twenty. By tipping his glasses forward on his nose,

Alex was able to sharpen his vision to a slight degree, and doing so now, he could just make out the thing on the road as an animal. He could not tell what kind. He shrugged and headed toward it, drawn by a slightly morbid curiosity and a reluctance to turn back quite so soon.

In truth, he hated to go back, since there was nothing to go back to. Well, there was home, of course, but what was that except a lonely one-bedroom apartment with the sole distinction of being a half block from the beach, a dubious advantage in the off-season.

The animal was a dog. He could see that now. Dead and ... mauled. But still, at ten yards, too far to make out details.

He supposed he was just feeling sorry for himself again. He didn't care. He was used to it. The world, he had long ago decided, was divided into winners and losers. And don't give Alex Driscoll any BS about the winners being self-made. Some people made it, some didn't, it was as simple as that. A crapshoot, that's all. One throw of the genetic dice and one stop along the random flight pattern of the stork. Those with bright smiles, stiff handshakes, and social connections did not need subliminal suggestions on audio cassettes, or self-help seminars, or determination, perseverance, and the will to succeed, in order to climb the golden ladder of success. They were destined to climb it, destined to be among the movers and shakers. They were the lucky ones, the chosen few.

And then there were the losers, the vast majority, the pathetic hopefuls who took the dress-for-success courses and read the *How to Make Your Fortune in Tupperware* books and sent in their $12.95 for offers of instant wealth beyond their dreams.

He was one of them, a loser superior to all the other losers of the world in one way only. He'd peeked behind the curtain. He'd read the playbook. He was in on the con.

No illusions, not for him. He knew the game of life

was rigged and only suckers played to win. It was his sole claim to wisdom. He might be a nobody going nowhere, he might be a cosmic accident of no significance, but at least he wasn't one of the chumps on the midway who ponied up their wages to take a chance on fortune's spinning wheel.

If he had to be numbered among life's losers, at least he had the good grace to own up to it and the dignity to take it in stride. It wasn't a lot, maybe; but it was all he had.

Alex reached the dog and stood over it, staring down.

The dog was a collie and it had been ripped open and turned nearly inside-out.

# 2

"WYLIE. EAT your Fruit Loops, dear. Before they get soggy."

"Not hungry."

"Don't be difficult."

"Not."

"We don't want a spanking this early in the morning, do we, young lady?"

Wylie Elizabeth Gaines, eight years old, dipped her spoon morosely into her cereal bowl, then stuffed it into her pouting mouth. Her cheeks expanded like pink balloons. Her lips puckered. She did not chew.

"Swallow it," said Barbara Gaines. Her gray eyes had narrowed, aging her still-pretty face, unlined at thirty-one. A bright red spot stood out on her forehead between strands of chestnut hair like a smear of rouge.

Wylie hesitated, contemplated the probable consequences of refusal, and swallowed. The air went out of her cheeks, and her eyes were once again hooded by lowered lids. She stared down at the cereal bowl. She did not take another mouthful.

Barbara Gaines looked at her husband with *that* expression on her face. Paul Gaines sighed and put down the two-week-old *U.S. News* he had been pretending to read. He supposed he should do something. The trouble was, he didn't know what. He never knew. Barbara was the disciplinarian of the Gaines household. She had always said that Paul was too soft, too willing to give in, to spoil the child. She was right. He wanted nothing more than to give in right now. He glanced at Barbara, standing by the open door of the dishwasher with one of last night's plates in her hands. Her gunmetal eyes read his mind and dared him, just dared him to do it.

Paul Gaines was not one to take his wife up on a dare. He was a tall man, but slightly built, with stooped shoulders and sagging jowls that made him look older than thirty-five. His eyes were a very pale blue that seemed faded, like worn denim. They were nervous, wandering eyes—like his hands, slender, long-fingered hands always looking for a pencil to tap or a paper clip to bend.

He had failed as a lawyer in Aberdeen and now made a comfortably dull living as a partner in Sea Cove's only law firm. Normally he left the domestic duties to Barbara, an arrangement which, though old-fashioned, suited them both. Today, however, a little fatherly discipline seemed called for.

"Wylie," he said tentatively.

The big eyelids were lifted. The gray eyes, so like her mother's, peeked up forlornly.

"You understand why we we're being ... why we're being kind of rough on you. Don't you, kiddo?"

"I was bad."

"You were."

"I'm sorry."

"I hope so."

"Now can we go look?"

Paul felt his resolve, such as it was, melting away. Barbara saw indecision in the drumming of her husband's knuckles on the table.

"No," she said with quiet firmness, "we will not go look."

"But ..."

"You remember what we said last time." Wylie's eyes were downcast again. "Don't you?"

"We said Buster is my dog. And I have to take care of him."

"Which means?"

"Lock the gate."

"Or else?"

"Buster will get out."

*You're leading the witness,* Paul Gaines observed silently. He had often thought his wife would make a better attorney than he had. Prosecuting attorney, of course.

"And why did we agree to do that?"

Wylie said nothing. *Take the fifth, kiddo,* Paul advised. *It's your only chance.*

"Because," Barbara said in reply to her own question, "Buster has gotten out through that gate five times. And every time it's because Someone We All Know forgot to lock the gate. And every time your daddy and I have had to go out in the middle of the night and look for Buster. Until finally we informed That Certain Party that if she forgot, one more time, she would just have to hope Buster found his way back on his own."

"But, Mommy, he's lost!"

"He'll be all right," Paul said soothingly. He patted his daughter's arm. He remembered when her whole body had barely been bigger than that arm. "He'll be back by tonight. Dogs always find their way home."

"Then why'd you and Mommy go out looking for him all the other times?"

Outwitted by an eight-year-old.

Secretly he had an answer, but it was not admissible in this court. Buster would be home by tonight because, once Wylie went off to school on the little yellow school bus that arrived every weekday morning at 8:15, Paul would hurry off himself. But not to the office. He was going to drive the Tempo down the back roads, honking his horn, till he found Buster loping along with his tail between his legs. "Hey, honey, guess what! The animal pound called me at work and ..."

There were holes in his story. Why would the pound call him at work when Buster's tag was inscribed with their home phone number? *Answer the question, please, Mr. Gaines.* What would he say if Barbara had called him at work in the meantime and learned he wasn't there? Or if Gary, his partner, called her, asking where in the hell was Paul and what in Christ's name was going on with the Larson briefs? *How does the defendant explain this contradiction in the testimony?*

Paul Gaines looked at his daughter. Wylie's pleading eyes still gazed at him with her unanswered question. They were huge and almost perfectly round, a doll's eyes. His little doll. Really, they were not her mother's eyes at all. He knew he would carry out his plan despite the risks.

There was a fleck of milk on Wylie's chin from her single mouthful of cereal. Paul dabbed it away with a corner of his napkin.

"We went out looking because it was night," he answered, perjuring himself, "and dogs have trouble finding their way home at night. But now that it's daytime, Buster won't have any trouble at all."

"Oh."

She seemed dubious. He smiled, an easy lying smile that reassured her.

Barbara, putting away the cereal boxes and milk, regarded her husband with pursed lips and narrowed eyes.

*She's on to me,* Paul realized with a sinking feeling. Then he saw that his daughter was eating, actually chewing and swallowing, her soggy Fruit Loops, and suddenly he just didn't give a damn what Barbara Gaines thought.

# 3

KARL MASTERSON had been up for more than two hours when the telephone rang at 7:45.

He was a man of regular habits. Every morning he awoke at precisely 5:30. He never used an alarm clock. His body was its own clock, ticking off seconds with Teutonic efficiency. At the stroke of the half hour, he simply opened his eyes, took a deep breath, and got out of bed.

Fifty push-ups to get the blood circulating. Twenty sit-ups in the modified-bent-knee position. Then he dressed in a jogging suit, quietly, because he did not wish to disturb the lady still fast asleep in his bed. He blew her a kiss, a romantic vanity but a negligible one, before leaving the bedroom.

Then it was down the curving staircase, under the crystal chandelier, and out onto the grounds of his ranch. His dogs were still asleep in their pens in the long gray kennel building as he broke into a trot, then a jog, then a run. He covered the perimeter of the ranch eight times, which made four miles, in twenty-eight minutes.

He thought of nothing as he ran. He let the cold air wash over him, wash him clean. He breathed out bad thoughts and drew in fresh, healthy, living air. He felt renewed and vital and strong.

He *was* strong. It was the first impression Karl Masterson made on people, and the lasting one. There was his size, of course, two hundred forty pounds of hard muscle spread over a six-foot-six frame. He seemed to be constructed out of solid blocks—the immense cylinders of his legs, the square torso, the jutting shoulders, and the square-jawed, hairless, bullet-shaped skull. His head, people said, was like a battering ram. Masterson was inclined to agree. He had spent most of the fifty-two years of his life butting down obstacles, and he had used his head to do it.

After the run he let himself into his private gym, where his forty thousand dollars' worth of equipment awaited him like a collection of Erector Set assemblies cast in stainless steel. He worked the Nautilus and the rowing machine and did some bench-pressing, light work. Then he showered, scalding hot water followed by icy cold.

In a terry-cloth robe and bare feet he walked from the gym to the explosion of white light and curving Formica countertops that was his kitchen. Breakfast, at 7:00 precisely, was a glass of orange juice, fresh-squeezed; a bowl of wheat bran and wheat germ sprinkled with fresh sliced fruit and skim milk; whole-wheat toast with a dab of honey; 1,000 mg. of vitamin C in two time-release capsules; and a yogurt-and-egg shake, flavored with a mashed banana.

At 7:25 he ascended the stairs. Nikki was groaning irritably in bed.

"Wake-up time," Karl Masterson purred, his German accent barely noticeable after years of effort directed toward its eradication.

"God, you get up early," Nikki moaned. She buried her face in a pillow and let her ash-blonde hair stream around her head like the rays of a star. "I don't know how you do it. I need at least a good, solid, two hours' sleep every night. What time *did* we get to sleep last night, anyway?"

"It wasn't last night. It was this morning."

"That's what I thought."

"I don't see why you should be tired. I did all the work."

She lifted her head with some notion of a swift retort, but let it die. He was selecting his clothes from the closet, standing with his back to her, with only the robe to stress the outlines of his body. She liked to watch him that way. She rested her head in the crook of an arm and lay still, perfectly content, until he became aware of her scrutiny and turned.

The slow smile on her face answered his unasked question.

"Thought you were worn out," he said softly.

"Uh-uh. Well rested now."

"We'll see what we can do about that."

He stripped off the robe and tossed it aside and crossed the space between them in two strides. His giant hands closed over her shoulders, thin and trembling, then drew her up, half out of bed, as he bent from the waist and kissed her, in a way that was gallant and mocking at once. Her hands were rubbing his chest, making slow, expert circles. Ordinarily he would have taken his time, but he found as she touched him that he wanted her now, urgently, and he took her without preliminaries, with only the squeeze of his hands on her buttocks and the grinding of his chest against her breasts and the sudden meeting of their hips in a series of shudders that rose to a racking eruption. He rolled off her and lay by her side, his eyes closed.

"Sorry," he said, catching his breath. "Too fast."

She kissed his shoulder. "Just right," she whispered.

"No. It wasn't good. Not for you, I mean. Come here. I know what you like."

He did know, if anybody did, and he was just beginning to prove it with the slow, practiced probing of his tongue when the phone rang.

"Goddammit." He had to answer it. They both knew that. He rolled away from her and picked up the black telephone handset. "Masterson."

She rubbed his back, enjoying the ripple of corded muscle under her hands.

"What are you talking about?"

She noted the concern in his voice. She rubbed harder.

"All right. I'll get on it."

He cradled the phone and stared into space. She felt the tension stiffening his muscles, drawing the massive plates of his shoulder blades closer together like drifting continents on a collision course.

She did not have to ask. He would tell her. She was his assistant, wasn't she? *Don't laugh,* she told her friends. *I'm a damn good one.* She was.

"The four dogs we trucked to Manhattan never arrived," he said finally. "Warehouse manager wants to know where they are. That's what I get for hiring free-lance."

"You didn't have much choice with Delgado out sick and Prentice doing the drive to Atlanta."

"Yes. Right."

Her reassurance hadn't helped. She stopped massaging and swung her long legs around to sit next to him on the edge of the bed.

"So where are they?" she asked meaninglessly.

Masterson did not answer.

# 4

RAZOR WAS tired. He had not slept in twenty-four hours. His paws were sore and his bruised shank was stiff. His companions, trotting behind him in a ragged line, were in no better shape.

They might have rested early this morning, but the Bad Dog had spotted them first. The dog had come ambling down a dirt road when Razor was guiding the pack across. The world was still dark, with only the hint of a sunrise on the blue-black horizon, and Razor could not see the dog clearly. But he could see well enough to know that the dog was padding forward, tail wagging, ears pricked up alertly, in a way that Wylie Gaines would have recognized. *Buster wants to play,* she would have said. And when Buster barked—*woof*—and wagged his tail harder, Wylie Gaines would have giggled, knowing it was only a game Buster played with all unfamiliar dogs, a silly doggie game, because her big, fluffy collie would never hurt anybody or anything.

Razor knew nothing of games. He did not know how dogs like Buster made friends. Razor had never made friends with any animal. The concept itself was beyond his capacity. The pack at his heels were not friends, merely comrades bound to their leader out of the common instinct of survival. This new dog was an outsider, an intruder, and he was challenging the pack with his wagging tail and his *woof woof woof.* He was a Bad Dog. He was an enemy.

Razor slunk toward the collie with his head low and

his eyes dangerous, his black velvet coat rippling sensuously. The other three stayed back, held in place by some unspoken command. Razor had claimed this kill for his own.

The collie named Buster seemed to sense the sudden danger. He took a step back, confused, fully prepared to back off if this particular dog did not want to make friends. All the other dogs Buster had ever met had made friends with him easily. The Cobbs' Dalmatian, Barney, would romp and bark at him all day in playful combat. The Whittakers had two big old mutts, Jake and Jasper, who liked to roll around with Buster and slobber on him. But this dog here, this stalking, catlike shape, all liquid tension and crescent-moon fangs, this dog was different, and Wylie's dog Buster felt a slow, prickling sensation of fear. He took another step back.

Razor smelled the Bad Dog's fear and liked that smell. It was nearly as sweet as blood. The association made him salivate. Without further thought he tensed down on his haunches, tightened his buttocks, and drew his head back, till he was coiled like a steel spring, like a rattlesnake.

He hesitated for one moment, not from any flicker of doubt, but merely to drink in one more tantalizing whiff of the retreating collie's fear and to taste the delicious moisture in his mouth. Then he leaped.

His body arced through the air, slicing distance like a knife, and landed directly on top of the collie, and then the two dogs were a dissonance of yelps and barks, a frenzied blur of black-on-white, till the purity of the stark tones was shattered by a jet of scarlet.

Razor's teeth had found the collie's throat and split it open and now Buster lay on his back, strangling on his own blood and still wagging his tail, piteously, as Razor's claws dissected the white belly as neatly as a scalpel. Then the Doberman was pawing at the collie's entrails, spilling them onto the road, and nosing in deeper, drowning his muzzle in gore, tearing at heart and lungs and intestines, wrenching them loose, until the dead collie was hollowed out, a shell of bone and bloody fur, its vital parts hanging out like the wires and clock-spring gears of a wind-up dog pulled apart by a curious child.

Razor rubbed his snout on his paws and licked them clean, enjoying the fresh blood taste. The other three, Bigfoot, Cleo, and Mr. Dobbs, still stood waiting and panting raggedly when Razor returned to them and led them on.

Now they were deep in the pine forest and the pred-awn kill was only a vague memory. The sun had been up for some time and the day was unseasonably warm, and Razor knew his need for rest could be postponed no longer. He stopped and drew in several deep smells and listened warily. No danger signals reached his senses. This was a safe place. A place to sleep and restore his energy. He padded into a leafy glen, settled down in a sphinxlike pose, and was asleep in the instant when his head touched his front paws.

The other three did likewise. They slept in a tight circle under the trees. Cleo's stomach muttered and Bigfoot kept on drooling sloppily and Mr. Dobbs woke up from time to time to change position, none of which was unusual.

Razor did not stir. He slept without cares, without dreams, his eyes shut tight, a splash of dried blood darkening the skin around his mouth.

# 5

JESSIE BLAIR stood on the front porch of the Oceanview Inn, her hands on the railing, looking out to sea.

Past the boardwalk, the narrow jetty jutted into the Atlantic, knocking back the waves in bright splashes of foam. A fisherman stood on a rock at the end of the jetty, waiting resolutely for a tug at one of his lines. Jessie would be willing to bet he had been there since dawn. She felt a stab of empathy with him, as she glanced self-consciously at her watch for only the fifth time.

He was late and she, for no logical reason at all, was irritated. After all, for God's sake, it wasn't as if he had an appointment with her. She just happened to be out on the porch every morning when he turned down the corner of her street, that's all. Just ... happened.

She brushed reddish-blond curls from her eyes and turned her profile to the sea to glance down First Avenue again. An observer, had there been one, would have noted the high forehead revealed in that profile, with the hair cut short and swept back, the nose that turned up just slightly too much and the mouth which never looked more than an instant away from a smile. Then she turned back to the sea, gazing at its mysteries with dark green eyes, wide-set in a freckled face scrubbed red by the wind.

The observer might well have concluded that she was younger than her age, twenty-eight, and pretty in a girl-next-door sort of way, which was not far from Jessie's own opinion.

The sound of a car drew her glance back to First Avenue. *Well, what do you know, there he is. And speeding, too, going forty at least, must be late for work. Oh, hell, does this mean he won't have time to stop?*

She waved to him, feeling foolish and flustered, as always, and hating the way her heart thumped at her eardrums.

The Pinto turned the corner and braked at the curb, and Alex Driscoll got out.

"Howdy, stranger!" he yelled.

"Top o' the mornin' to ye, Mr. Driscoll," she called back in a put-on Irish accent as she hurried gratefully to the side railing.

It was a ritual of theirs, this exchange of greetings, a ritual that had been going on for eight months now, long enough to make it a tradition almost. Well, that was appropriate. The Oceanview Inn was a place for traditions, if for nothing else.

The hotel had gone up in 1920, in the age when Sea Cove had emerged from nowhere to become the mecca of the Northeastern seaboard for the restless rich, who migrated here each summer in their chauffeured motorcars. By day they splashed in the surf in the one-piece swimsuits that had looked so very chic then, so ridiculous now in the faded photographs that hung on the lobby walls; by night they twirled in the ballrooms of the town's great hotels. The Oceanview had never been one of them, never the equal of the Suffolk with its Doric columns in the neoclassical style, nor of the Wellington House, its high-ceilinged lobby awash with the candlelight of a dozen crystal chandeliers. But still, her grandparents' place had been popular and crowded and oh so very exclusive. Scott Fitzgerald and Zelda had stayed here for the month of August in 1922, in Room 39B, a small room with wide bay windows framing the gray Atlantic. Perhaps in that room, as he sat in the overstuffed armchair staring out to sea, Fitzgerald had conceived the character of Jay Gatsby. Jessie had no proof, but the fancy pleased her.

The hotel sat on a hill. To the east it overlooked only First Avenue, the boardwalk, and the sea. It was a sprawling, ungainly heap, three stories piled on top of each other like the layers of a cake, with rococo dribbles of icing and a chocolate frosting which was the black-shingled roof, currently in need of only minor repair. There were forty-four rooms, all cramped, not including the restaurant downstairs, closed for years, and the game room, a shadowed hideaway of pine wall panels, green baize billiard tables, soft lights in tinted shades, and bookcases that concealed what had been liquor cabinets. Prohibition had never been more than a nuisance in Sea Cove.

Jessica Blair was now the third generation of Blairs to hold title to the Oceanview Inn. She loved the old place for its memories, which were not even her memories, mostly, but memories belonging to guests long dead, memories of poker games played in clouds of pipe smoke for lunatic stakes, of the pop and fizz of bootleg champagne and the distant, answering echo of firecrackers on the Fourth of July, of women with long suntanned legs and Clara Bow eyes who gathered around the swimming pool to laugh and chatter while the band played "I've Got a Crush on You."

For the sake of those memories she had kept the Oceanview alive, fighting a desperate, hopeless battle. The Suffolk had been leveled ten years ago, rows of houses stood on the land now, and the Wellington was being renovated and made into condos. The glory days of Sea Cove were long past. Today and for many years the restless rich went to Monte Carlo or Malta or wherever the wealthy went, and the crowds of less affluent vacationers who flocked to the Jersey Shore either headed down to Atlantic City and Beach Haven or holed up in the Howard Johnson, the Ramada, or the Marriott out on the highway.

They preferred the motels, the tranquilizing sameness of the abstract wall prints and sterilized toilet seats and complimentary soap. They did not want the drafty, musty charms of an era that had come and gone before they were born.

She did have some guests, fewer each summer, none—almost none—in the off-season. She made a marginal profit in the summer, took a serious loss in the winter, and was going bankrupt very fast. She would have to sell the place after next season, she knew. They would tear it down and put up condos, if the town council approved, or houses, otherwise. Then there would be nothing left of that dead past, nothing save her faded photographs and, somewhere, the fading memories of ghosts.

"I tell you, it's been one of those days." Alex Driscoll flashed the crooked smile that said he wasn't complaining because one could expect no better.

"Already?" She glanced at her watch, pretending it was for the first time. "It's only eight thirty. That's hardly enough time for it to be one of those days."

Alex told her what he had found on Potters Road and how he had called the police from the Andersons' farm. She listened attentively and let herself look at him, as he stood at the crest of the hill on the other side of the porch rail.

She did not know if he could be called good looking. She doubted it, but he had a kind, slightly sad face she liked, a face that captured some quality of the photos in the lobby. He was a head taller than she, which was not tall, since in her stocking feet she stood barely five foot two. The eyes behind his thick glasses were intelligent, dryly humorous, a shade cynical, and a very pure blue. They were his best feature. The rest of him, all narrow shoulders and unkempt brown hair, was hardly the stuff of a lady's dreams. Well, most ladies, anyway.

Each morning he stopped to talk on his way back to

his apartment down the street, before hurrying off to work at the Sea Cove *Citizen,* the weekly newspaper. He seemed to enjoy talking with her, but he had never asked her out. There was a barrier between them, dividing them as neatly as the porch rail, a barrier she did not understand and could not cross.

"So whose dog was it, do you think?" she heard herself asking.

"Ben Harper told me it belonged to the Gaines family. You know, Paul Gaines, he's a lawyer, has an office on the South End."

"I've heard the name."

"I interviewed him once. Nice enough."

"It's a shame. About the dog, I mean." She ran a hand through her hair and added, more brightly, "But I still think it's a beautiful day."

"I'm not arguing. Too bad the leaves fell early, though. The trees seemed a lot more colorful when I was a kid. Didn't the shore used to have better autumns then?"

"I think so. Maybe it's just ... memories. Like, sometimes I think the ocean used to be bluer." She chuckled. "Crazy."

"Tell you one thing, the beaches used to be a lot bigger."

"God, yes. That beach out there shrinks a little more every year."

"Everything changes. You ever think about how much has changed in this town? The way it must have been fifty, sixty years ago?"

*All the time.* "Sometimes."

He seemed to have heard the answer she hadn't given. He rapped the railing, once. "I guess living here, it's hard not to."

"I won't be living here much longer."

He looked at her. She had not meant to say it, and instantly she regretted it. The words were too much an admission of defeat. And she hadn't liked how her voice had cracked.

"Business that bad?" he asked carefully.

"Worse."

"Heating bills must eat you alive."

"Well, thank God, I can close off the upstairs and let thirty rooms freeze. Otherwise I'd have sold out ten years ago." *When I was eighteen. Then I could have had a life. Now I've got ten years of memories that aren't my own.*

She saw the look of honest concern on his face and loved him for it. He was, at least, her friend. She didn't have many. He cared for her, cared about her. He even let it show, sometimes.

She smiled and added with false cheerfulness, "I do have a guest now, though. One."

"In October?"

She nodded, amused at his astonishment, and lowered her voice. "Kind of a strange one, actually. Ragged-looking guy. Checked in at seven this morning—woke me up. No car, no luggage, just a backpack. He must be traveling around the country or something. Anyway, his credit card is good."

"What's his name?"

Jessie thought for a moment. "Tuttle," she said. "Mike Tuttle."

# 6

WYLIE HAD left on her school bus ten minutes ago, and Paul Gaines was about to head off to the office—or so he said—when the doorbell chimed.

His eyes met Barbara's.

"Maybe someone found him," she said with an unmistakable note of relief.

Paul crossed the living room, too quickly, to the front door. He opened it.

Ben Harper stood there, lips pursed.

Paul's heart sank. The expression on Harper's face told the story, even before he spoke.

"Mr. Gaines. Afraid I've got bad news about your dog."

Paul let him in, and he and his wife exchanged mumbled hellos with their chief of police, whom they knew slightly, the same way everybody in Sea Cove knew Ben Harper. It was not that Ben was unpopular, just ... remote, a bachelor ten years past the age when bachelorhood is envied, a man with a tomcat, a cottage on Peach Street, and a fondness for old movies; you could see him sometimes, alone, at the Rivoli when they had Nostalgia Night, seated in the back row, watching Bogart and Tracy and Paul Muni, his face expressionless.

He was a short, squat fireplug of a man with a nose badly busted—how, nobody knew—so that it lay crosswise on his face like a shapeless lump of flesh. The nose made his eyes look small and slitted, but still kindly, with cheerful crinkles at the corners. Ben played Santa Claus every Christmas for the kids at the medical center in

Asbury. The kind eyes and the snowdrift of false beard he attached via rubber band made the impersonation work, but in his ordinary line of duties he looked more like a boxer in one of those old movies, the gutsy little guy, Cagney maybe, who had been pummeled too many times in too many rings, who had taken a lot of beatings but never a dive. People didn't socialize much with Ben Harper, but they trusted him, and maybe that was enough.

Ben told the Gaineses how their collie had been found on Potters Road early this morning and how he had identified it by the tag on the collar. Paul remembered, for no particular reason, the way Buster used to chase his little girl, squealing in delight, around the backyard till finally she gave up and hugged him and they rolled over and over in the grass, her squirming body lost in the collie's black-and-white blur. He felt his eyes burning.

"Was he hit by a car?" Barbara asked. She looked suddenly pale. Her lips kept moving even after all the words were out.

Ben Harper hesitated. "No. He was ... mauled ... by an animal of some sort. Lots of animals in those woods, you know. Foxes. That's probably what did it. They raid the Andersons' henhouse some nights."

"I've never heard of a fox attacking a dog," muttered Paul, who had never heard anything at all about the subject, truthfully, but whose mind was replaying a movie scene of a foxhunt across the British moors. "Aren't foxes scared of dogs?"

"Mostly, yes. But there's always rabies. Rabid animal will attack anything. I want Dr. Simpson to look into that." Dr. Simpson was the local veterinarian, the same one who had given Buster pills to prevent heartworm. Buster was outside a lot—in the backyard, rolling in the grass with Wylie—and Paul had worried about heartworm.

"It's awful," said Barbara, her voice so low it was hard to hear. Paul took her hand reflexively and squeezed it, while inside he vacillated between sympathy and vindictiveness: *Got what you wanted, Miss Discipline?* Sympathy won. He knew this was not what she had wanted.

"I'm sorry, folks," said Ben heavily. "I know a pet is like ... like part of the family. I'm sorry for your little girl too."

Paul told him it was all right and Barbara thanked him for coming over to give the news in person, and they all shook hands and Paul let Ben out the front door. Then he and Barbara watched Ben Harper drive away in the green-and-white squad car. They stood in the doorway a long time, watching, even when there was nothing more to watch because the car was long gone and the road was empty and silent.

- — -

Ben Harper drove down to Route 35, then cut over to 71 and turned east on Hampton Avenue, heading into town. The railroad tracks buffeted the car, and looking down the tracks he could see the retreating square of the Jersey Central 9:05, next stop Manasecon, then Belmar. Then he was on Main Street in Sea Cove's downtown.

His mind, however, was not on the passing scenery. No, his mind was on a dead collie and a lie about a rabid fox. Fox, hell. No fox had done that. Foxes went after chickens. A rabid fox might conceivably attack a dog, though Ben had never heard an instance of it. But rabid or not, it surely would not, could not, mangle a pooch the way the Gaineses' dog had been mangled. No, the thing that had gone to work on that dog was bigger game. Something like a mountain lion, except there were no mountain lions in Jersey. Were there? Or a bear, but in his forty-eight years spent in Sea Cove, his whole life, Ben Harper had never heard of a bear in these parts. Maybe he should check around and see if any animals had escaped from a zoo or a circus or that Lion Country Safari out by Lakewood. It was a hell of a long shot. But something had taken the insides out of that dog, that was for damn sure.

He passed Johnson's bakery and Sam Tirelli's barbershop and the Gentle Reader Book Store, and there, squeezed between Gladys Rumson's ice cream parlor and the Carroways' clothing store, was the glorified shoebox that Ed Clancy had long ago designated the editorial and publishing offices of the Sea Cove *Citizen*. This week's edition was due out today. That thought stirred another worry in Ben Harper's mind.

Alex Driscoll had found the dog, and Alex was Ed Clancy's entire editorial staff, juggling the roles of reporter, copy editor, and errand boy. Ben read the *Citizen,* of course; everybody did; and about half the articles in it had Alex's byline. Ben's worry was that Alex would make a page-one headliner out of dead Buster and scare folks half to death: DOG HORRIBLY MAULED. WILD ANIMAL ON THE LOOSE. POLICE HELPLESS.

But Alex wouldn't do that. Would he?

Ben had gone over to the Andersons' as soon as the desk sergeant on the day shift had gotten the call. Alex was there waiting for him. Together, in the squad car, Alex and Ben had crawled a mile and a half up Potters Road till Alex pointed out the dog. They got out and looked it over and Ben had felt like puking, and would have if he'd been alone, but he restrained himself in the presence of the press. Then Ben had checked the ID tag that confirmed his suspicion. It was the Gaineses' dog. He told Alex as much, though in hindsight that was a mistake. Never tell a reporter anything he doesn't ask. Well, too late now.

Ben had carefully bundled up the dog in heavy plastic and loaded it into the trunk of the squad car, and he and Alex had driven back to Alex's Pinto in silence. But before letting Alex out, Ben had asked him not to play up the story too big, please, because hey, Alex, it could get a lot of people worked up. Alex had shrugged and said sure, he wasn't going to sensationalize the thing, just a small item in today's edition. He wasn't trying to get on the wire with this one, not to worry, Chief.

Ben Harper worried anyway.

MYSTERY MAULER MANGLES MUTT.

Oh, hell, Alex wouldn't do that.

Besides, Ben Harper had bigger worries on his mind.

There was a thing out there in the woods, a thing that had already struck once. And as he pulled the squad car into its parking space behind the police station, Ben felt suddenly, deep in his gut where the warning signals always came, that soon, very soon, that thing would strike again.

# 7

THE KID lay in his bed in the Oceanview Inn, staring up at the ceiling, thinking.

Things had gotten pretty damn messed up last night, that was for sure, and for a while he had been depressed, until he realized it wasn't his fault. No. It was all the fault of the driver, Tuttle. The son of a bitch refused to cooperate, even with a knife at his neck. He had fought back, nearly gotten both of them killed—and what for? To protect his stinking little Tonka Toy truck and whatever worthless crap it was hauling. The kid shook his head, his lips twisted tight in contempt. Some people just didn't know how to be robbed.

If Tuttle had played the game like he was supposed to, he wouldn't have gotten hurt. Probably. Although you never could tell. That knife had been awful sharp. It would have been fun to watch Tuttle's eyes bulge as the blade slit his throat.

The kid had not killed often—only three times—but whenever he did, he enjoyed it. Especially the first time. He sighed. He guessed your first time was always the best. Like your first car or your first love.

Mary Ann Foster had been his first love, and his first kill. He had asked her out and she had laughed in his face and said he was a creep. Said she didn't like a guy who was a shoplifter with a police record. Said she wouldn't go out with him if he was the only guy in school. And she had walked away down the hallway, leaving him stung and humiliated and close to tears. People had heard her, too. Everybody had heard. That only made it worse.

The hurt didn't last long. By evening it had been replaced by quiet rage. Who was she to turn him down? Laugh at him? Criticize? She was nothing. She was worthless. He could kill her so easily, easy as stomping on a bug.

He began to make plans.

When Mary Ann Foster went into the girls' restroom on a Thursday afternoon three weeks later, she found him waiting for her. He had pried loose the faucet from one of the sinks and was tapping it slowly, methodically, against his open palm. She tried to run. He grabbed her. She almost had time to scream before he bludgeoned her face. He could still hear the satisfying meat thud of the steel pipe against her forehead. She sprawled half-conscious on the tile floor, and he battered her again and again until her rouged cheeks were streaked with blood and bits of broken teeth spilled out from her puffed lips.

He beat her to death, then fled.

The police came to his parents' house two days later and arrested him. Somebody had found the bloody faucet, which he'd dumped in a trash bin near the school. The fingerprints on it matched the prints in his police file.

He wasn't scared. His lawyer told him just what to do. He claimed that the murder was an act of impulse. He hadn't known what he was doing. He felt remorse. All bullshit. But they bought it, all right, they ate it up, and when he broke down and cried on the witness stand there wasn't a dry eye in the house, except his.

He was declared not guilty by reason of temporary insanity and remanded to the custody of an institution for rehabilitation. He was good at rehabilitation. He quickly learned what the doctors wished to hear him say. After fifteen months the experts diagnosed him cured. He was set free to assume his normal place in society.

He had done so. His normal place, as he saw it, was as an outsider, a drifter, a loner. He had no patience for rules, for routines, for work. The very thought of a nine-to-five job made him sick. He wanted excitement. The kind of excitement he'd felt when Mary Ann's pretty face caved in. The excitement he felt, in smaller doses, whenever he slipped a can of Bud under his jacket or a carving knife up his sleeve and strolled out of the store, so cool, so casual. Like a gambler, he lived for the thrill of risking everything on one spin of the wheel.

Last night, the odds had worked against him; but what the hell, there would be other nights.

After the truck had crashed, he'd panicked. He had to admit it. He was so wired, he could have sworn he heard wolves howling, like in the horror movies. He had to get away. He glanced at Tuttle's motionless body, pronounced him dead, lifted his wallet, and ran.

He stumbled raggedly through the woods to Route 35, then trudged east, toward the pale promise of a sunrise, and ended up three miles later on First Avenue in Sea Cove. Dawn was breaking over the ocean. He felt the need to be indoors, out of sight. He walked north along the boardwalk for more than a mile before he spotted the peeling vacancy sign outside the Oceanview.

The doorbell summoned a pretty young lady who seemed to be the manager, a lady who was sleepy-eyed, wearing a tossed-on blouse and blue jeans and a bird's nest of uncombed reddish-blond hair. She was astonished that he wanted a room. She let him in the way one might let in a long-lost relative, believed dead.

The credit card was good, thank God. She asked for payment in advance, and he fumbled with the wallet, hoping it contained something other than yellowed snapshots and a driver's license. It was a calculated risk, using a card with Tuttle's name; it could lead the police straight to him, if they found the truck and identified the body. He didn't care. He liked risks. Just one more spin of the wheel.

He made some kind of senseless conversation with the woman, whose name was Jessica-Blair-but-everybody-calls-me-Jessie, while she processed the card, handed it back, and turned to a rack behind the desk. The room keys hung there, each by a different mail slot. She scanned the keys, deciding which room to give him. He looked idly over her shoulder and noticed that all of the keys were there, none taken, and he remembered her surprise at having a guest check in, and with a sudden mental click like the tumblers of a lock falling into place, he realized that the hotel was empty, that he was the only guest, that there was almost certainly no live-in staff, that he and Jessica Blair were alone together in this great, dusty, echoing cave of a building, where no one would ever hear her screams.

His eyes, studying her as she plucked a key from the rack and turned, rose from the slender hips to the small rounded breasts outlined in the pastel blue of her blouse, to the sunburst of freckles on her cleavage, to the delicate arms, the smooth skin of her neck, to her mouth, moving as she talked, saying something about his room number, and to her eyes, bright and wide awake now. How her mouth would twist and her eyes bulge—like Mary Ann Foster's, he thought—when she was spread-eagled under him and his knife was making red slash marks every-where ...

He smiled politely as he took the key and reached into the pocket of his corduroy jacket, where he kept his knife.

The pocket was empty.

The knife was gone.

He had left it in Mike Tuttle's dead body.

He could not carve up the woman without the knife, so the desire had left him, just like that.

But now the desire was back.

After all, he could always get himself a new knife—couldn't he?

# 8

THE SEA Cove *Citizen* was a tradition which, not unlike Sea Cove itself, persisted for no very logical reason, out of sheer obstinate resistance to what people called progress. The *Citizen*'s resistance took the form of one man, Edward Drinker Clancy, editor-in-chief, a robust seventy-seven-year-old with a mane of white hair and an imperious manner that gave him a passing resemblance to Frank Lloyd Wright.

Ed Clancy stood in a corner of the *Citizen*'s editorial offices, studying his staff, whose name was Alex Driscoll.

Alex's chance discovery on Potters Road had forced a last-minute insert on an inside page of today's edition. Two paragraphs, composed on the typewriter by Alex in his straightforward style, had given all the relevant facts. No mention was made of the details of the animal's condition. Anyone reading the piece would no doubt assume that the Gaineses' dog had been hit by a car. That was fine. People read the *Citizen* while eating lunch, and there was no cause to make anybody sick. Besides, Ben Harper had asked Alex to play down the gory stuff.

At the moment, Alex was building a rather elaborate structure out of pencils and bottles of Liquid Paper. The Liquid Paper, stacked precariously in three-bottle columns, supported the pencils, which ran as crosswise beams. Alex picked up another pencil and chewed on the eraser while contemplating possible improvements in his design. There was nothing else to do till the *Citizen* was run off.

"Alex."

"Ummm." Still concentrating on his creation.

"You look at me when I talk to you."

Alex looked. There was no resentment in his face. There never was, no matter how his boss snapped at him or ordered him around. There was only the hint of a smile, that slow, sad, cynical smile of his. Ed Clancy didn't like that smile. A young man shouldn't wear a face like that. That was an old man's face.

Ed hesitated. He hated to ask a personal question of Alex or of anybody, but he hated even more to be kept in the dark when there was something he wanted to know. *Well, ask it, then.* Ed Clancy was not a man for preliminaries.

"Alex, what the hell kind of life is this for you?"

The suggestion of a smile did not waver. "Come again."

"You're a young man. You should be out dallying with the ladies, seeking fame and fortune, *doing* things. When I was your age I went out west to Hollywood, California. Nineteen hundred and thirty-eight, it was. I had failed at everything else so I decided to be a movie star. I starved. Never worked once in a picture, not even extra work. Lived in a loft with six other starving young hopefuls just like me. Nothing ever became of any of us, far as I know. It was the Depression and we were all out of work, hiding from the landlord, guzzling nickel booze we couldn't afford. They were great times.

"I met a girl. She wanted to be a starlet, every girl did, prettiest little thing you ever saw. Rose Ashton she called herself, though her real name was Peggy Ann Mulligan, from Sioux Falls, South Dakota. I used to swipe flowers from the graves of dead movie stars at Forest Lawn so I could have roses to bring her. I wrote poetry on little cards. 'A rose for Rose'—oh, God, such dreadful stuff ..."

He realized his memories were carrying him away again, back to the past, when all the colors had been so bright, and now you looked at black-and-white movies from those days on the Late Show and it wasn't the same. He shook his head slowly. "My point is, boy, you should be out in the world, having adventures, falling in love, while you're young and you've got the chance."

"Maybe I should sign up as a cabin boy on a tramp steamer," said Alex dryly.

"Maybe you damn well should."

"Sorry, Ed. I get seasick."

He was still smiling, that half-hidden smile that said he was onto the biggest joke in the world, and the hint of despair that said the joke was on him.

"You know," said Ed slowly, "if I were your age, I don't think I would sign up on a tramp steamer. But I'd ask Jessie Blair out to dinner. That, I'd do."

"Jessie ...?"

"Don't play dumb with me. Every damn morning you two are out there in front of her hotel making a public spectacle of yourselves, but I've never once seen you try to press your luck."

Alex's smile was gone, replaced by the self-conscious pursing of his lips. "How do you know these things?"

"Birds tell me."

"What makes you think Jessica Blair would want to go out with me?"

"What makes you think she wouldn't?"

"She could do a lot better." The half-smile was back. Ed hated it, in that moment, more than ever.

He shook his head sadly. "Boy, you need to do yourself some good hard thinking."

He disappeared behind the closed door of his office, and Alex was left alone with his pencils, his Liquid Paper bottles, and his thoughts.

The clock on the wall said 11:35. At that very moment, though Alex didn't know it, Ben Harper was on the phone with the assistant manager of the Great Adventure amusement park near Lakewood, who was earnestly assuring him that no animals had escaped or could escape from the park's Lion Country Safari attraction; and Karl Masterson was calling every police station and hospital along the route that Mike Tuttle was presumed to have traveled, a route that did not include a detour to Sea Cove, to inquire if there had been an accident involving a GMC Van-dura last night; and Stu Holland, watching his line bob in the waters of Morrison Lake, was thinking very seriously about taking a leak.

# 9

HE HAD been fishing for a good two hours with no luck. His knees were stiff and the seat of his trousers, planted in the damp earth at the water's edge, had been soaked clear through. About an hour ago he had propped the fishing rod between his legs and shrugged off his light jacket as the day warmed to about 65. Unseasonable for October, but he wasn't complaining, especially since, on the way over, the car radio had said tomorrow would be cold and overcast, with a chance of snow by evening. Snow, of all things, and Halloween still ten days away. He shook his head wonderingly. You never knew what to expect, this time of year.

But today was a fine day, and this was a fine place to spend it, in the shadowed stillness of the woods. The sky had blossomed into a flawless blue, cupped by the mirror of the lake, a mirror pitted in spots by clumps of algae-encrusted rock and rippling with slow, random currents, like waves of distortion in the glass. The trees hung like a lacework of bare branches around the lake, hemming it in, closing it off from the outside world in a way that seemed jealous and protective.

But that protection was an illusion. Someday these woods would be cleared and rows of duplexes or a nice neat office complex would rise where the trees had fallen. Stu Holland felt vaguely guilty about the prospect. He and his wife, Betty, lived in Parkfair Homes, a modest middle-class retirement community about a mile east of Denham's Wood. The community had a recreation hall where canasta games were played two days a week and bingo every Friday night. It had a babbling brook and a shuffleboard court and a bus that took the residents up to the Monmouth Mall in Eatontown. And every apartment had cable TV. It was a nice, quiet place, and he and Betty had been happy there, ever since they moved in three years ago.

Still, Stu Holland felt a tad uneasy about all that when he looked around at Denham's Wood. Parkfair had gone up five years ago, on land that had been a pine-shaded forest like this. He would hate to see these woods go too.

He shrugged. He was sixty-four. He would enjoy the woods while he could. With luck, when they were finally cleared away, he would not be around to see it.

Besides, at the moment he had a far more pressing concern on his mind.

He had to take a leak.

Oh, more than a leak. He had to piss like a racehorse, as his friend and occasional tennis partner Tom Watson would say. Stu had no idea where that expression had come from or what it meant, and he doubted Tom did either. But dammit, it sure fit. He *did* have to piss like a racehorse. He felt like bolting out of the starting gate right now.

Another nice thing about being alone in the woods, Stu reflected as he reeled in his line and laid down his pole, was that there was no call for modesty. A man, needing to relieve himself, simply stood up and did so.

Stu stood up, took a few steps back so as not to contaminate his immediate surroundings, unzipped his pants with a burst of mental fanfare ... and did nothing.

He was trying, but ...

He got this way in public restrooms. Never used the urinal. Always went and sat on the potty, just to make water. He got uncomfortable with people watching.

Well, holy hell, there was no one watching here.

He redoubled his efforts, without success.

All right, face it, he felt uncomfortable here too, whether it made any sense or not. Somehow it just didn't seem right for a man to perform his bodily functions out in the open like this. He felt almost like ... for God's sake ... like he was exposing himself.

Now, watering the bushes, that would be an entirely different matter. There was something private and rather manly, in an outdoorsman's sort of way, about that.

Stu zipped up his fly and headed into the woods, intending to take his leak where even the sky could not see him.

- — -

Razor slept, as always, without dreams. His consciousness was too uncomplicated for such subtleties. It simply switched on and off, like a machine. Now it was off and Razor was in a humming darkness that tingled faintly, pleasantly, with the odor of blood.

A low sound penetrated the background hum. A crunching, snapping sound ... the crunch of dry earth and dead leaves ... the snap of twigs ... a slow, regular sound. Footsteps.

Razor was awake instantly.

He raised his head and sniffed the air with his ears pricked up. He caught the human scent. A Man was coming.

Razor was on his feet in the span of a single heartbeat. His body stood waiting, quivering slightly, nostrils flared and twitching.

*Crunch.* Pebbles shifting under a boot.

*Crack.* A sapling's branch, breaking.

The Man was much nearer now. One by one Razor's three companions awoke. Cleo looked around drowsily, perhaps unsure if she were still in a dream. Mr. Dobbs rose to a sitting position. Bigfoot lay on his side with his head tilted up and a bright streamer of drool hanging sideways out of his mouth.

Crunch.

Snap.

Abruptly the sounds stopped.

Razor and the others listened. Razor drew in the scent. It was strong and intoxicating. The Man was close. Only two or three yards away. Hidden by the dense underbrush and trees.

Then ... a sound Razor could not recognize, a brief tearing sound, like a sheet of paper torn neatly in half.

Silence.

Somewhere, a bird chirped frantically, then was still.

And ...

Razor's ears trembled to catch a new sound. The sound of ... rainfall. But it was not raining.

A running-water sound.

Razor breathed in a warm, salty, living-body scent. He recognized that scent. He had smelled his own urine and that of other dogs many times. But, mixed with the human scent, this meant something more—an association, very strong, that set him salivating.

One time during training at Karl Masterson's ranch, Razor had lunged for a Bad Man who was taunting him and had knocked him down, biting savagely through the foam chest pads, and suddenly there had been *that* smell, the urine smell, rising strong and rancid from the Man's lower parts. Then the other Bad Men had dragged Razor away and muzzled him. He did not understand that the trainer had wet himself in terror.

Razor did not actually remember the incident. It had blurred together with all the other memories of home, memories now so distant and unreal they might have been flashes from a previous life.

But he did remember the Bad Man's urine smell. And with that memory came vague images of the Man's helpless, struggling figure and Razor's fangs chewing and his claws slashing and other good things.

Razor padded forward, noiseless as a shadow, and the other three followed.

- — -

Stu had nearly finished his business, and he was just making sure with a few final forced squirts when he saw the Doberman.

He had walked a little ways into the woods to find a spot shaded by trees. He enjoyed the walk. It was a fine day and the woods were bright with fallen leaves and the mottled trunks of sycamores against the pearl-blue sky.

So he had found his private spot and piddled, as his father used to say, and now he was standing there with his fly open and his dick hanging out and a big black Doberman looking at him from out of a dead laurel bush three feet away.

The dog growled.

Stu Holland experienced a slow sinking feeling which, roughly translated, would have read: *Holy shit.*

His first act was to fumble with his fly, tuck his valuables back into his underpants, and seal up the family jewels with a jerk of his trembling wrist.

Then his privates were protected once again and, like a woman caught in the nude who covers her breasts with her hands, Stu felt a little better. But not much.

The dog was still growling.

Behind the Doberman, three more dogs, two other Dobermans and a German shepherd, crept into view. They made a dirty, miserable band, and part of Stu couldn't help but think that they ought to be bathed and fed and given their shots and provided with good proper homes, because they were obviously just poor strays lost in the woods. But that was only a small part of his mind, because the greater part was frozen by terror. Two words kept reverberating in there like a shout bouncing off the walls of an empty room.

Wolf pack.

That was what they were, not poor, orphaned dog-gies, but wild animals, prowling the forest, dangerous as coyotes or wolves. And they were three feet away and they were ... watching him.

He had to get out of here.

He took a cautious step back.

The dogs did not move.

He took another step.

Four sets of red eyes glowered at him.

He took another step, and there was something behind him, Jesus Christ, reaching out for him—a tree, a pine tree. He had backed into a tree, that's all, *get hold of yourself.*

Still the dogs had not moved. He was six feet away from them now.

Carefully he maneuvered around the tree while his eyes remained fixed on the dogs.

Eight feet away.

If he could get back to the lake ...

Yes? What then?

He didn't know. He knew only that out *there,* past the maze of leafless trees and shafts of mote-dusted sun-light, lay the cold, clear waters of Morrison Lake, and his fishing pole, and his reel of thirty-pound monofilament line with a worm-baited hook, and it had been so nice out there and so peaceful and safe, and if he could just get back ... get back ...

Then the first Doberman slunk forward, with the others at its heels, and Stu Holland knew with sick cer-tainty that he would not get back, that his fate was sealed, that he had, in his wisdom, chosen the worst possible place and time to take a piss.

The dogs were creeping closer and he was backing up. For every step he took, they advanced, keeping the distance of about two yards between themselves and their prey unchanged. Stu found himself thinking of Betty. The words *I love you* would not leave his mind. He wondered if he had kissed her cheek before he went out this morning. Of course he had. He always did. He wouldn't forget a thing like that, not on today of all days, but then, who had known that *this* would be the today-of-all-days? Sure, he had kissed her, he remembered now, and she had said something, too, as he was leaving. What was it? It seemed vitally important to know exactly what Betty Holland had said, what her last words to him had been. He could not remember.

The dogs were fanning out, with the first Doberman directly in front of him and its three companions creeping forward on both sides, ringing him in. The lead Doberman had stopped growling, disdainful of the need to intimidate. The four dogs were silent, as grimly silent as executioners. They would simply keep closing in, drawing that circle smaller and smaller, until they could close in no more, and then they would kill.

Stu Holland took a final step and felt another tree at his back.

The dogs inched nearer.

There was no place for him to go. Except ...

He glanced up. An oak tree. Bare branches. One branch was low enough to be just within reach. It looked like a good strong branch, strong enough to take a man's weight.

The first Doberman was two feet away. It growled again, softly, and showed its fangs. Yellow fangs flecked with blood.

*Betty, I love you.*

He turned and grabbed hold of the branch and hoisted himself up, his boots scrabbling on the tree trunk, searching for a foothold as he pulled his chin level with the branch. And then the dogs were on him, all of them at once, their teeth shredding his trousers, their claws slashing at his shirt. He hung on, clinging to the branch with one hand while with the other he reached for a higher branch, and the dogs were pulling him down, scratching and clawing and barking, until finally, with an effort that nearly exploded his heart in his chest, his free hand closed over the higher branch and then miraculously the other hand joined it. He pulled himself up, kicking wildly to shake the dogs loose, but one dog still clung to his right leg, its teeth caught in his calf, drawing blood. He looked down. It was the Doberman, the leader of the pack. He swung his leg hard to one side and the Doberman slammed against the tree and was stunned by the blow and fell, releasing the leg. Stu hauled himself up to a squatting position with both hands still on the higher branch and his boots balanced on the lower one. Below, the four dogs had crowded around the base of the tree and were glaring up at him with cold, angry, cheated eyes.

He had done it. He had climbed the tree. Jesus Christ. Sixty-four years old and he was out in the woods climbing trees.

His heart pounded. He fought to catch his breath. Black specks pulsed before his eyes. It occurred to him that he might be having a heart attack, and if that were the case, then he would fall in a moment and the dogs would finish him. He pushed the thought out of his mind, gripped the tree branch tighter, and blinked to clear his vision, until he felt almost healthy again.

Six feet below, the first Doberman drew back low on its hindquarters, like a jack-in-the-box squeezed down, tighter, tighter, and then it sprang.

The dog shot straight into the air, an arrow targeted at the branch where Stu Holland's feet were balanced. It clawed at the branch, taking one vicious swipe at the apex of its leap, then fell back.

Stu hung on as the branch shook and the dog leaped at it again and again. Finally its talons sank into the branch, digging in like steel hooks, then slid down slowly, haltingly, leaving long, twisting grooves in the wood, and finally came loose, and the dog fell.

It landed on the ground, jerked to its feet, and readied itself for a new assault.

"Betty," said Stu Holland between gasps of air. "Love you." The words had almost no meaning anymore.

The Doberman leaped, and this time its foreclaws caught solidly on the branch and the dog hung there, kicking and struggling and making hideous guttural noises, and the branch creaked treacherously under the combined weight of man and dog.

Stu kicked at the dog with his boot. The Doberman snarled and lunged for the boot and Stu kicked again, smacking it hard on the snout, then stomped on its paws till the dog, whining, lost its grip and tumbled down to land in a heap.

Stu prayed it had broken its leg or its spine, but no, it was on its feet again, with a new strategy. It leaped not for the branch but for the tree trunk, and its front and rear claws momentarily found footholds in the flaking bark. It fought to shimmy up the tree like a man shimmying a telephone pole, while Stu Holland watched in dumb horror and disbelief, until the Doberman lost its footing halfway up and went sliding down to the bottom once more.

The Doberman shook its head, stunned, then glared up at Stu Holland.

It would keep on trying. Stu knew that. He knew it in a way that went beyond observing the Doberman's actions. He knew it from looking into the Doberman's eyes.

They glinted red in the sun and brown in the shade, shifting from the tones of fresh blood to dried blood, the fresh blood trickling down Stu Holland's leg, the dried blood on the Doberman's fangs. Those eyes burned with inhuman intelligence and a ruthless bloodlust that would not be denied.

Stu clung to the tree in a half-crouch. His leg hurt like hell and he knew he could climb no higher. His only hope was to wait it out.

The other three dogs seemed to sense this also. They settled around the tree, sitting or sprawling, content to rest and wait for what might be a long time.

Only the Doberman, the leader, remained standing. It stared, motionless and obsessed, at the man in the tree.

Stu Holland gripped the tree branch tighter, planted his boots more firmly on the lower branch, and thought random thoughts about Betty and what she must be doing now and when she might begin to worry about why he hadn't come home, until these thoughts were interrupted by a new thought that was, quite simply, absurd.

He had to take a leak.

# 10

IT WAS 3:00 in the afternoon—and somewhere out in the woods by Morrison Lake, a sixty-four-year-old man was clinging to a tree with failing strength, still trying to remember the last words his wife had said to him that morning—when Wylie Gaines trudged out of the New Bridge Public School, fought her way through mobs of kids, and climbed onto her bus.

She dropped heavily into her seat, by a window, with nobody else nearby. She hugged her books and her writing tablet and her Princess of Power lunchbox close to her chest. The bus was a madhouse of kids ranging in age from seven to seventeen, all talking and yelling and shrieking at once.

The bus driver, Mr. Frenzell, a horse-faced man of indeterminate age and unpredictable temper, cranked the door shut and drove slowly over the five-mile-per-hour speed bumps that lined the school driveway.

Wylie sat very still, oblivious of the maelstrom around her, and looked out the grime-streaked window. Her mind was on Buster, as it had been all day. She had not been able to concentrate on class, and when Mrs. Larchmont had asked her to *answer the question, Wylie,* she had not even known what the question was. Recess had been spent alone, in a corner of the echoing lunchroom, as she picked moodily at the peanut-butter sandwich her mother had made for her and sipped dispiritedly from her milk carton through the little plastic straw, till finally she was only sucking air and the straw was making that dry, scraping sound. She felt just like that sound, dry and empty. She did not finish even half her sandwich, though she did manage to eat the Hostess cherry pie that had been included as dessert.

She was sure Buster would be all right, because her daddy had told her so, and her daddy never lied.

But still ...

Even daddies could be wrong. Couldn't they?

Why, heck, even old Mrs. Larchmont, who knew *everything*, could probably be wrong, at least some-times. At least ... once.

Wylie stared out the window and waited for the bus to groan all the way out to her house, one of the last stops, while hoping with quiet feverishness that Buster would be there to greet her, like always, barking and wagging his tail, when she finally got off.

Three rows back, a gang of boys from the sixth grade were passing around today's edition of the Sea Cove *Citizen* and glancing toward Wylie's seat and whispering. The whispering had a nasty edge to it, and their angels' faces, at this moment, were not pretty to see.

Billy Turnbul, twelve years old and in grave danger of being held back if his grades did not improve, had stolen the paper from the desk of his homeroom teacher at the end of the day. Billy did not really want the paper, and he figured his teacher, Mr. Cunninger, probably didn't want it either, but then he calculated that he wanted it even less than Cunninger; so he took it.

On the bus, for want of anything better to do, Billy had thumbed through the paper with his three friends. Matt Murdoch, Sam Letterman, and T.W. Brolin, real name Theodore Wesley, but call him that and he'd beat your fucking face in, and fast. They giggled at the stupid news stories about the crummy hick towns they lived in, and Sam, who had something of an artistic bent, drew a long, limp penis drooping out of the mouth of Police Chief Ben Harper, whose photo appeared next to a story about the purchase of a new patrol car, and they were having a pretty okay time.

It was T.W. who found the small item on the bottom of page four and pointed it out to his buddies in a low voice.

That was when the ugly whispers and the stupid, leering smiles aimed in Wylie's direction had begun.

Now the four figures rose as one and found new seats around Wylie, with Billy sitting right beside her, uncomfortably big and close.

"Hey, Wylie," said Billy with mock pleasantness, and the others echoed the words in a way that turned her name into a drawn-out sneer.

She turned her big eyes on them. The eyes were gray and dark and cold, and in that instant they were very much her mother's eyes. "What do *you* want?"

Wylie had been pushed around by these guys before. They pushed every little kid around. She was afraid of them, a little, but right now she was more annoyed than afraid. She was in no mood for their dumb jokes today. She would yell for Mr. Frenzell to stop them if they started up calling her names like Silly-Willy Wylie and No-Brains Gaines and Little Fatso and Piggy-Wiggy and all those other, even worse names. She had Buster on her mind right now, and that was enough.

"We just wanted to say hi," said Billy.

Matt Murdoch giggled and waved his hand girlishly, with the pinkie extended. "Hi, Wyyyy ... leeeee."

They all laughed.

"Get away from me," Wylie mumbled as she turned back to the window, her face flushed.

"How's your dog, Wylie?"

The voice was Billy Turnbul's.

Wylie heard it, but she could not quite believe it. She

felt as if the big pimple-faced jerk had looked right inside her and read her mind, almost. None of these guys had ever said anything about Buster before.

She turned, despite herself, and looked up at Billy Turnbul. He was smiling down at her. She saw teeth cruddy with bits of chewing gum, a nest of blackheads around his nose, and two dimwit, pig-slit eyes regarding her with dark amusement.

"My dog's fine," said Wylie bravely.

Across the aisle, Sam Letterman laughed.

Wylie swallowed. "What's so funny?"

"You are, Wy-lee," said T.W. "We think you're real funny. That's why we like you."

"Yeah," said Matt Murdoch. "That's why we're your friends."

"You're not my friends." Wylie's lower lip was trembling. "Leave me alone."

"You seen your dog lately?" asked Billy slowly.

Wylie was scared now. Not scared for herself. Scared for Buster. She stared up at Billy Turnbul and his oh-so-amused eyes, then at the others, T.W. and Sam and Matt, all watching eagerly like spectators at a ball game.

"Sure I did," said Wylie.

"When?"

"What d'you care?"

"Seen him this morning?"

She felt real terror now. For a moment the idea flashed in Wylie's mind that Billy and his gang had done something to Buster, kidnapped him, or even ... *hurt* him. No. No, they couldn't have. Her daddy wouldn't let them.

With all her courage she lifted her chin and said, "'Course I saw him."

Then they were laughing raucously, and T.W. was singing, "Liar, liar, burn in hot hellfire, Wy-lee Gay-yaines, lies about her own nay-yame ..."

"Not a liar!" she shouted, her voice choked. "Buster's

my dog and I saw him ... this ... morning ..."

"You lie, you die." It was T.W., offering yet another example of his penetrating wit. "Roll with the pigs in a dirty pigsty."

"We don't like liars," said Billy ominously.

"'Specially fat, ugly little liars," snarled Sam Letterman.

"We thought you were our friend, but we don't make friends with liars," said Matt Murdoch.

Wylie was crying now, tears of shame and fear, shame at herself, fear for Buster. Because the big kids knew something about Buster. Something bad.

Then Billy Turnbul's face was close to Wylie's, his breath a hot stink on her cheek, his spit stinging her eyes as he said savagely, "You didn't see your dog this morning, 'less you was out on Potters Road! 'Cause that's where he was! See?"

Page four of the Sea Cove *Citizen* was thrust into Wylie Gaines's trembling hands, and Billy Turnbul's triumphant finger was stabbing at a modest item in the lower-right corner: STRAY DOG FOUND DEAD.

Wylie was a good reader for the second grade, even the omniscient Mrs. Larchmont said so, and as her blurry vision stumbled over Alex Driscoll's two brief, understated paragraphs, she was able to understand that the "collie belonging to Mr. and Mrs. Paul Gaines of Vista Lane" was Buster, *her* Buster, her friend, the tail-wagging bundle of black-and-white fur that flew at her when she stepped off the bus, flew at her and nearly knocked her down in his eagerness to welcome her home, the dog who rolled over with paws limp in the air and tongue lolling when she told him to, who snapped Pet Snax out of midair and licked her hand in gratitude, who flopped and flounced in the backyard to shake himself dry after she sprayed him mischievously with the garden hose. *Her* Buster.

" ... found dead shortly after sunrise ..."

Found dead.

Found ...

Dead.

Billy was chortling. "Like that, Crud-for-Brains?" and T.W. was singing "How Much Is That Dead Doggie in the Window?" but Wylie didn't hear it, didn't even hear Mr. Frenzell finally take note of the situation and snap at the boys to leave Wylie alone.

Wylie heard nothing..

Buster was dead.

She looked at the words again, and suddenly they were not mere words any longer. They were reality.

Wylie Gaines screamed.

Not the laughing shriek of the playground—this was a grown-up's scream, interrupted only for a wheeze of air, then renewed at higher volume. Her eyes were wide and her mouth was open and she was screaming as Billy and his gang backed nervously away, afraid they might have gone too far this time. She was screaming as tears flooded her chubby cheeks and streamed down her neck, as her books and lunchbox crashed to the floor, as her legs kicked and her arms flailed. The other little kids burst into tears for no reason, while the high school kids stared in horrified fascination at the Gaines girl. Then the bus pulled over and Mr. Frenzell went back and shook Wylie and yelled at Billy's gang, "What the hell did you say to her?" Billy and company looked blankly innocent, and Mr. Frenzell kept on shaking Wylie and wondering if he was supposed to slap her or what, and all the while, and for a long while to come, Wylie Gaines went on screaming and screaming and screaming.

# 11

BETTY HOLLAND'S eyes were on the twenty-one-inch Sylvania color TV, but her mind was elsewhere, as it had been for most of the afternoon. Around 2:00, during *As the World Turns,* she had gotten out this week's *TV Guide* and done the crossword puzzle, so imbecilically easy it consumed all of fifteen minutes. Then at 2:45 she had decided to do her needlepoint. She did not really like needlepoint, but it kept her hands occupied, and her hands had been starting to shake. Twice in the last hour she had put the needlepoint aside, gotten up from the sofa, gone to the phone, and actually dialed O for operator, before hanging up. Now she was thinking of dialing again, and staying on the line this time. *Hello, Operator, would you connect me with the Sea Cove police department, please? No, no, not an emergency ... Hello? Yes, I'd like to report ... well, that is ... my husband went fishing and he hasn't come back.*

Oh, Stu would kill her, just simply kill her, if she did that. She could imagine his face when he walked in the door with his rod and bait box in one hand. *I go out to do a little fishing and nod off for a nap, and next thing I know the whole Sea Cove police department is tramping around the woods looking for me. I woke up because I thought I had a tug on the line, except instead it was a cop shaking my arm and asking me my name. Said my wife called to file some sort of missing-persons report. Never been so embarrassed ...*

Yes, he would say all that, and he would be right.

Still, she was tempted to call. Just for her own peace of mind.

He might have fallen asleep. Betty remembered how he'd done that, once, last year. He had slept half the day in the woods and gotten back at 3:30, when she was starting to worry herself sick. More than likely, the same thing had happened today.

But suppose, wondered Betty Holland, now just suppose Stu hadn't fallen asleep. Suppose he was ... ill, say. Suppose he'd fallen in the woods and turned his ankle. Suppose he'd been in a car accident on the way home and no one had called her yet. Suppose ...

She dropped her needlepoint decisively, rose from the sofa, and walked to the phone. She hesitated. Maybe just another half hour or so. It would be getting dark soon. Daylight saving time was over and the sun went down by five. If he was not back by, say, 4:30, she would call.

- — -

Stu Holland was cold. The woods' noon warmth had slipped away as late-afternoon shadows stole in, and now he was wishing he had his jacket, the jacket he had shrugged off so casually and left by the lake. Most of all, he wished he had gloves. His hands were numb from gripping the cold tree branch. Every so often he would release one hand to blow on it, flex the fingers, and watch the blue veins pulsing under gray liver spots. His legs were numb too, not from cold but from having remained motionless for so long. He was afraid to move them. His balance on the branch was too uncertain. His left leg had stopped bleeding and seemed to have fallen asleep. Pins and needles were shooting up his calf.

The dogs had not stirred. Well, that was not quite true. The big Doberman had finally consented to sit. That must have been two hours ago. But the Doberman's blood-red eyes still gazed up fixedly at him from out of the pool of shadow at the base of the tree. And every now and then the Doberman would growl softly, as if to say: *I've got you, old man. I've got you caught like an animal in a trap, and you make a nice catch, too, such a nice …*

*Catch.*

"Catch one for me."

The words popped into Stu's mind, just like that. He turned them over in his head, just four words strung together, that's all, but his mind handled them lovingly, the way he would have handled a string of pearls. *"Catch one for me."* Yes, that was it. That was the last thing Betty had said. He could hear her calling the words cheerfully after him as he stepped out the door.

He smiled, pleased that he had remembered, and gripped the tree branch tighter.

Below, the Doberman was growling again.

# 12

BEN HARPER had thought he'd known what fear was. Sure. Fear was trying to break up a drunken brawl on the boardwalk on a hot August night with your gun holstered—stupid, so stupid, but you were young then, just a kid—and suddenly a straight razor was shaving your cheek and a punk was shouting obscenities while the crowd chanted, "Cut the pig." And fear was feeling the road squirt out from under your tires on that long drive down from the Berkshires, and seeing the whirl of snow in the windshield and the guardrail clawing at your side door, while your mind said calmly, implacably, like a tape recording, *Turn into the skid, into the skid,* only it was too late and the car spun around on the mountain road, accordioned against the guardrail, and nearly went over the side. Fear, yes, *that* was fear, wasn't it?

Oh, Ben knew all about fear. Sure he did.

He knew nothing.

Tonight was fear.

This was what people meant when they talked about terror—this slow death march into the fading dusk, this advance through the crackling brush toward something bestial and murderous and unknown.

Betty Holland's call had come at 4:30, on the dot, and ten minutes later Ben Harper had parked his car on Potters Road and led two officers, Tilby and Garrick, into the darkening woods.

His reassuring lies still hung heavily in his memory. *I'm sure there's nothing to concern yourself about, Mrs. Hol-*

*land. But just to be on the safe side, I'll be happy to take a look. You sit tight and we'll have your husband back home in no time. Oh, no, Mrs. Holland, it's no trouble at all.*

The twilight was cold. The sky was a drab, pale purple brightening to a red fireglow on the horizon that shot sudden rare sparks through breaks in the trees. Hickories and white elms and cedars swayed in the breeze, their branches scraping together. Dead leaves papered the ground. They crunched like potato chips under the boots of the three men who advanced slowly with Ben at the lead. Then the men reached a spread of pine needles which absorbed their footfalls and made them aware of the eerie stillness of the woods, the silence of the birds and insects.

Tilby and Garrick said nothing. Unusual for them. But then again, hardly unusual under the circumstances.

The day was dying, the last embers of the sunset flickering feebly in the mirror of Morrison Lake, when they found Stu Holland's fishing gear. It lay undisturbed, a rod with a baited hook, a bait box, a discarded jacket. All very normal, except for the fact that Stu Holland was nowhere in sight.

Ben Harper switched on his flashlight. Tilby and Garrick did likewise. The three beams probed the ground, dancing like three full moons under the blank, blue-black, moonless sky.

"Chief."

Danny Garrick pointed. Ben saw a footprint in the damp earth near the water's edge, a footprint leading away from the lake.

"Okay." Ben swallowed. "Let's go."

Ben walked toward the line of trees with his men flanking him. There were no more footprints. The ground a few yards from the water was hard, cold, and thick with dead brown grass.

Where the trees began, Ben stopped abruptly. He

peered into the woods. The lacework of pines, maples, cedars, and their branches intermeshed crazily, faintly luminous against the night, and seemed to form a sort of pattern. Like a spiderweb, he thought. The pattern shifted. It was only the branches creaking in the wind, but Ben saw it as a network of gossamer strands shifting under the spider's slow crawl. *Come into my parlor,* said the spider in a voice as low as the whisper of the wind.

Ben knew all that was crazy. But beneath the craziness there was the redeeming sanity of a fact.

Stu Holland had gone into these woods and had not come out.

"Draw your guns," said Ben Harper quietly.

Tilby and Garrick exchanged a glance. Tilby had been on the force a year, Garrick three. They were both local boys. They'd known Chief Harper for a long time, since before he'd even been promoted to chief. Neither of them had ever heard that particular tone of his voice before. And neither had ever heard him give the order to draw a gun, except in training sessions.

Both guns were unholstered instantly. Like Harper's, they were .38s, Smith & Wesson Police Specials with four-inch barrels, glinting blue, and checkered walnut grips.

Harper nodded to his men, and the three of them walked into the woods, following, by Ben's best guess, the path Stu Holland had taken. Ben had no trail to guide him, but he figured the man would have chosen the line of least resistance—the wide spaces between the trees, the stretches of bare ground traced in white streaks by the trio of flashlight beams. He moved forward, sweeping his flashlight from side to side in a wide, protective curve, straining to see into the shadows that surrounded his group on all sides.

The wind set the trees creaking again, and Ben tried to brush aside the thought that he was now inside the web, tangled in its silken threads, struggling and shaking the webwork and summoning the spider for its kill.

He kept moving forward.

It was odd how time slowed down when your life was on the line. Each step came with molasses slowness. He felt like he was slogging through quicksand. Odd, too, how everything was magnified. The flashlights seemed to burn much more brightly than normal. The slow, regular crackle of the leaves with each new footfall was deafening in the stillness. His breath was loud in his throat, a hoarse, rasping sound. Oddest of all was the way certain things just disappeared. The cold, for instance. He was certain it was cold out here, bitterly cold with the sun gone, and yet he could not feel it anymore.

If death in some incomprehensible shape came lumbering out of the dark to split his belly and spill his innards out, would he feel that?

He took another step forward, into a narrow glen ringed with dead shrubbery. He froze.

Because ... he had felt something on the back of his hand. His left hand. Something warm. Something ... wet.

He aimed his flashlight at it and saw a perfect teardrop of blood.

He watched, fascinated, as another drop fell, and then the two drops rolled slowly down his hand, leaving long, curving cherry-red trails.

Slowly, with infinite caution, Ben Harper removed the flashlight's beam from the back of his hand, lowered the beam to the ground at his feet, and saw a thick, dark puddle.

Time had slowed still further, and his mind was working creakily, like one of those ancient computing devices of the early postwar years, the kind jerry-built out of vacuum tubes. His mind added up the data and analyzed it and ground out the logical conclusion in a clatter of gears.

The blood was dripping down.

The thing, the *bleeding, dripping* thing was … above him.

He wet his lips and raised the light, letting the beam sweep along the trunk of an oak tree to the lowest branch, where it came to rest, shaking slightly, because the hand that held it was shaking.

Framed in the circle of light was a face, which could not be a human face because the eyes and mouth were all wrong, reversed, in fact. No human face was made that way. And then Ben grasped that the face *was* human. Only it was hanging upside down, and the throat had been slashed open, and a river of blood had washed over the face and left it a crimson mask. The mouth hung open and the tongue protruded from between the teeth. Ben could see the silver fillings in the bottom molars. The eyes were wide, pupils dilated and rolled up in their sockets, eyeballs white and round as eggs. The hair, which might have been silver-gray once but was now blood-soaked to a muddy red, hung down in thick, gooey, vertical streaks, dripping like melting icicles.

Ben stared at the face and was mildly surprised to see that its expression did not register horror or anguish or shock or any particular reaction at all. It was the face of a man who had spent his last moments trying to find a way to breathe without a windpipe or a throat and, failing, had surrendered to unconsciousness, his facial muscles going lax and blank, erasing whatever final message might have been recorded there.

It was really a rather peaceful face, if you ignored the torrent of blood that had altered its complexion and the steady *drip-drip-drip,* like a leaky faucet, from the tips of the hair to the spreading puddle below.

"Jesus Christ," said Danny Garrick, and George Tilby choked.

Ben couldn't say how long he stood staring at the face of what must have been Stu Holland. Probably it was not longer than a second or two. Then he swept his flashlight along the tree branch where the dead man's body hung awkwardly, arms and legs twisted. He did not know if the man had been killed and placed on the branch for some obscure reason, or if he had taken refuge in the tree, or ... He did not know. That would have to wait.

He had a more immediate priority.

He swung around and flashed the beam over the clearing, probing the shrubs and surrounding trees. Tilby and Garrick collected themselves and did the same.

Nothing stirred in the woods but the wind. The trees creaked again, and the branch supporting Stu Holland's corpse groaned softly under the strain.

The clearing and the woods around it betrayed no other sign of movement, no hint of life.

"All clear," said Ben Harper finally. He hoped his voice did not sound as weak and drained to his men's ears as it did to his own. "Whatever finished off Mr. Holland is gone."

George Tilby nodded, then half-turned and retched dryly.

Danny Garrick was pale and looked not too far from puking, himself.

"What d'you think did it, Chief?" he asked in a voice so low as to sound almost awestruck.

"I don't know."

"You ... you sure it's gone?"

"Yeah."

"Where to?"

Ben Harper looked away from Garrick, stared into the darkness, and felt the webwork of bare trees shiver around him. He noticed that he was feeling the cold again. At least he thought it was the cold.

"I don't know," he said gruffly. "How the hell should I know?"

"Well," said Danny Garrick, "somebody better."

# 13

RAZOR'S MOUTH burned with that feeling he knew so well, the feeling he'd always had when they dragged him away from a Bad Man and muzzled him, the feeling that said he had been cheated of a kill.

The Bad Man in the tree had been killed, true; but that was small consolation, because his body had stayed in the tree, wrapped around the branch, twisted like a rag doll, and even though Razor and his three companions had done their best to shake it loose, it had stubbornly refused to budge.

Still, there had been that one moment.

Razor had lain still for an untold stretch of time while the Bad Man clung to the tree. He had not ticked off minutes and hours as Stu Holland had done. He had merely waited with inhuman patience as the sun swam lazily across the sky, until finally dusk's lengthening shadows began to swallow the woods, in meager nibbles at first, then great bites, and at last the forest floor was eaten away by darkness. That was good. Razor liked the dark, because in darkness he could strike without warning.

Concealed in an ink-spot shadow at the base of the tree, he had drawn down on his haunches, slowly enough to ensure that even if the Bad Man did chance to look down, he could detect no movement. Razor tensed his hind legs. He squeezed his buttocks painfully tight and let his head shrink into his shoulders as his back arched, until he could not tense his body any more, because his eve-

97

ry corded muscle was as taut as piano wire, and as finely tuned.

Then, with a snarl, Razor leaped.

He sprang up out of the darkness and his right fore-claw caught hold of the lowest branch and he felt his nails dig into the wood as the branch shook and the Bad Man, startled, lost his grip and fell.

But he did not fall all the way. He sprawled facedown on the branch and hung on and Razor had a glimpse of the Bad Man's eyes, level with his own and wide with terror. Then Razor took one vicious swipe with his left paw, a swipe guided by months of training and generations of instinct, guided directly to the Bad Man's throat.

Razor's face was sprayed with blood as his talons ripped the throat open as neatly as scissors slitting an envelope.

And in that moment—as the Bad Man's blood showered down on Razor, as Razor inhaled its sweet fragrance and tasted the red rain on his panting tongue—in that moment Razor felt a surge of ecstasy. The long, patient hours of waiting were forgotten. There was only the intoxicating thrill of drawing blood.

Then Razor's hold on the branch was lost and an instant later he was on the ground again, with the Bad Man dying but still in the tree.

The moment of euphoria was over. Razor wanted more. The other three, Bigfoot and Cleo and Mr. Dobbs, had been snapped alert by their leader's surprise attack and by the smell of blood. They sensed Razor's racing bloodlust, sensed it and shared it. They must pull down the body and shred it and feast.

But despite all their efforts, they had failed. Even in death the Bad Man mocked them. Finally Razor, frustrated and sensing that this kill could bring him no further satisfaction, had turned his back disdainfully on the tree and trotted into the woods. The others had followed.

Razor had no plan or destination. He knew only that his snout was wet with blood and the smell was maddening in his nostrils and he had to have *more.*

When the pack emerged from the woods they found a sagging fence, a row of posts leering like gapped teeth, with wider gaps where the posts had rotted and fallen and had not been replaced. Razor led his comrades through one of the holes, into a stretch of open field.

The pack crossed the field. They ignored the house a few yards away, a small two-story house standing desolately alone under the black overcast sky. Razor had no interest in the house. Had he been interested, he might have pricked up his ears and detected the faint murmur of conversation and the clatter of dinner dishes from inside. But none of that could penetrate his consciousness now.

He had caught a scent, the warm scent of many living bodies packed together, close and hot and vulnerable, and this smell, mingled with the fresh blood crowding his nostrils, had blanked out all other thought. He must kill. He had not had enough. Not nearly enough. Not ever enough.

He picked up his pace, and Cleo, Bigfoot, and Mr. Dobbs followed. They passed by the house and padded hungrily toward the henhouse of the Andersons' farm.

# 14

MAGGIE ANDERSON was circling the dinner table, ladling a steaming glop of mashed potatoes onto every plate, with a double helping for Owen and a measly morsel for baby Melissa, and Owen Jr. and Will were arguing amiably about whose turn it was to say grace, when the squawking started out in the henhouse.

"Oh, hell," said Owen Anderson. He scraped his chair back and rose to his feet in one swift, sure motion. He was a strong, broad-shouldered man with hands as brown and callused as tanned leather and a narrow face marked by sullen stoicism. Looking at him, you might have guessed he was forty or sixty-five, or anywhere in between; he had the kind of ageless energy that was not youthful. He was in fact only one year to the day older than his wife, which made him thirty-nine by her calculations and forty-one by his own.

"Whassa matter, Daddy?" asked Will, five years old and in love with questions of all kinds.

"It's the chickens, stupid," snapped his older brother with the authority of one who was nearly seven. "Fox in the henhouse again."

"I've told you, Owen, you've just got to keep that fence repaired." Maggie's voice was low and toneless and long-suffering.

Her husband had already marched into the living room and pulled the Remington rifle down from its wall mount. He checked the pump action and snapped four 6mm cartridges into the magazine and a fifth into the chamber. He grunted what might have been a reply.

"Fox," said two-year-old Melissa. "Fox, fox, fox!" She banged her fists on the arms of her high chair, threatening to upset the tray balanced there.

"You stop that, now," said Maggie. She touched the child's head tenderly.

"Fox," said Melissa once more, with a wide, mischievous grin.

Owen headed resolutely for the front door. Outside, the panicky cackling was louder.

"Lemme watch," said Owen Jr. "I wanna see Daddy shoot the fox!"

"Me too! Me too!" It was Will.

"Too," echoed Melissa, who punctuated the thought by spitting up a piece of carrot.

"Nobody leaves this table," said Maggie. She sat down in her chair and unfolded her napkin for emphasis. "Your daddy has a job to do and he doesn't need our help to get it done."

The two boys groaned and Melissa made a raspberry sound. Maggie glanced through the dining-room doorway into the living room, hoping for Owen's moral support, but all she saw of her husband was his broad back, retreating out the front door. The door slammed shut, heavily enough to make the glass knickknacks tinkle on the end table by the living-room couch.

Maggie Anderson loved her husband. She loved him very much. She found that she had to remind herself of that fact with increasing frequency.

"What about dinner?" asked Owen Jr. in a sulking tone that reminded her, somehow, of his father.

"Not till your daddy gets back."

"It'll get cold."

"Then you'll eat it cold."

There was a long silence around the table. Outside, the hens were still raising a ruckus, and Maggie thought, with a touch of irritation, that Owen ought damn well to have bagged that fox by now.

Then there was a shot—as loud and startling as the door slam had been.

"Got him!" yelled Owen Jr.

"Blammo!" shrieked Will.

"Blu-blu!" agreed Melissa.

"All right," said Maggie. "That will be enough. Could we please have—"

Another rifle shot echoed in the night, then another and another, and then, piercing the still October air, a single agonized scream.

Maggie's chair was on the floor and she was running for the front door, with only enough presence of mind left to yell, "Stay in your seats and don't budge, any of you!" Then she was outside, on the porch, down the front steps, her blouse too thin for the night chill, her eyes wide as she peered into the darkness. Then she saw it.

Owen Anderson, her husband for better or worse for eleven years, came stumbling out of the shadows near the henhouse, fifty feet from where she stood. Stumbling because of the weight he carried—the weight of four dogs that were all over him, like leeches, and like leeches they were drawing blood, so much blood. A Doberman clung to his back, and another hung on to his chest with its fangs buried deep in the flesh under his collarbone, and a third had its mouth locked on his arm, and the fourth dog, a German shepherd, was biting his legs again and again.

Owen was not even struggling. That was the worst part, to Maggie, the really horrible part, that he was just stumbling along, dragging the dog pack with him, and Maggie thought wildly and sacrilegiously of Christ bearing his cross without protest through the streets of Jerusalem while the centurions' whips crisscrossed his back and the crowd pelted him with stones. Owen still carried the rifle, but he was not trying to fight off the dogs. It was no use. They were slashing his face and arms and legs into rivers of blood. She doubted he could see with the red tide washing over his eyes from his bleeding scalp. As she watched, he fired his last bullet blindly into the air. It was less an act of defiance than of surrender.

Then he was on the ground and the dogs were rolling him over onto his back and the Doberman that had sunk its teeth into his chest now brushed the others aside, slashed Owen's throat, and lapped up the spurting blood. Maggie stood frozen, paralyzed by horror as the dog took a short leap backward, landed between Owen's legs, and bit deep into his crotch and tore him apart down there, castrating him, and even though Owen was dead, *must* be dead, that sight was finally too much for Maggie Anderson to bear, and she screamed.

With that scream, the dogs saw her, smelled her, and the Doberman with its muzzle in Owen Anderson's groin raised its head, very slowly, and its eyes locked on Maggie's as they had locked on Stu Holland's not so very long ago.

The Doberman broke into a run, straight for her, with the others following, and Maggie turned and tried to take the five stairs to the porch in two giant steps, and failed. She fell on her knees, scrabbled at the banister, and pulled herself up, getting splinters in her palms. Then she was on the porch and at the door, which, thank God, had not closed behind her, and she threw herself inside and spun around to slam the door shut and almost succeeded, but not quite, because ...

The dogs were there.

They thrust their snouts and claws through the crack in the door and fought to force the door open as Maggie leaned against it with all her strength and fought to force it shut. From the dining room she heard the children shouting questions and from some greater distance she heard herself screaming at them to shut up and stay where they were.

The crack in the door was widening. The combined strength of the four dogs outmatched her own. Maggie strained against the heaving wood with every reserve of energy in her body. Still the crack widened. An inch ... another inch ... She felt a knife-cut of pain as a swiping claw caught her arm. The four faces leered at her. One Doberman's mouth was bright with chicken feathers, pasted with blood. They looked ludicrous, like false whiskers.

Another Doberman rammed its head farther inside and bit her hand. She moaned and whacked it hard on the ear till it drew back, and now the crack in the door was wider, the four dogs cramming their necks and shoulders through. She could not close the door. She could not keep them out.

"Mama, what are they?"

It was Will, at the doorway to the dining room.

"Stay back!"

She wanted to tell him to run, but there was no place to run, and no time to think about it.

The door was opening and at any moment the dogs would make a final thrust and she would be flung back helplessly against the wall. They would kill her and kill her children, and there was nothing she could do about it, nothing. Except ...

One hope.

The chain.

The door had a chain.

She reached for the chain and jerked it taut, trying to force the hook into the socket bolted to the door, but it would not reach.

Another dog took a swipe at her, slitting her wrist, and she nearly dropped the chain in the burst of agony that followed, but somehow she hung on.

With a final effort, she shoved her full weight against

the door and knocked it back an inch, and the hook slipped into its socket, the chain was secured. She backed away as the dogs rammed their muzzles through the crack and snapped and barked and pawed, straining to break open the door.

For the moment, the chain held.

Maggie ran through the living room and grabbed Will, standing stunned in the doorway, and dragged him into the dining room. She thrust Will at Owen Jr., who had grasped something of what was going on and looked ready to scream or cry or both, and yelled, "Take care of your brother!" Then she snatched Melissa out of her high chair as the baby cried and hiccupped.

The dogs were clawing at the door and barking savagely and throwing their weight against it with echoing thuds.

There was a phone in the kitchen, and Maggie thought of using it to call the police. She had just taken a step in that direction when the chain burst and the door exploded inward and the dogs were in the house.

"Come on!" she screamed, and some part of her was briefly astonished at the ferocity of her voice. She was running to the guest bedroom down the hall with Melissa in her arms and the two boys behind her. She shoved the boys inside, flew in after them, and slammed the door and locked it in the instant before the dogs were there.

She hugged the door with one hand and Melissa with the other, hearing howls of fury from the other side and feeling the door tremble with each smack of the animals' paws. But the door was solid, it did not give. She did not think they could break it down.

She found the light switch and flipped it on. The lamp by the bed cast long shadows across the room. The lampshade was yellow and the light filtering through it seemed pale and sickly.

She put Melissa gently on the bed and let her cry.

The boys were huddled together in a corner with their hands clasped, eyes wide. She looked at them, trying to show no emotion.

"Is Daddy dead?" asked Owen Jr. in a voice that wavered on the edge of hysterics.

"He's hurt," she lied. She ripped off a sleeve of her blouse, wound it painfully tight around her slashed wrist, and knotted it in place. The tourniquet was soaked through almost instantly. "He's just hurt, that's all. Now do what I tell you."

"Yes, Mama."

"We're gonna drag that dresser by the clothes closet over in front of the door. You understand me?"

"Yes, Mama."

"Will, you gotta help too."

Will nodded manfully and sniffed back tears.

The two boys got on one side of the dresser and Maggie got on the other side and, holy Christ, the damned thing weighed a ton, but she strained till she thought she would bust a gut, all the while a trickle of red escaping from her bound wrist and her two boys struggling as best they could, and together they slid the dresser across the floor in slow, zigzagging jerks, till it stood before the door, a barricade.

Maggie leaned on the bed, her head lowered, and caught her breath, while waves of gray faintness washed over her and Melissa cried.

The faintness passed. She raised her head and knotted the tourniquet tighter, tight as she could stand. Then she sat on the bed, no energy left. Will and Owen Jr. ran to her and she hugged them both and said in a hoarse, quavering voice, "Good job. We got 'em locked out now."

Outside the bedroom, the dogs were still barking and pawing and scratching, but she felt certain they could not break down the door with the dresser blocking the way.

Then she heard another sound, beating a slow, regular counterpoint to the dogs' howling frenzy.

A telephone ringing.

The phone in the kitchen.

Oh, damn. An extension. Why didn't they have a telephone extension in any of the bedrooms? *Because Owen was too damn cheap, that's why*—She stopped herself from even thinking such thoughts.

The phone rang eleven times. She counted. It was a kind of self-torture. With every ring she wanted to scream for help, scream loud enough to knock that phone right off the hook, so that whoever was on the line would hear her.

Mercifully, the phone fell silent.

The dogs were still working at the door, but their barks had turned to growls and frustrated whines. They could not get in.

Maggie looked around the room, a room she rarely entered except to dust and vacuum. She saw it as if for the first time. There was that oil painting of the ocean at sunset she had picked up at the Allaire Village flea market. A framed photograph of Owen's grandfather as a young man. An armchair with a quilt draped over the seat cushion. A curtained window, shut tight against the cold ...

A window.

It occurred to her that she could open that window and then she and the children could easily climb out. They were on the ground floor, after all. She would lead them to the station wagon out front and gun the engine and be out the driveway, spitting clouds of gravel, while the dogs still sniffed uselessly at the bedroom door.

She turned the plan over in her mind and regretfully discarded it. To reach the wagon, she and the children would have to pass by Owen's ... remains. She couldn't have them see that. And anyhow, the way Melissa was crying and carrying on, there was no chance for them to sneak away. The dogs would hear them and follow and they would be ambushed on the front lawn and ... and wind up like Owen.

No, they just had to stay here where it was safe and wait it out and figure that somebody, somewhere, would come by to help them. And if not, well, sooner or later the dogs would figure out they were beaten. They would leave and go back to wherever in the name of God they had come from.

One way or the other, things would work out. The children were saved, that was the main thing. And Owen ... well, she would think about Owen later. And probably she would mourn for him too.

She hugged Will and Owen Jr. tighter and said very softly, "Melissa, honey, please stop crying," but Melissa didn't, and outside, the dogs were still growling and scratching at the bedroom door.

# 15

CALVIN BENNETT hesitated for a moment with his hand on the telephone. He was certain he had heard shots, four or five shots, and what might have been a scream. And he was pretty certain the sounds had come from the Andersons' farm. And he had gotten no answer when he called. All in all, things just didn't sit right.

He thought about driving over to his neighbors' place to check on them personally. Then he remembered the scream and decided this was the sort of thing the police earned their paychecks for.

He picked up the phone and dialed the operator.

- — -

Assistant Police Chief Sullivan found his job moderately boring most nights. He took the graveyard shift from 6:00 PM to 6:00 AM. True, statistics proved that the majority of crimes occurred at night, but in Sea Cove, especially in the off-season, there was so little crime that statistics ceased to matter.

His job was promising to be moderately less boring tonight, however, since barely five minutes after he sat down and took his first sip of coffee, he had received Cal Bennett's phone call. He thanked Mr. Bennett, hung up, and was about to dispatch a car to the Anderson place when his boss's voice came over the radio.

"Frank? This is Harper."

"Getting in some overtime, Chief?"

"You could say that. Betty Holland over at Parkfair reported her husband missing. We just found him. He's dead."

The small thump was the sound of Frank Sullivan's coffee cup hitting the desk.

"Natural causes?"

"Very unnatural. Something killed him. Something in the woods. Ripped the poor son of a bitch to pieces."

"Shit." Frank Sullivan was all business now. Suddenly his job was as far from boring as he ever wanted it to get. He condensed Cal Bennett's phone call into two matter-of-fact sentences. "I was just going to send Kane and Lowden."

"Do it." Ben Harper's voice crackled like static. "We might need backup. Out."

The radio went dead, and somewhere in the night on Potters Road, Ben Harper was speeding with officers Tilby and Garrick toward the Andersons' farm.

- — -

The dogs were gone.

Maggie Anderson had been listening intently for the last two minutes. Melissa had stopped crying and the room was quiet. And from the other side of the door ... nothing. No pawing and scratching, no barks or growls, no ragged animal breathing. Nothing. They were gone.

Maggie rose from the bed and let go of Will and Owen Jr., who had been hugging her and trembling. They looked up at her with round, scared eyes. She put a finger to her lips and they nodded.

She crept to the dresser blocking the door and crouched down, on hands and knees, with her head nearly on the floor. She listened for the faintest sound from outside.

Nothing.

She got to her feet, letting out a long sigh, walked back to the bed, and sat down heavily. Her two boys were instantly in her arms again. Melissa sniffled, then was still.

"It's all right," Maggie said softly, almost wonderingly.

"They've gone away. We're safe now."

She let a moment pass for the enormity of that statement to sink in.

Then Owen Jr. raised his head.

"Mama. Was it true—what you said?"

"Yes, dear." Her voice was gentle. "We're safe."

"No. I mean ... about Daddy."

She stroked his head and tried to figure out what to say. A lie would be wrong, and useless, but the truth was too hard. "Your daddy ..." She swallowed. Owen Jr. waited, watching her. She took a breath and decided on a compromise, a half-truth. "I saw your daddy get hurt real bad. And ... from what I could tell ..."

Owen Jr.'s eyes brimmed with tears. He knew what was coming, what she meant to say, whether she came right out and said it or not. She felt, in that moment, that he had known it all along. Then maybe it was best to just get the words out, clean and honest.

"Owen. Listen to me, dear. Your daddy is—"

The room exploded.

For a split second Maggie was sure the entire outside wall had been blown apart. *A missile,* her mind said wildly. *A bomb.* Then she saw it was the window, that's all, just the window that had shattered when the Doberman dived through.

The dog landed on the floor in a shower of ringing glass. It was tangled in the curtain and spent a moment shaking the drapery off its head, then took a step forward, dragging the white lace behind it, and Maggie thought crazily of the wolf dressed in Granny's nightgown to fool Red Riding Hood.

The Doberman growled. Its muzzle was streaked with blood, the blood it had lapped up when it slit Owen's throat, and stringy with strands of gore, the gore it had chewed when it tore into Owen's groin.

The other three dogs climbed in through the open

111

window and stood flanking their leader.

Maggie gathered up Melissa in her arms. The baby was crying again. She glanced at the door but the dresser was there, the heavy oak dresser meant to keep the dogs out, but which was just as effective at keeping her and her children in.

The first Doberman took another step forward, trailing the curtain like the train of a bridal gown.

Maggie clutched Melissa tighter and scrambled over the bed into the bedroom's far corner, away from the door and the window, where she was trapped and she knew it, but she had no choice. A second later, Owen Jr. and Will stood huddled with her, hugging her legs and waist.

The four dogs moved in slowly. Broken glass crunched under their paws. The lace curtain now lay in a heap on the floor. A cold wind blew through the open window.

"What d'we do, Mama?"

It was Will. His voice was low and pleading. His chubby fingers clutched blindly at her blouse.

Maggie choked back a sob. Melissa was whimpering. Owen Jr. looked hard at his brother and hissed, "Shut up, stupid."

Will started to cry.

Now the four dogs hemmed in the tight cluster of their victims.

"Take your sister," said Maggie to Owen Jr. with sudden firmness. Cautiously she lowered the hiccupping baby into the boy's hands.

The first Doberman was growling and showing its fangs.

"All right," said Maggie Anderson. "Now, you boys listen up, and you listen good. You two are going to get out through that window. Owen, you be sure not to drop your sister, now."

"The dogs. Mama ..."

"I know about the dogs. You just wait till ... till ..." She licked her lips and was astonished at how dry her tongue was, dry as sandpaper. "Till I shout at you to run. Then you do it. You run, do you hear me?" Her voice was breaking. "Run and don't stop and don't look back. Run to Mr. Bennett's place. And tell him what's happened."

Owen Jr.'s voice was barely audible. "What about you?"

"You just do as I say. And don't look back." She looked hard at Owen Jr. "You understand me?" He nodded. She looked at Will. "You?"

"Yes, Mama."

She ran a shaking hand through Will's hair. She did not know if what she was feeling was terror or grief, terror at the prospect of dying in a minute, or grief that she would never see her children again. Whatever it was, it was like a series of dynamite charges rocking her insides, threatening to blow her apart.

"All right, then," she said. *I love you both very much.* She did not say that. Could not. Her mouth was too dry and her tongue wouldn't let her, and anyway, she couldn't lose control, not now, and if she said those words, she would lose control.

She took a step forward, out of the corner. Her plan was brutally simple. She would run for the bed and the dogs would swarm over her as they had swarmed over Owen, and she would yell to her kids to run, and with God's grace they would be out the window and fleeing into the safety of the night while the four dogs were busy with her. She would keep them busy, too. She would put up a struggle. She wouldn't go down without protest the way Owen had. She would fight them as long as she could, no matter what it cost her in blood and pain, because every second she fought was one more second of distance between her children and this house.

She tensed, and the words *though I walk through the valley of the shadow of death* ran through her mind. *I will fear no evil, I will fear no evil* ...

"Mrs. Anderson!"

Her head jerked up at the sound of footsteps in the house.

"Mrs. Anderson! Police!"

*"In here!"* she screamed. *"In here, oh God, in here!"*

Then Owen Jr. and Will were screaming too, and Melissa was wailing like a siren.

The dogs heard the voices outside and drew back anxiously with their ears standing up and their eyes darting from the bedroom door to the corner and back.

There was a heavy banging of fists on the door, a curse, a gunshot to blast off the lock, and finally, a tremendous crash that sent the door pitching forward off its hinges, carrying the dresser with it to the floor, under the combined weight of Chief Ben Harper and officers Tilby and Garrick.

The dogs lurched away from Maggie and her children and squared off against this new threat.

# 16

BEN HARPER jumped off the slanting wreckage of the door, into the bedroom, and froze.

His eyes swept the room and took in the relevant details instantly. In the corner, the woman who was the widow of the man they had stumbled across out front, clinging to her terrified brood; on the floor, a litter of glass from the broken window; and creeping out from behind the bed, one by one, their appearance preceded by contorted shadows cast by the lamp onto the wall ... the dogs.

"Christ Almighty," Ben Harper breathed. Behind him, Danny Garrick let out a low whistle.

"What in hell ...?" whispered Tilby.

Ben Harper shook his head for quiet. He raised his .38 in both hands, aimed it at the pack, and prepared to fire.

- — -

For the first time tonight, Razor sensed danger.

He did not know fear. But he knew survival. It was the instinct of survival that had guided him into the tangle of woods last night. It was the instinct of survival that guided him now, as he took a sideways step toward the window.

The Bad Men challenging him were afraid—Razor smelled their fear and liked it—but they had power, too. Some sort of power Razor sensed but did not understand. A power that permitted them to stand there, not to back away or run as the other Bad Men had done. Razor respected power. He took another cautious step sideways.

A yard away, Mr. Dobbs was growling.

Mr. Dobbs had fed well in the henhouse. Perhaps too well. He had pounced on the flying, tumbling, scrambling chickens and torn them to bits, till the Bad Man had barged in and the dogs had turned on him in a surprise attack too powerful to resist. Mr. Dobbs had sprung onto the Bad Man's back and bitten deep into the meat between the Man's shoulder blades. He had been wild. Perhaps bloodlust and the riot of scattered feathers and squawking hens had crazed his mind.

He was growling louder now. Razor knew that growl. It was not a warning. It was the prelude to attack.

Razor prized a good kill, but he prized survival more. He took another step closer to the window.

Mr. Dobbs leaped.

- — -

Later, Ben Harper remembered only one image out of the ten seconds that followed—the vivid freezeframe image of a Doberman wearing a chicken-feather mustache, frozen in the instant of its leap, filling his field of vision like a close-up filling an eighty-foot movie screen, its mouth open in a snarl, its red eyes fixed on his.

He knew, later, that his index finger had squeezed the trigger of the .38 and the bullet had caught the Doberman directly between the eyes and the impact had knocked the animal back onto the bed in a spasming heap, to die almost instantly.

He was faintly aware that the children were screaming.

And when he heard more gunshots, he realized that he and Tilby and Garrick were all firing on the remaining dogs as they scrambled out the window.

The first dog to escape was a Doberman that arced into the night with a move so graceful and perfectly timed as to be almost balletic. That dog was gone before the Doberman that Ben Harper had shot had even hit the bed, and there was no hope of stopping it. But the other two dogs, a Doberman and a German shepherd, were confused and a fraction slower, and somebody's bullet caught that last Doberman in the hind leg as it was perched on the windowsill. The dog whined and almost slipped back, and if it had, the next shot would have finished it, but no, it tumbled forward, out of the window, and was loping away into the darkness before Harper and his men could get to the window and squeeze off their final, useless rounds.

Those were the ten seconds, but when Ben tried to relive them later that night, only that single image remained, clear as a frame of movie film cut from the strip of action and mounted as a slide. The Doberman, leaping, and those red eyes that spoke to him in a language plainer than words, and what they had said was: *I am Death.*

- — -

It was only after the ambulances had come and gone—taking with them Owen Anderson's body and his traumatized family—that Ben had time to take a good look at the Doberman.

The dog was sprawled on the bed. Its forehead was a bloody crater. Around its head, the bedspread was littered with chicken feathers and stained a deep burgundy. The animal lay on its back with its paws in the air, like a dog playing dead. Ben ran his thumb over the gleaming claws spread wide like the talons of a bird of prey.

The dog's jaw hung open. With morbid curiosity, Ben touched the yellowed, blood-smeared fangs. He was amazed at how sharp they were. They reminded him of the screwdrivers with sharpened tips he had confiscated from those kids the summer before last, kids who had been prying open video-arcade games to steal the quarters. The thought passed through his mind that if his bullet had been off-target or an instant late, those fangs would have been in his throat. He withdrew his hand.

Still he did not move away. He stood over the Doberman, looking at it and seeing ...

A collar.

Around its neck, a light chain-metal collar. The collar was caked with blood and half-buried in the dog's matted fur, but it was still there, glinting like a necklace of diamonds.

Ben reached for the collar and gently tugged on it, turning it till a silver tag came into view.

He remembered the tag on the Gaineses' dog: MY NAME IS BUSTER. IF I AM LOST, PLEASE CALL ...

His hands trembled a little as he lowered his head and squinted to make out the inscription on the tag in the bedroom's dim light: MASTERSON SECURITY SYSTEMS, WOODSBORO, MARYLAND.

# 17

GAZING INTO the fireplace, lost in the hypnotizing dance of flame, Nikki Grant did not quite hear the phone for the first few rings. Besides, she thought dreamily, Karl would get it.

Then she remembered that Karl Masterson was out talking to the trainers after having spent the entire day in a hopeless quest by telephone for the lost Van-dura and its cargo. She jumped up and crossed the room to the phone.

When she answered, she heard a man identifying himself as Ben Harper, chief of police of the town of Sea Cove, New Jersey, calling for Masterson Security Systems—but what she actually heard was a man who wanted to kill somebody, a man who would have strangled her with the telephone cord, via long distance, had it been possible.

"Mr. Masterson is in a conference right now," she said crisply, but somewhere beneath her surface cool was the premonition of disaster.

"I don't give a damn where he is or what he's doing," said Ben Harper. "Get him on the line. *Now.*"

She thought of requesting an explanation, but decided against it for the obvious reason that only one explanation was possible. They had found the dogs.

She asked Harper to wait for one moment, and then she had put him on hold and was running into the cold night without a coat, running across the lawn to the long gray expanse of the kennel. Somewhere, a dog was barking.

- — -

Karl Masterson took a moment to compose himself before pressing the button to release Ben Harper from hold.

"Chief Harper? Karl Masterson. What can I do for you?"

"You can explain, for starters, why the hell one of your Doberman pinschers was running around loose in my town."

Masterson closed his eyes. Loose. They had gotten loose.

"You have captured the animal, Chief?"

"I killed the fucker."

Masterson allowed a beat of silence on the line. His voice was steady but too quiet when he asked, "Was that necessary?"

"I'd say so. Considering that this animal and its three friends, who are also running around loose and who are also, I assume, your property, have killed two people within the last twelve hours. No, let me take that back. They didn't just kill them. They folded, spindled, and mutilated them. You ever see how a pumpkin looks after it's been smashed on the sidewalk? I've seen two faces that looked like that ... Hello? *Hello?*"

Each new sentence had hit Karl Masterson with the force of a blow. He sank into the nearest chair, grateful for it, knowing that without it his knees would have carried him unresisting to the floor.

At the doorway Nikki watched tensely. She could not hear Ben Harper's end of the conversation, but she could see its effects in the sudden unnatural paleness of Masterson's face.

"I am here ... Chief." Masterson gritted his teeth and gathered up the reserves of inner strength he had discovered as a child and had called on many times since. "Two people, you say?"

"So far. The night is young. And three of the bastards are still out there."

Masterson's strength was back now, surging through him like fresh oxygen during a run, filling his body with clean, hard energy, leaving no room for fear ... or guilt.

There would be plenty of time for both. Later.

"Very well, Chief," said Karl Masterson slowly. "I cannot explain what has happened. I don't know how the dogs escaped."

"Great. That's a big help."

"I am *trying* to help you, Chief. But I can't give you information I don't have."

"Well, you must know something, for Christ's sake."

"I know that the dogs were being transported by truck to New York City—and that the truck never reached its destination."

"Why not?"

"I don't know. I've been on the phone all day trying to track it down." Masterson had a thought. "Have you had any traffic accidents in your area? Involving a GMC Van-dura, license plate—"

"No. No accidents. Just a pair of corpses—oh, and a dog, not one of yours, a family pet, slaughtered."

"All right, Chief. Our first priority must be to find that truck. It must be somewhere in the vicinity of Sea Cove. If you could send out a helicopter to search for it or for its wreckage—"

"I hate to break this to you, Masterson, but our department was lucky to get a fifth squad car last week. We haven't got a helicopter."

"I do. My assistant and I will fly to Sea Cove tonight." Masterson glanced at Nikki, who nodded. "We can be there in minutes. We'll find the truck, if our searchlight can pick it up from the air."

"Gee, that's darn nice of you, under the circumstances, but isn't it a little bit like locking the barn door after the horses have bolted?"

"Chief Harper. In order to catch these dogs, it is necessary to think like them. To anticipate their next moves. Otherwise they will not be found. They have your whole town and its outskirts in which to hide. Our only hope is to outthink them. I can do that. I trained them. I know how they think."

"And what does all that have to do with the truck?"

"The dogs are wandering in the night. They are lost, cold, confused. Possibly injured ..."

"My men got one of the Dobermans in the leg."

Masterson nodded. "They will begin to wish they were back where they were safe and warm and taken care of. They will want to go home. In their minds, the truck is associated with home. It is their last connection with the place where they were born and raised. They will return to it, instinctively, if they can. When they do, we must be there."

"You think they can find this truck again?"

"They will try. Therefore, so must we. It's our best hope."

"Yeah. Well ... you may be right. Okay, Masterson, I can't say you're not being helpful. I'd like to say it, but I can't. In fact, to be perfectly honest, when you picked up the phone I would have liked to break your fucking jaw." He added slowly, without humor, "I still would."

"Chief Harper," said Karl Masterson softly, with the quiet dignity of a man unaccustomed to taking insults, "if beating me up would help you to catch those dogs—or would bring those two people back—I would let you break every bone in my body."

# 18

RAZOR HAD no idea what had become of Bigfoot or Cleopatra, and he did not care. He had a dim sense, more a feeling than a thought, that something bad had happened to Mr. Dobbs. He remembered, vaguely, a blast of sound and the Doberman's body hurtling back in a spiral of blood. Then Razor had been out the window and running and his mind had no space for thoughts of anything but survival.

He was cutting a straight line through the woods, loping along tirelessly, covering ground as swiftly and silently as the racing shadow of a cloud. Then suddenly he stopped, nostrils quivering.

He had caught a scent. Not the scent of Men or blood. He had never smelled anything like this. It was overpowering, intoxicating, maddening.

He followed it, rushing blindly, his tongue lolling, eyes wild. Razor had spent his entire life at Karl Masterson's ranch, and all of Masterson's female dogs had been spayed. He had never smelled a female in heat. Until now.

He loped into an open field and followed the scent to a doghouse where a Weimaraner named Lucy stirred sleeplessly.

The dog's amber eyes met Razor's as he stood blocking the doorway of the doghouse. Lucy got up slowly. Her smooth silver-gray fur shimmered like velvet moonlight. She growled. Razor crept inside the doghouse. The female panicked and tried to run and Razor launched himself on her, mounted her, penetrated her, impelled by a need he had never felt before and could not resist.

Lucy whimpered, growled again, then barked hysterically as Razor's legs pumped up and down like pistons and his body shuddered and he spattered her fur with drool. The barks rose to ululating howls. Razor panted raggedly, oblivious of anything but the consuming urge to force himself even deeper inside.

Then, somehow, a noise did reach him, past the female's howling, past the fever in his brain. The sound of a door slamming. And then ... a Man's voice, yelling, growing louder as the Man drew near.

These were danger sounds. Razor had never ignored a warning of danger. But now he almost did. His mind was crazed. The female's scent was so strong, so close, it was driving him to frenzy.

Lucy's howling went on. The Man was approaching at a run. He was nearly there.

At the last moment Razor's survival instinct flared up, and his mind cleared. He pulled free of the female, bolted out the door, and ran. He had a brief glimpse of the Man, lone and startled and defenseless, an easy kill, but Razor had killed enough Men for one night. He streaked past the Man, over the field, and let the woods swallow him up.

His body was still on fire. His nostrils burned. His brain buzzed. He had not had enough. He stopped once and almost turned back. By sheer effort of will he ran on. He was not fleeing the Man. He was fleeing this madness within him.

Only after he had covered long miles and left the last traces of the female's scent behind was he finally free.

# 19

AT 9:45, as Karl Masterson and Nikki Grant were lifting off in an Aerospatiale chopper with Masterson at the controls, the night DJ at Sea Cove's number one, original—and only—radio station took Ben Harper's call.

The DJ, whose professional name was Stevie Stevens but whose birth certificate identified him as Morton Thomas Tillinger, got lots of phone calls on the air, since his was a request show and, if the caller was lively enough, could just as easily double as a call-in talk show. Every night he sat alone in the studio and took the calls and played the songs people wanted to hear, till eventually, past midnight, the calls stopped coming because most of his listeners were asleep, at which point he just played whatever he felt like. To break the monotony he had a standing order for an extra-large pizza with the works to be delivered every night at 10:00, free of charge, in exchange for an occasional friendly plug of Antonio's Pizza Palace on Route 71. He was getting a little antsy, waiting for the kid to show up with the pizza, when Ben Harper called.

Very calmly Harper explained over the phone, on the air, that there were three trained attack dogs loose in town, that they had taken two lives, identities of the victims withheld at this time, and that while the people of Sea Cove and surrounding communities should *not* panic, they should take reasonable precautions.

"Don't go out of your house tonight unless it's absolutely necessary," he said. "If you need to go somewhere and you don't have a car, call your local police station and a squad car will be provided to escort you."

He gave out the phone number of the Sea Cove police department, then added that he would greatly appreciate any information that anyone might have about a missing GMC Van-dura truck that had been hired to transport the dogs, and which might have been involved in an accident or otherwise incapacitated. The state police, he said, had been notified and were keeping an eye out for strays that matched the descriptions. The Department of Public Health in Trenton was expected to send experts to the scene first thing in the morning. And the man who'd trained the dogs was en route from Maryland. Help, in short, was on the way.

Finally he repeated what Karl Masterson had told him at the end of their conversation.

"If you do see a dog," said Ben Harper to the radio audience, "stay perfectly still. Frozen. Like a statue. Any movement will provoke the animal. Do *not* attempt to approach the dog or feed it or pet it or talk to it or treat it as you might treat any other dog. And don't try to run away. No matter how fast you think you are, the dog will chase you down. It can cover ten feet in one leap. It can run like a greyhound and pounce like a tiger.

"I'm not exaggerating or trying to be melodramatic, and believe it or not, I'm not trying to scare you—not much, anyway. I'm just telling you what the man who trained these things told me. Attack dogs are different from ordinary guard dogs. A guard dog is trained to bark and make noise and scare people. An attack dog is trained to kill. Manstopper. That's what it's called.

"This is obviously a difficult situation for our community, but we are getting it under control. In the meantime, please don't take any chances," Harper concluded in his calm, flat, oddly reassuring voice, the voice of an airline pilot informing his passengers that the plane had a minor problem with its landing gear but everything would be taken care of shortly.

Stevie Stevens, aka Morton Tillinger, shifted his corpulent bulk in his creaking chair and felt suddenly uneasy in the deserted building. He thanked the chief and promised to repeat the bulletin periodically throughout the night. Then he went on with his show, though without his usual quota of levity and with a noticeable shortage of the bad puns that were his closest approximation of humor. He was glad when the delivery boy arrived with the pizza and sorry to see him go, and to be left alone again with only a telephone switchboard and a broadcasting tower to keep him in contact with the outside world.

- — -

In Sea Cove and Manasecon and New Bridge and all the other little coastal towns within reach of the station's signal, people in their cars, in their apartments, and in their houses heard Ben Harper's phone call and Stevie Stevens' bulletins. Those in their cars drove faster to get home, those already home checked and double-checked the locks on their doors and windows, and those with children looked in on them anxiously as they slept.

# 20

WYLIE GAINES lay in bed, motionless but for the slow rising and falling of her stomach, her eyes wide, staring at the ceiling. She was not crying. She had cried herself out.

Mr. Frenzell had gotten her to stop screaming, eventually. Then she had sat crying while all the other kids looked at her and the bus drove her straight home, bypassing its regular stops. Her mommy and daddy had been waiting when the bus pulled up, and when she saw their faces she understood that they already knew about Buster. They both said a lot of things to her, but none of it made any difference.

She did not ask how Buster had died. The question did not occur to her. He was dead, that's all, and that was enough. She did not know how grateful her parents were that she did not ask.

During dinner—Wylie's favorite, sloppy-joe hamburgers, which she barely touched—her daddy had said the one thing that caused her to perk up momentarily.

"Maybe tomorrow, kiddo," he said gently, "we could all go out together and get you a new dog."

Wylie's face almost brightened. Then her mommy put down a fork laden with potato salad and said in a low warning tone, "Ohhhh, no," and Wylie's face was dark and brooding once more.

Her mommy had explained, not to her but to her daddy, that she no longer felt a pet was necessary to a child's healthy development. In fact, she now believed that the emotional attachment involved was positively dangerous. Wylie was not sure what any of that meant, but she noticed that her mommy's eyes looked drained and almost guilty, and her words sounded like something she had read someplace and memorized.

Her daddy had not pursued the matter.

Wylie had left her hamburger uneaten except for a few reluctant nibbles and had gone to bed at 8:00, to lie awake and think.

Her parents had been quiet downstairs. There had been no sound of the television or the stereo or the radio, not even the sound of conversation.

Around 10:00 she heard their slow footsteps on the stairs and pretended to be asleep when they peeked in through the doorway. Her mommy had whispered, "She'll be all right," and her daddy had said, "Sure, she will," and neither of them had sounded very certain.

Then they had gone to bed too, and now the house lay dark and silent.

Almost silent.

Outside, in the backyard, the gate was creaking in the wind.

The gate that A Certain Person had forgotten to lock, and because of it, Buster had run away and now he was dead.

The thought almost made Wylie cry again.

The gate creaked a little louder, with the rusty, groaning sound it made when it swung open wide.

Wylie listened, suddenly fascinated, not knowing why.

Faintly she heard a jingle-jangling sound, like the jingling of Mommy's keys in her purse or Daddy's coins in his pants pockets or ... Buster's dog collar.

The gate creaked, opening wider, and then was silent.

Wylie, heart pounding, got out of bed and padded in bare feet and pajamas to the bedroom window and looked down at the backyard.

She gasped.

There was a dog in the yard.

*Buster had come home.*

No. That was impossible. Buster was dead. The newspaper had said so. Mommy and Daddy had said so. But maybe ... just maybe ... they were all wrong. Maybe some other doggie had died, and all the grown-ups had gotten it mixed up with Buster, and Buster was alive, after all, and he had come back. Maybe.

She pressed her face to the cold glass, straining to see the dog more clearly, but all she could make out was an obscure four-legged shape, a shadow lost in shadows. Then her breath fogged the glass and she could see nothing at all.

Well ... there was one way to tell.

She crammed on her slippers, belted her robe around her waist, and slipped silently along the hall, past the closed door of her parents' bedroom, then down the stairs, artfully avoiding the third-from-last step that squeaked, then through the kitchen to the back door.

She unlocked the door, opened it, and stepped outside into the backyard, hugging herself against the cold. She stumbled forward, peering ahead.

The dog stood just inside the gate, near the toolshed.

"Buster ...?" she inquired in a faint, tentative, breathless voice.

The dog made no sound.

She crept closer. Then, ten feet away, she stopped. Her heart sank. She could now see the dog clearly. It was not Buster. It was just some poor stray, looking all dirty and raggedy, its brown fur splotched all over with mud, she guessed, or anyway, with something dark and messy.

- — -

Bigfoot stood motionless, watching the girl.

He and Cleo and Razor had fled from the Bad Place

and scattered into the woods, and he had lost the others. For hours since, he had wandered aimlessly, until he caught a dog-smell, a curiously familiar smell, a smell he associated in a dim way with Potters Road. The smell had led him to this fence, this gate, and he had poked the gate open with his snout and crept into the yard.

But there was no dog here, only this Girl who stood swaying back and forth on her stout legs, staring at him with wide innocent eyes.

Bigfoot was very tired. He had done enough killing for one night. He did not wish to kill again.

But the Girl was so small and awkward, such easy prey. He thought of the chickens—how simple it had been to slaughter them—how good their warm meat and salty blood had tasted.

This Girl would be no more difficult to kill. Easier. She was not squawking, not trying to escape.

She was, in fact, coming toward him, step by step.

He drew back slowly on his hindquarters.

- — -

Wylie felt a little silly about having thought that it could be Buster in the backyard. Of course it wasn't Buster. She was a big girl, in the second grade, and when her mommy and daddy and the newspaper all said something was true, then it was true, just as surely as if Mrs. Larchmont had said it.

But there was something else her daddy had said ...

*"Maybe tomorrow, kiddo, we could all go out together and get you a new dog."*

No, her mommy had said.

And Wylie had felt so sad.

Because she wanted a new dog so much. A new friend to play with in the grass in summertime. A friend to snatch Pet Snax out of the air. A friend who would let her tickle his tummy and scratch him behind the ears and cuddle him, till he licked her all over and made her laugh.

A new Buster.

And now, here was a poor, lost, homeless, hungry dog who had showed up practically outside her bedroom window.

She took a step toward the dog, cautiously, so as not to frighten it away.

"Don't be scared," she whispered. "I won't hurt you."

The dog did not move.

She took another step.

The dog shifted back on its hind legs. To Wylie, it looked like it was lying down, making itself comfortable. That was good. Maybe the dog wouldn't run. Maybe it would stay and make friends.

She took another step.

The German shepherd looked at her with brown eyes glinting red in the dark. An adult would have seen menace in those eyes. Ben Harper would have seen death. Wylie Gaines, eight years old, saw nothing there at all. She had never been afraid of dogs. She was not afraid now.

She moved closer.

"I bet you're hungry," she said.

The dog made a low purring sound, too indistinct to be a growl.

- — -

The Girl was very close. Bigfoot could smell her. The scent of live flesh was strong, dizzying. His mind spun with images of hens, wings flapping, and the Bad Man in the tree, his neck shooting up a fountain of blood, and the Man outside the henhouse, and the Man from the truck, and the Bad Dog on Potters Road.

He was tired. But he wanted this kill. But he was tired. He was confused. He could not decide.

The Girl took a step closer and Bigfoot dug his claws into the dead grass and stared at her and waited.

- — -

Wylie was so close now that, with just one more step, she could extend her hand and touch the dog, pet him, stroke him gently as she had stroked good old Buster.

The dog showed its teeth. Its growl was louder, unmistakable now. Wylie giggled. She thought the dog was funny, to growl like that. That was how Buster had always wanted to play. He would bark and growl and show his fangs, and then he would chase her and she would chase him, and they would end up together, squirming madly and delightedly in mutual surrender.

She guessed that this dog wanted to play too.

She took a final step.

She hesitated.

Then, very slowly, Wylie Gaines reached out to the dog with one pudgy, helpless hand.

-—-

Bigfoot opened his mouth. He felt the sizzle of electric tension in his haunches, the tingle of anticipation in his claws, and the sharpness of his teeth against his drooling tongue.

-—-

"Nice doggie ..."

# SECOND DAY

# 21

SHE DREW in a lungful of frozen air and exhaled steam. Her Reeboks thudded on the boards in a light, steady rhythm. It was exactly two miles from the start of the boardwalk at the South End, at the edge of the inlet which gave Sea Cove its name, to the North End pavilion near the town's border with Manasecon. She always ran the two miles up, rested briefly with a walk on the beach, then ran the two miles back—every morning, rain or shine, even on bitchingly cold mornings like today.

She hated it. She hated the ringing of her alarm clock at 6:00 AM, the painful half-light of dawn, the stretching exercises and jumping jacks, and most of all, she hated running. The monotony of it, day after day, the agony of the last quarter mile, and the trembling exhaustion at the finish. She hated it, but she did it, because she liked the way her body looked since she'd started working out. She liked the long, slender, taut-muscled legs, the hard, slim buttocks, the trim waist. She liked the way her breasts bounced as she ran, and she liked the stares she drew from male joggers, the way they smiled too broadly when she smiled at them, though she had yet to see any other joggers this morning. And she really liked the smart navy-blue jogging suit that showed off the long lines of her figure and made her look taller.

Most of all, of course, she liked the fact that Bobby Tyler, a senior at Monmouth College and a star basketball player, was going out with *her*, Stephanie Carruthers, eighteen years old, a mere freshman, but a freshman who was more than willing to please—within certain limits.

Yes, she had let Bobby feel her breasts and she'd helped him to get off a few times, but as for actually having sex ... no. Not yet. And that was how the trouble had started last night in Bobby's car. He wanted to go all the way, and she said no. He got pushy, so she shoved him off her and called him a creep, and neither of them said another word during the long drive back.

She passed the gazebo that marked the halfway point of the first leg of her run, while reflecting that if Bobby was extremely repentant today, then over the weekend, when her parents were out of town, she might, just might, let him stay over. Maybe.

Stephanie kept running north, while part of her wondered without much interest why the boardwalk was so totally empty, and part of her contemplated with vastly greater interest the prospect of Bobby Tyler's naked body entwined with her own, and no part of her at all was aware of the Doberman that padded silently under the boardwalk, directly below her feet.

- — -

Razor was cold. The night had been cold, too, but he had kept warm then by running.

After outracing the Weimaraner's scent, he had reached a wide road bright with headlights. He had huddled in the shadows until the road was clear, then darted across and continued east. Another scent had drawn him, one by no means as powerful as the last, a scent that merely teased his memory and his curiosity. It was the damp, salt-air smell he had first sniffed in the rear of the Van-dura.

Razor crossed another road, narrower and less traveled than the first, and then he ran down the streets of a town—lightless, deserted streets walled in by rows of sleeping houses and columns of telephone poles. At last he could run no farther, not because he lacked the strength—Razor never lacked strength when survival or a kill was at stake—but because there was nowhere left to run. He had reached the sea.

He crept under the boardwalk and onto the beach, a pale strip of desert beneath the starless sky. He made his way warily across the sand, his paws crunching seashells and clambering over driftwood, until he reached the surf. He stared, fascinated, at the waves as they rolled in slowly. Each one glittered like glass, then shattered into bright fragments of foam that bubbled down into the sand and were gone, to be replaced by the crash of another wave a moment later. Razor breathed in deeply and his nostrils buzzed with fresh salt air and suddenly he understood that this strange, roaring, pulsing spread of foam was the source of the mystery scent.

Then a wave splashed up higher onto the beach, lapping at his front paws, and he drew back, sniffing his damp feet and growling. He barked, once, at the ocean. He thought about biting it. But the thought flickered and vanished because there was nothing solid enough to bite, and besides, now that he had stopped running and his feet were wet, he was getting cold.

He crept back under the boardwalk, curled up in a tight fetal ball, and slept.

The thumping over his head had awakened him. He had jerked upright, scented the air, and caught a living-body smell. He was instantly alert. The thumping grew louder, till it was directly overhead, a regular sound, *thump thump thump,* like the sound of Bigfoot's nervous pacing on the roof of Razor's cage. Then the sound began to fade. The prey was escaping.

Razor followed swiftly, till he was directly beneath the source of the sound again, and then he kept pace with his victim with a steady, effortless trot.

The day was bright but the rising sun was hidden behind heavy clouds. Morning had brought no relief from the cold. Razor felt the chill ocean breeze sweeping through him. Gradually he became aware of a new sensation, more powerful than cold. Hunger. He had killed, and killed well, but in the last twenty-four hours he had eaten nothing but one chicken in the henhouse of the Andersons' farm.

In his mind he saw himself ripping flesh, ripping and chewing and swallowing. He remembered the Bad Man who had been his first kill, and the Bad Dog on Potters Road. The memories blurred together into an unbroken stream of images and smells. They made him salivate.

He looked up, catching flashes of white sky through gaps in the boardwalk planks, but he could not see his victim. He could hear the steady footfalls, though, and he could smell the perspiring warmth, the body heat, and he could follow, step by step, and when the moment came, he would strike.

And then he would feed.

-— -

She reached the pavilion at the North End and slowed to a brisk walk, feeling exhausted already and dreading the run back. Ahead, just past the pavilion, was a short flight of wooden steps leading down to the beach, where she always took a quick walk to gather strength for the rest of the workout, most especially that final grueling quarter mile. She half-walked, half-jogged toward the stairs, holding her gloved hands outstretched above her head to let the blood flow down into her chest, feeling the hard, rapid pulse of the veins in her palms.

She did not see the shadow that stole along the ground under her feet, amid the discarded beer bottles and lost pocket change, the shadow that hesitated, waiting, then lay hunched beneath the stairs as she stood poised at the top, still moving her feet up and down mechanically as she prepared to descend.

The beach, like the boardwalk, was empty. There

were no fishermen on any of the jetties laid out in long parallel lines, shrinking with distance, until the farthest rocks merged into a mist of sea and sky. There was nobody, nobody anywhere. That really was unusual, and for just a second it gave Stephanie pause, but then she shrugged and chalked it up to the weather—cold and bleak and threatening snow. She watched the waves smashing against the jetties and a few sea gulls dipping and gliding through the air like scraps of wastepaper flung against the cloud-scudded sky.

Something about the desolation of the scene frightened her; she could not say what or why.

Six feet below, the shadow waited.

She took the first step down the stairs.

The shadow coiled tight on its haunches.

She took another step—and stopped, in time with the blast of a car horn.

She turned. A police car had pulled to a stop on First Avenue. The cop at the wheel gestured to her and hit the horn again.

What the hell? Stephanie frowned. They had already made it illegal to bicycle on the boardwalk. Were the damn cops cracking down on joggers too?

Feeling a mixture of bewilderment and irritation, she ran back up the stairs, across the boardwalk, to a ramp that led down to the street. She strode up to the police car, swinging her arms briskly, partly to keep the blood circulating but mainly to keep her breasts bouncing. She was rewarded by what appeared to be a look of plain openmouthed admiration on the cop's face, till she got closer and saw that he was merely yawning. He rubbed his red eyes and asked her what she was doing out alone, and she leaned in the car window and said she was jogging, at which point the officer, named Tilby, observed that obviously she had not heard The News. She hadn't. Tilby briefed her on the night's developments, then offered her a ride home. It was clear that the offer was not subject to refusal.

Stephanie had no intention of refusing. She was only too happy to slide into the warm, safe confines of the car, sink back in the passenger seat, and shudder a little as she thought about what the cop had said. Two people dead ... killer dogs ... running wild, could be anywhere ... and she had been out jogging, for God's sake. No wonder the boardwalk, the beach, the jetties, and even the streets were deserted. And last night, when Bobby had let her off at her parents' place at two o'clock, he hadn't waited, as he usually did, to see that she got in the house all right. Oh, no, he'd driven off with an angry squeal of tires, and she had walked up the path to the front door and fumbled with her keys, all alone, defenseless and vulnerable, while the night rustled and whispered around her, a night that concealed, somewhere in its vast darkness, a pack of wild animals seeking blood ...

With that thought, she resolved that no matter how repentant Bobby Tyler might be after class today, she would not let him go all the way with her, uh-uh, not after his thoughtlessness had nearly gotten her killed.

No, she would not let that big dumb jerk anywhere near her, and that was final.

At least ... not this weekend, anyway.

The police car executed a U-turn on the wide, empty street and sped back to Sea Cove's South End. In the darkness under the boardwalk, twin pinpoints of red glinted in frustration, watching it go.

# 22

TWENTY MINUTES later, Alex Driscoll stood at the edge of the vacant lot at the corner of Fairburn and Fourth, rubbing sleep out of his eyes and waiting with Ben Harper for the helicopter to set down.

Alex had not been listening to the radio last night. Somehow he had sensed that he could not tolerate the DJ's chatter, the inevitable request for "anything by the Boss," and the pathetic friendliness of the telephone callers, lonely people reaching out for the illusion of companionship with a faceless man in a broadcast booth.

Instead he had climbed into bed and read for a while, without interest, and drifted off to sleep.

He was awakened by the frantic ringing of the telephone at five o'clock. He groped for the phone, blinking, while his tongue probed his mouth and tasted cotton.

"Hello?" His voice was a croak.

"Alex?" It was Ed Clancy. "Aren't you up yet?"

"I am ... now."

"Well, dammit, better late than never. Don't you know we've got the biggest story this town's ever seen?"

"Let me guess. Martian landing? Invasion of Russian paratroopers? Or is it something really big?"

"It's two people dead, and don't give me any lip, son."

Ed had explained brusquely, and Alex had said he would be right over. Ten minutes after he cradled the phone he had arrived at the *Citizen*'s offices, and now, an hour and a half later, he was standing next to Ben Harper and watching the helicopter emblazoned with the logo

MASTERSON SECURITY SYSTEMS as it descended like an immense buzzing insect onto the dead brown grass.

The engine whine abruptly shut off and the blades slowed, cutting lazier circles in the air. Other than Ben Harper and Alex himself, there were no spectators. The people of Sea Cove had been given good reason not to venture out-of-doors; those who had not heard the news on the radio had been informed via the grapevine of gossipy telephone calls or by the police officers themselves, tirelessly patrolling the streets. The town was now locked and shuttered and huddled in silent fear.

The day was fiercely cold, and the overcast sky promised worse. Alex shrugged his jacket collar up higher around his neck and wished he had remembered to wear his wool hat.

He was waiting for Harper to approach the copter. The police chief did not move. Alex glanced at him and saw Ben's eyes squinting against more than the stinging wind, his lips pursed, his arms in their fur-lined parka sleeves wrapped tightly across his chest.

Portrait of an angry man. A man who blamed this whole godawful mess on Karl Masterson.

The helicopter door opened. Alex tensed, and he felt Ben Harper tense beside him. They were both anxious to get their first look at this man who made his living—and a damn good living, it appeared—by training animals to kill.

The first person to step out the door and duck under the blades was a young woman in knee-high boots, a white pantsuit, and a fur jacket that had to be mink. One gloved hand swung a briefcase, while the other swept strands of ash-blond hair from her face.

The woman was walking toward them, covering ground in brisk, long-legged strides, when Karl Masterson emerged from the helicopter.

He was tall, so tall he had to nearly double over to

avoid the dying spin of the overhead blades. The immediate impression he gave was of immense, raw, physical power. It was there in the wide chest, the jutting shoulders, and the square-jawed hairless head, a head like a blunt instrument, hatless in the cold, its scalp mottled red. A huge leather carrying case was slung easily over one shoulder. Binoculars bobbed on a strap around the collar of a coat that was unostentatious, exquisitely tailored in consummate taste, and which, by Alex's impromptu calculations, had cost at least twice his own monthly salary.

Masterson walked swiftly, with the effortless dignity of a man accustomed to rapid movement, and caught up with the woman halfway across the field. A moment later he was extending a gloveless hand to Ben Harper and Ben was shaking it cautiously.

"Chief. Karl Masterson."

Alex focused on the handshake and noted how Ben's hand was swallowed whole by Masterson's. It was a good, stiff, manly handshake, the sort of handshake the All-American Boy would give the dean while accepting his diploma to his classmates' loudest applause.

Masterson was introducing the young woman as his assistant, Nikki Grant, and Harper was nodding curtly, but Alex was not aware of it. *The born winner,* he was thinking as he stared, fascinated, at Karl Masterson. *Oh, yeah.*

Then Masterson glanced at him, and Alex remembered that he was a reporter, the only one on the scene. Under any other circumstances, he would have been fighting for a place in a mob of media people, but not today. Early this morning, while he slept, another news story had broken, sucking up all the oxygen in the tri-state area. A jumbo jet coming in from Amsterdam had overshot the runway at Newark Airport and crashed into a residential neighborhood, blowing down row houses like dominoes and scattering wreckage and bodies everywhere. It was the biggest story in the country, running nonstop on every TV channel and consuming all available ink. The media, as Ed Clancy liked to opine, was a many-headed beast, but it could digest only one large meal at a time, and the Newark crash—PLANE-AGEDDON, one of the tabloids had dubbed it—was more than a meal; it was a veritable banquet. No one had time for killer dogs on the rampage in a town nobody had ever heard of, not when rescuers were still digging survivors out of the debris while the FAA, state police, and a dozen other agencies descended on the scene.

Which made this Alex's show, and as Ed had forcefully reminded him, the Sea Cove *Citizen's* best chance to get on the wires and on the journalistic map. If Alex didn't blow it, of course.

"Mr. Masterson," said Alex briskly enough to almost cover his nervousness, "I'm Alex Driscoll, reporter for the—"

"Sorry," said Masterson, turning away. "No time for interviews. Chief, is there somewhere we can talk?"

Ben shrugged. "My office."

Harper led Masterson and Nikki Grant to his squad car, and Alex was left standing behind.

He shook his head with sudden determination. Ed Clancy had ordered him to get a comment, any comment, something for publication. He wasn't going to give up without a fight.

He ran to his Pinto and pulled away in pursuit of Karl Masterson and a story.

# 23

THE KID had slept fitfully and awakened at dawn. He showered, a rare luxury, then pulled on his jeans and boots and corduroy jacket. He brushed his long hair back into place with his hands. Then he lay in bed, waiting.

Around 7:00 he heard footsteps, running water, and the clinking of pots and pans. Jessie Blair was up. Good.

He could have killed her last night. Once she had gone to sleep, it would have been easy to sneak into the kitchen, steal a knife, and find her bedroom. But he had restrained himself. Once he killed her, he would have to leave the hotel. To linger at the scene of a crime was too risky a spin of the wheel, even for him. Besides, he didn't like hanging out with dead bodies. They made him nervous.

And he had not wanted to leave last night. He'd spent too many nights shivering in roadside bushes, huddled against the cold. His bed was warm and soft and it didn't creak too loudly even when he masturbated, thinking of what he would do to Jessie Blair. In the morning ...

Now he rose from bed and left his room.

He found Jessie in the kitchen, cracking eggs into a pan steaming with bacon grease. Music from the radio played in the background. At first she didn't hear him, and he thought he could grab her from behind, throw her to the floor, and pour the hot grease over her face. It would be different. But not as satisfying as cutting her. Anyway, she had a pretty face. It was always a shame to spoil a pretty face.

He tapped her shoulder and she turned, startled.

"Oh ...!"

"Sorry," he said in his politest tone. He could be real polite when he wanted to be, which wasn't often. He smiled, the faggoty, bashful smile women always went for. "I didn't mean to startle you, Miss Blair."

"It's all right." She swept stray hairs off her forehead and smiled back. "You can call me Jessie, you know."

He gave her the smile again and was pleased to see color tinge her cheeks, making her freckles stand out girlishly.

"I was just wondering ... since I heard you fixing breakfast ... if you could make me some too. If it's not too much trouble."

She hesitated. "The Oceanview isn't really a bed-and-breakfast sort of place."

He dug into his empty pants pocket. "I'll pay."

"No," she said quickly, embarrassed. "No, it's okay. A couple of eggs won't break me."

"I really appreciate it. Thing is, I wasn't feeling so hot yesterday and I didn't have anything to eat." Except for some candy bars in his pack, this was true.

"Well, we can't have that," she said briskly. "How would you like your eggs?"

"Any way is fine. Whatever's easy."

"I usually just fry 'em."

"Sounds great."

They made small talk while the eggs fried. She asked if he was seeing the country. He said yes. He gave her the story of how he'd taken a year off from college to travel around America, meet people, broaden his horizons. People loved that shit. It was like something out of *Easy Rider.* It appealed to their own frustrated yearnings to say fuck you to the boss and the bills and the system and take off for parts unknown.

By the time he and Jessie Blair sat down to breakfast, she was asking him breathless questions about places he'd never been and he was fielding them like a pro.

The eggs weren't bad. He ate quickly, ravenously, while keeping up his end of the conversation. But his thoughts were not on the food or the talk. He was thinking about the knife. Just an ordinary table knife, not ideal, but he ran his thumb along the blade and it was sharp, nice and sharp. He would clamp one hand over her mouth to stifle her screams, then cut her up good. After she was dead he'd rob the place—there had to be money in that cash register in the lobby—and go. With luck, nobody would find her body till he had hitched a ride on the parkway.

He was planning to make his move when Jessie interrupted one of her own questions and turned to the radio. "Oh, wait a second. The news is coming on. I always listen to the local news."

*You're gonna make a pretty big news item yourself, call-me-Jessie,* he thought coolly, *front page news, when they find you.* He put down his fork, gripped the knife tighter, and prepared to spring out of his chair—

Something in Jessie Blair's face stopped him. She was staring wide-eyed at the radio. Her mouth hung open in shock. She looked like she had just heard the president announce a nuclear war.

Curious, he focused on the DJ's voice and heard the details of the one and only local news story in Sea Cove today.

Suddenly he felt cold. He remembered having thought he heard the baying of wolves after the truck crashed. Now he understood. Not wolves. Attack dogs. That was the cargo Tuttle was hauling. Fucking Dobermans. They must have escaped from the wreck, and now they were depopulating this hick town while the cops searched everywhere and ...

The cops.

They would find the truck. If they hadn't already.

And when they found it, they would launch a manhunt for Mike Tuttle's killer.

The knife clattered on his plate. He rose. Jessie glanced at him.

"You okay?" She seemed to have trouble speaking. Her face was unnaturally pale.

"Yeah. Just ... a little scared, I guess. You know, I thought this was a nice quiet area."

"It usually is." She swallowed and looked down at her plate. "These eggs ... I bought them from Owen Anderson ..." Her voice trailed off.

"Listen ..." His words came out in a mumbled rush. "I think I'm gonna be moving on. Thanks for the food. Appreciate it. Really."

"I don't think you should be out there alone. The radio said to stay indoors."

"I'll be okay."

He hurried to his room and grabbed his jacket and pack, then said a hasty goodbye to Jessie Blair.

He looked back once as he walked away down First Avenue. She stood on the porch of the Oceanview Inn, watching him go. She waved to him and called out, "Be careful!" He smiled and waved back and kept walking and wished to God he had killed her last night when he'd had the chance.

# 24

THE DOOR to Ben Harper's office had barely swung shut, leaving Karl Masterson alone with the police chief, when Masterson unshouldered his carrying case, zipped it open, and spilled the contents onto Harper's desk.

Harper saw four blue-black Walther .22's customized to fire tranquilizer darts; four sets of seven darts, each one tipped with an ampule of pentobarbital; a plastic bag containing hypodermic needles, gauze, bandages, antiseptics, and painkillers; four Tekna Micro-Lite miniature flashlights; two coils of rope; three muzzles; an Uzi 9mm semiautomatic pistol fitted with a Redfield Accu-Trac infrared scope; ten 32-round magazines for the Uzi; and an Auto Ordnance Thompson Model 27A-1 semiautomatic rifle with ten 30-round .45-caliber magazines.

*Jesus. This guy's a fucking one-man army.*

Harper was not too sure he liked that idea.

Masterson scanned the equipment, then picked up a Walther and began to load it. Harper circled around to his desk chair and sat down, feeling dazed and suddenly weary. He hadn't slept all night. He supposed Masterson hadn't either. You'd never know it to look at him. The man radiated strength, energy, certainty.

"You wanted to talk," said Harper. "So talk."

Masterson did not look up as he snapped another dart into its chamber. "I found the truck. About half an hour ago. Wrecked. Ran right off the road, into a ditch, and flipped over on its back. Hard to see. We must have passed over it once or twice during the night, but our searchlight couldn't pick it up. In daylight, from the air, it's visible; but I'm certain no one could see it from the road. And there are no houses nearby. No other vehicles were involved, from what I could tell. It's not surprising the accident went unreported."

"You think the driver was killed in the crash?"

Masterson hesitated. He snapped another dart into place. "He was killed. But not in the crash. His body was lying near the wreck. As if he had crawled out. He was ... mangled. Torn open and ... and pulled apart."

"Okay," said Harper, remembering the collie and Stu Holland and Owen Anderson and feeling mildly sick to his stomach. "I get the idea. Chalk up another one for your furry friends." Masterson pursed his lips and said nothing. "So where is it?"

"West of here, on a back road. We determined its location as accurately as we could, but we didn't have a map of Sea Cove itself. My assistant is going over the maps in your outer office right now to pinpoint it." Masterson finished loading the first tranquilizer gun. He picked up a second one. "Have there been any more ... incidents?"

"None we know of."

Masterson nodded.

"I called the state police," Harper went on, feeling the need to justify himself, to show that he hadn't been sitting on his ass all night while Karl Masterson was out scouring the countryside with his helicopter's searchlight beam. "Unfortunately there's not a whole lot they can do, unless I want to call in extra manpower for patrols."

"I doubt that will be necessary."

"You're pretty damn sure you can handle this, aren't you?"

"Yes." Another dart. Snap.

"Well, I'm not."

Harper waited for Masterson to challenge him or

take offense. Masterson showed no reaction. He was concentrating on the gun and the darts.

"So," Harper went on, "after I got off the phone with the state troopers, I called the Department of Public Health in Trenton. Got through to somebody on the emergency line who told me they could get some Animal Control people out here by morning. But nobody's shown up, and now the phone lines to Trenton are jammed. It's all because of that goddamned plane crash. Every state official is either in Newark or on the way there. But I'll keep trying to get through. With any luck ..."

Masterson looked up from the third tranquilizer gun with the first of seven new darts in his hand. It was poised there, between thumb and forefinger, and he looked momentarily like he was aiming it at some invisible dartboard behind Harper's head. Then he loaded the dart—snap—and put down the gun.

"Chief, let me tell you a story. Two years ago a dog, a Rottweiler, escaped from my ranch. The one and only time such a thing has happened. A hole in the fence had gone unnoticed, a minor hole, but large enough for the dog to squeeze through. The moment I learned there was a dog missing, I had my men comb the ranch to find him or his escape route. That's how the hole turned up. Then at least I knew in what direction the dog had started off. I went out after him, into the woods at night, armed with a gun like one of these"—he swept his hand over the Walthers—"and a dozen extra darts and a flashlight. I went alone. I wouldn't allow any of the trainers with me. Too dangerous—for them and me. Six men make more noise than one.

"I cannot tell you how I did it, because I don't know. But somehow I followed the precise path that dog had taken. I did not track him. I did not detect any paw prints, any spoor. I simply made myself *think* his way. And I found him. He was hiding behind a bush, and as I approached I could sense him there. I aimed the gun just as he leaped. I got him. One dart. A clean hit, right in the neck. He was out cold in a half second. I carried him back in my arms. Like a baby. His name was Blood, incidentally. And he was a good dog. I never punished him, though I did fire the groundskeeper who had failed to notice the hole. The dog was doing only what he'd been trained to do. The groundskeeper had been trained also, but he had not done his job."

"There's a point to all this, I imagine?"

Masterson sighed. "The point, Chief, is that I understand these dogs. Each one has his own distinct personality, his own unique way of acting and reacting. Every dog is special. Don't let anyone tell you that we humans merely read our own emotions into our animals. A dog has more brains and more cunning than most humans care to admit. And these dogs are *mine.* You can't expect a crew of professional paper-pushers and desk jockeys from Trenton to track them down. You have to ask the man who trained them. Who ... made them what they are."

"For better or worse."

Masterson met Harper's eyes. His voice was level as he answered, "Precisely."

Ben Harper drummed his fingers on the desk, then leaned forward, pushing some of Masterson's equipment away, and folded his hands in front of him.

"So tell me about your dogs, Masterson. And their winning personalities."

"There are—were—three Dobermans and a shepherd. You ... killed ... a Doberman?"

"Don't take it personally."

"Was the dog male or female?"

Harper thought for a moment. He had to force himself to bring into focus a mental picture of the dead dog on the bloodstained bed.

"Male."

"That was Mr. Dobbs, then."

"Mr. Dobbs?"

"Short for Mr. Doberman." Masterson was loading the third gun again.

"Oh. Cute. Didn't he make some movies? Mr. *Dobbs Takes a Vacation, Mr. Dobbs Goes to Town ...*"

"We have to name them something," said Masterson impassively. Snap.

Harper rubbed his forehead. "Right. Sure. How the hell do you know which Doberman it was, anyway? Are the other two both females?"

"One is male, one female."

"Then—"

Masterson shook his head. "It wasn't Razor."

Ben Harper allowed a beat of time to pass in the silent room.

"Razor."

Snap.

Masterson started work on the fourth gun. He shrugged. "The other male Doberman. He would not have been killed so easily."

"Easily?" Harper half rose from his chair. "We're talking about three cops, myself included, busting into that room and firing maybe twenty-four rounds of .38-caliber ammo in less than ten seconds ..."

Masterson held Harper's gaze. "Was the dog killed in the act of attacking or escaping?"

"The son of a bitch jumped right at me!"

"Then it could not have been Razor. He places a very high value on self-preservation. He would not fight a losing battle. Against overwhelming odds, he would be the first to cut and run. Not out of cowardice, but cunning. And you couldn't stop him. His reflexes are quicker than yours—or mine."

He went back to the gun. Snap. End of discussion.

Harper was still fuming as he settled back into his

chair, but through his anger and resentment he did remember the Doberman that had leaped through the open window like a rainbow of black, a vision so fleeting and dreamlike it was gone almost before it could be perceived.

*Razor ...*

"Why don't you check out the carcass before you leap to any conclusions?" Harper said, without conviction.

"Fine. I will. But I know what I'll find. Mr. Dobbs was well trained—but impulsive. Precisely the sort to panic under duress. To let bloodlust get the better of him. Not a leader. Razor led the pack. If they're still running together, then he is still their leader. If they've scattered ... well, that would be better for us."

"Better? Why? I'd rather have all the bastards in one place."

"No." Masterson snapped in the last dart and tossed the gun back onto the desk. "We need them to find their way back to the truck. As long as Razor leads them, they won't go near it. He's too smart to fall for such an obvious trap. And too independent to want to go home. So we have to hope the other two are cut off from him."

"They've got names too, I gather."

"The female Doberman is Cleopatra. I called her that for the way she turned her snoot up as a puppy. Haughty, like a queen. Arrogant. But that's only appearances. Inside, she's nervous. Sometimes she has bad dreams. She's the most likely to weaken."

"And the German shepherd?"

"Bigfoot. As a pup he had such big clumsy paws." Harper could swear he heard a note of tenderness in the man's voice, of affection. "He's the least intelligent of the four. That makes him less dangerous, in some ways, but also more unpredictable. He may return to the truck. He may try to find it, and fail. Or he may have forgotten about it entirely. My hope is that he and Cleo are still together, but separated from Razor. Then she may lead the shepherd back."

Ben Harper rose from his chair and went to the window, to stand looking out at the deserted Main Street. He kept his back to Karl Masterson and his eyes on the shops that would not open for business today.

"I've got a cat," said Ben Harper thoughtfully. "Alley cat named Henry. Hank to his friends. He's spent his whole life, just about, in my home."

Harper turned abruptly. "But you know what? I couldn't tell you what that cat would do tomorrow if he ran away tonight. I can't analyze him, for Christ's sake, or think like him. He's an animal. And these goddamn dogs are no different. You can't know what they'll do next or where they'll do it or why or how. You can't know a goddamn thing!"

"Yes, I can, Chief," said Karl Masterson. "Because I trained them. They're mine. I raised them and disciplined them and taught them everything they know. They're not my pets. They're my ..."

"Children?"

Masterson raised his eyebrows, letting them burrow deep into his hairless scalp and shatter his forehead into a webwork of wrinkles, and Ben Harper enjoyed the thought that he had managed to get some kind of reaction out of the man. But his enjoyment lasted only a second. In the next moment Masterson's brow was calm and unlined, and he was shrugging his huge shoulders and saying quietly, "I hadn't thought of it that way. But ... yes. You could say so." He blinked, as if fascinated by the admission, like a man unaccustomed to self-revelation, intrigued by the novelty of it. "My children," he said softly.

"The children of the night," whispered Ben Harper, without even realizing he had said it aloud till the words were out.

The two men stared at each other across the length of the office.

"They aren't devils, Chief," said Masterson finally. "And neither am I."

*I wonder,* thought Ben Harper as he watched Masterson's bald head bent over the cache of weapons and supplies. *I wonder, Mr. Karl Masterson, just what you are.*

# 25

IN THE outer office, Alex Driscoll had been pursuing an answer to that same question, persistently but without success—until he said the magic words.

He didn't know they were the magic words or that, like "Open Sesame," they would open the door to Karl Masterson's past. All he knew was that he had spent the last fifteen minutes pestering Nikki Grant as she sat in a corner with a large map of Sea Cove spread out on her lap. She was comparing it with her own map of New Jersey, a map littered with penciled arrows and dotted lines that traced the crisscrossing pattern of the helicopter's search. One spot had been marked with a large, triumphant X. The truck, obviously.

"Miss Grant, I get the definite impression you don't want to talk about your employer."

"Not right now." Her head was bent close to the map as she studied the back roads west of Route 35, the roads running parallel to Route 33.

"I understand," said Alex casually. "Successful people, such as your boss, generally don't like having other, less successful people pry into their backgrounds."

"Um."

"You know, the average person would assume that that's because they have something to hide."

"Karl Masterson has nothing to hide." Her voice was flat, without emotion. She might have been aware that Alex was trying to goad her into revealing something, anything, but if so, she didn't let on and probably didn't care. Alex pressed ahead anyway.

"Sure, he does. Don't get me wrong. I'm not suggesting corruption or scandal or anything like that. The truth is, I sincerely believe that the vast majority of success stories don't depend on any of those things."

"Then what are you suggesting?" Her head was still bent over the maps, but there was a hint of irritation in her voice, which pleased Alex, because at least it was a sign of interest.

"Only that Mr. Masterson, like most other rich, successful people, has a secret to hide. Or maybe I should phrase it differently. He has a myth to perpetuate. The myth of the self-made man. It's as American as apple pie, but you know, if you leave a pie out too long it'll get stale and eventually you'll have to throw it away."

For the first time—yes, it was, Alex realized, the very first time—Nikki Grant raised her head to look directly at him.

"Just what are you driving at?"

Alex leaned against a file cabinet, feeling relaxed and in control of the situation, because he had Nikki Grant's attention now.

"I've got a theory. I think all these self-made Horatio Alger types are successful not because they worked hard and struggled and persevered and overcame adversity, but because they were lucky. That's all. Just plain, dumb luck. And that's the big, dirty secret all these big shots are hiding. If I really probed into the background of somebody like, say, your boss, you know what I'd find? A nice, decent, outgoing, good-looking guy who was born into the right family at the right time, made all the right social connections, got plenty of help from his rich friends and relatives, and wound up rich himself."

Nikki Grant held Alex's glance for a moment, then said, "Wait just one minute, will you, please," and looked down at the map of Sea Cove. With a final moment's deliberation she drew a large red X in pen on the road immediately south of Route 33. Pine Shadow Road. Then she folded the map, put it in her attaché case, and snapped the case shut. She rose and shrugged on her mink jacket and said quietly, too quietly, "Come outside."

Alex, baffled, followed her as she strode out the door with the attaché case swinging in one hand.

The cold air bit his cheeks and stung his eyes. The sky was blanketed in thick white clouds threatening snow. Alex and Nikki stood on the front steps of the police station as the wind whipped their hair. He watched her, saying nothing, while she stared at the empty streets. Then she turned to him.

"How much did you weigh when you were nine?"

Alex stared at her. The wind had plastered strands of blond hair across her face. She made no effort to brush them away. Her eyes peered out from behind the tangled net. They were intent and serious.

"What the hell ...?"

"You heard me."

"I don't have the slightest idea."

"Take a guess."

"You know, it's freezing out here."

"It's also private. Now, answer the question."

Alex sighed. His breath came out in a frozen plume. "Okay. I'll give it a shot. Guess your weight, win a prize. When I was nine I probably weighed in at about sixty, maybe sixty-five pounds."

"Quite possible. What do you weigh now?"

"One forty."

"Karl Masterson weighs two forty."

"He's a foot taller than I am, and about two feet wider, and it's all muscle, from what I could tell. So what?"

"Do you know how much he weighed when *he* was nine?"

"Surprise me."

"Forty pounds."

Alex opened his mouth, then closed it. Forty pounds. That was damn light for a kid who grew up into a big strapping son of a bitch like Karl Masterson.

"What was he, one of those kids who start out small and shoot up in high school?"

"He never went to high school. And no, he wasn't one of those kids. Karl was already tall for his age."

Alex's words came more slowly. He was intrigued in spite of himself. "So what was it, then? Childhood illness?"

"Karl Masterson was born in 1936 in Germany. But his name wasn't Masterson then. It was Karl Meyers. He was Jewish. His father was killed in a street brawl with some brownshirts when Karl was two months old. He grew up, an only child, in the ghetto, with his mother taking any job she could find. Scrubbing floors. Selling flowers on street corners. She might have been a prostitute, I don't know. Whatever was necessary to survive."

Alex heard her with part of his mind, while another part was replaying, like a tape recording, the speech he had made inside. *A guy who was born into the right family at the right time ... made all the right social connections ...*

"Damn," he said so softly that the word was all but inaudible, stolen by the wind.

"Things went on like that till Karl was seven," Nikki continued. "Then they came and took him and his mother away. They were separated. Karl found out later that his mother died at Ravensbruck. He was moved from camp to camp, but he wound up at Birkenau, the extermination plant of Auschwitz, the plant where the gas chambers were. But before the SS could get to Karl, the Allies liberated Auschwitz. You must have seen pictures of the children there, in their striped uniforms with their shaved heads, looking like ... like human scarecrows. That's how you get to be nine years old, tall for your age, and forty pounds."

Alex closed his eyes. He felt embarrassed—no, ashamed—to the point of illness.

"How the hell did he get from there to here?" he asked dully.

"Oh, it's a long, complicated story. You wouldn't want to hear it. It involves a lot of crap like hard work and struggle and perseverance and overcoming adversity, and, let me assure you, very little in the way of luck. Anyway, he did get here and he is rich and he's six foot six, weighs two hundred forty pounds, and keeps himself in excellent condition by working out every day, because he's never forgotten a certain nine-year-old boy whose eyes were too big for their sockets and whose ribs stuck out like pickets in a fence. Any questions?"

Alex said nothing. He looked down at his hands. His mind was blank. It felt like a giant bruise slowly turning black and blue.

He looked up when the door slammed in a gust of wind and found himself alone on the steps. He stood there, not moving, for a long time.

# 26

THEY HAD not arrived in Sea Cove until 7:30, well after Karl Masterson's helicopter had landed. The police were issuing no statements and providing no cooperation, and with the carnage in Newark, no one else had even picked up on the story. But that was all right. It gave them an opening. A chance for an exclusive, Deborah Bradbury decided—a breaking news story with a strong human interest angle.

"A town afraid," she told Johnny Kirk. "A town under siege."

They'd interviewed a few nervous locals who had locked themselves in their homes or reluctantly opened their stores to wait for customers who would not come. The whole job had not taken more than three hours, and all they needed now was the wrap-up.

"The beach would look good in the shot," Johnny said, and so they drove to the beach and crossed the sand to the shallow waters of low tide.

Deborah Bradbury had always intended to find work in one of the glamorous newscasting operations of Manhattan, but after too many failed job interviews she had settled—temporarily, she told herself—for starvation wages at one of New Jersey's UHF stations. The station ran reruns of *Mister Ed, Gilligan's Island,* and *Leave It to Beaver,* all of which received higher ratings than the local news. Still, she was getting experience and exposure, and one of these days she would move on to better things. At least she kept hoping.

Johnny Kirk had never wanted glamour or fame. He just liked cameras. He turned the focus ring on the hand-held video camera and brought Deborah's face into sharp relief against the gray Atlantic and cloudswept sky.

"Ready when you are, pretty lady."

"I'm ready. Let's get this over with. I'm freezing my butt off."

He rolled tape and aimed the mike at her. "Do it."

"Sea Cove," she said briskly in the inflectionless voice of a TV reporter. "A community facing a threat almost unheard-of in the civilized world. The threat of wild animals on the loose. Animals ... No, hold it." Johnny clicked the camera off. "That's no good. They're not really wild animals."

"More like party animals."

"Cut the jokes. It's too cold for humor. Roll again. I'll get it right this time."

"No hurry, sweet thing. I could watch you in close-up all day."

- — -

Razor peered out from under the boardwalk. The beach was narrow. The Man and Woman were only thirty feet away. He could cover that distance in seconds. They would have no place to run, no hope of escape.

He crept to the very edge of the boardwalk and glanced warily up and down the beach. He saw no other human beings. These two were alone.

Such easy kills.

His hunger was unabated. But not for long.

He tensed his body for a burst of speed.

- — -

Deborah had nearly completed the wrap-up on her second try when she caught a flicker of movement behind Johnny. She stumbled over her words and stared past him and then she screamed.

Johnny whirled, camera in hand, and froze at the

sight of the Doberman streaking toward them in a swirl of sand.

"Christ Almighty," he said softly. He dropped the camera. It hung from the battery pack around his waist for a moment, and then the power cable popped loose.

He looked back and saw Deborah break into a run. He followed. They splashed through the shallow water, racing north along the beach. The Doberman veered around and closed in on them, gaining easily.

"The water!" Deborah shrieked. It was their only chance.

She and Johnny rushed headlong into the ocean, kicking up a spray of rainbows.

Razor hesitated at the edge of the sea. He growled at the lapping waves. Then with a volley of barks he loped in pursuit.

The tide was going out, and even a hundred feet from shore the water was no more than hip-deep. Deborah and Johnny slogged through the surf, fighting the muddy sand that clung to their shoes like glue. Deborah looked back and saw the Doberman splashing toward them. They could not outrace it, not on foot. She dived into the water and swam.

The ocean was numbingly cold. She forced herself to concentrate on swimming, on each sure stroke of her arms, slicing the waves, propelling her forward while she sucked in lungfuls of freezing air. She looked to her side while taking a breath and saw Johnny, keeping pace with her but struggling, weighted down by the battery pack. His face was flushed a grotesque shade of red like boiled flesh.

After a long time she paused to get oxygen. She tried to stand and found she couldn't. She was far enough out that her feet no longer touched bottom. She gasped, treading water, and looked back, and there it was, the Doberman, dog-paddling furiously, its head and front paws raised above the waterline, the rest of it lost to sight. The dog could not make good time, but it seemed tireless, and Deborah felt her own strength fading.

It would swim till it reached her—her and Johnny too. They couldn't get away. There was no hope.

Johnny yanked her forward. "Keep going!" he ordered. She plunged into the waves once more, thrashing her arms, kicking wildly, too weak to guide her muscles in graceful, efficient action any longer. She was flailing at the ocean, fighting with it, beating at it with her hands and legs in a blind, exhausted effort to cover distance and leave the dog behind.

She and Johnny were a hundred yards from shore when she felt the sting of a jellyfish on her leg. Which was odd, because she was wearing heavy corduroy slacks and she hadn't thought jellyfish could sting through clothing. Then it happened again, worse this time, not a sting, *oh, my God*, a bite, deep, gouging, and she tried to scream and swallowed water instead. Then she was choking and gasping for air and seeing the stain of blood expanding like an oil slick on the ocean surface.

She looked around and did not see the dog and for the moment she forgot it in the flash of a single thought.

*My leg. Oh, God, what did it do to my leg?*

Deborah reached for her leg and had time to feel a long, jagged gash down her right thigh, and then the Doberman erupted out of the sea, jaws snapping wildly, fell on her, and sank its teeth into her breast. She was making incoherent sounds. It tore itself loose in the next instant and submerged. Her hands moved frantically over her chest and found the right breast intact and the left breast ... the left breast ...

*Where is it? Jesus, where is it, where did it go?*

Clouds of blood rose around her, out of the gored crater where her breast had been.

The ocean spun like a whirlpool. She was drowning

in a sea of blood, her own blood. She vomited. She yelled for Johnny, swallowed water again, and spit it up, coughing, and the Doberman surfaced behind her. She tried to turn, too late—its claws were slashing at her head, tearing out clumps of hair.

"Go away! *Go away!*"

Then Johnny grabbed the dog and pulled it back and wrestled with it like a man wrestling an alligator. She turned slowly and watched, dazed with shock, as the two twisted and rolled and finally disappeared under the ocean. She told herself this was her chance to escape, but she didn't believe it and the words had no meaning anymore.

Johnny Kirk had not had time to take a breath before the Doberman dragged him under, and already he could feel his lungs threatening to explode with the need for air. The dog would not let go. It had sunk its claws into his stomach and was forcing him down, toward the ocean bottom, as the light from the surface faded. Johnny wrapped his hands around the dog's neck and squeezed, pressing his thumbs deep into its flesh, until finally the dog ripped its claws free. He arrowed his body for the surface, with no thought but to breathe, now, immediately, before his chest burst under the strain.

The Doberman made a slow-motion lunge and buried its fangs in Johnny's throat.

Johnny Kirk kicked and struggled but he did not die, not until the last of his air had run out and his tongue had swelled up in his mouth and his lungs were waterlogged sacs.

Razor let go and launched himself with a beat of his hind legs toward the surface.

Deborah had seen the spurt of blood a few yards away and knew Johnny was dead. She was not even surprised when the Doberman shot out from under the water, panting raggedly, then paddled toward her, intent on finishing its work.

She did not flee. She waited, treading water, and hardly even struggled as the dog embedded its claws in her sides, locked its mouth on her throat, and twisted once, snapping her neck and killing her instantly.

Johnny Kirk's body bobbed up nearby.

Razor hesitated, uncertain which body to drag to shore, wanting vaguely to claim both kills. But the Man's body was already drifting away, claimed by the outgoing tide. Razor ignored it. He held on to the Woman with his foreclaws and kicked mightily with his hind legs, making no progress, fighting the undertow and losing. The body was awkward and the tug of the tide was too strong. He kept trying, anyway, and the strip of beach continued to shrink, until finally he understood that this was a battle he could not win. He could fight Men and he could kill them, but he could not fight this wet, frigid expanse of water with the salty scent.

He let go of the body but did not give up. He took a bite out of the Woman's arm, gulped it down, and lunged for another. But even that was denied him. Already the Woman was gliding away, shrinking with distance to join the Man.

Razor paddled back to dry land and staggered onto the beach, not far from where the camera lay, its sightless lens regarding him blankly. He shook himself vigorously, spraying the sand with brine.

When he was almost dry, he slunk back under the boardwalk and found a shadowed place that afforded some protection against the ocean breeze. He huddled there, shivering with cold, with hunger, and above all with rage.

He had killed twice and had little to show for it. His hunger was as powerful as before.

He gazed at the ocean and growled softly, hating it for having robbed him.

Far out to sea, nearly lost to sight, the remains of Deborah Bradbury and Johnny Kirk floated toward the thin gray line where the ocean met the sky.

# 27

WYLIE GAINES sat on the floor of her room in a patch of sun thrown through the unshaded window, surrounded by Charlie Bear, his wife Betty Bear, and Bobbie Bear, their baby, fast asleep in his crib.

Wylie ignored them. Her toys were out just for show, in case her mommy or daddy should look in. She was not playing. She was thinking. She had a difficult problem on her mind.

Oh, no, not the problem of staying home from school. That had been easy. As soon as she had brought up the matter at breakfast in her low, tearful voice, her parents had acquiesced. Even her mommy had seemed to understand that the wound left by Buster's loss would require time to heal. And then of course there had been the inexcusable incident on the school bus, which Wylie had once again related between sniffles. Both her mommy and her daddy had been in rare agreement that the best thing for Wylie would be to stay home, play with her toys, and rest.

Neither of them had guessed Wylie's real reason for skipping school. Neither knew anything about the stray doggie she had found last night, the dog she had fed and hidden in the toolshed.

He was a good doggie, all right. He had stayed perfectly quiet all morning. Wylie had been afraid he might start barking, locked up in that cold shed all alone, and give himself away. Uh-uh. So far there had not been so much as a peep of protest from the shed.

Wylie knew, of course, that she would have to reveal

the existence of the dog to her parents eventually, perhaps even as soon as tonight. But she was putting it off out of fear that her mommy would still say dogs were bad for a child's healthy development, whatever that meant.

The main thing now was that Wylie had to check on the doggie and give him some more to eat. He had been so hungry last night. He had wolfed down a whole can of Alpo Beef and Liver Stew—Buster's favorite—in half a dozen gasping swallows. Well, stray dogs probably didn't get much to eat.

The problem, as always, was her parents. They were both home today. She had heard her daddy say he was going in to work late, and then she had heard him on the telephone downstairs, talking angrily to Mr. Barnhoff, the school principal, and saying something about "legal action." She didn't know exactly what that meant, but from what she overheard she gathered that it had something to do with Mr. Frenzell and the big kids who had showed her the newspaper. Maybe her daddy was going to have the big kids thrown in jail. She hoped so. She hoped they got the electric chair.

As long as both her parents were around, it would be doubly difficult for her to sneak out to the toolshed unobserved. She really ought to wait, she thought as she picked up Charlie Bear and stroked his fur absently. In the afternoon her daddy would just have to go to The Office, where he worked, and her mommy would probably take a nap. It would be safer then. But Wylie was worried that the poor dog might be hungry and even more worried that he might bark, so finally, at a quarter past eleven, she decided to risk it.

The key to her decision was the sound of her mother's footsteps ascending the stairs, and then the soft click of the bathroom door and the whistle of running water in the pipes.

Wylie put down Charlie Bear, went to her bedroom

doorway, and peered out, gambling that her mommy would stay in the bathroom long enough for her to feed the dog. Cautiously she crept down the hall to the stairs. On the bottom step she paused, listening. From her daddy's study came the restless shuffling of papers.

Wylie took a deep breath, then quickly tiptoed past the open door of the study. Her daddy's head was bent low over the contents of a folder and he did not see her. She reached the kitchen and let out her breath slowly. So far, so good.

From the pantry she removed a can of Alpo Chicken Dinner with Gravy. She found the old-fashioned, hand-operated can opener she had used last night—the electric one would make a racket. She remembered how Buster had always come trotting in at the whine of the electric can opener, and how he would stand waiting with his tail swishing eagerly while the food was poured into his big plastic bowl. She sighed and pushed the memories away and told herself she should be happy, at least, that she had a new doggie to take care of, no matter what her mommy said.

Slowly, with effort, she began to cut open the top of the can.

- — -

Bigfoot was feeling mean.

He had slept through the night and most of the morning, a restless sleep from which he awoke at random intervals, his head throbbing. Whenever he woke up, he sniffed the dampness around him, shivered in the cold, and whined irritably, before curling up again with his muzzle tucked under his front paw. His mouth hurt and his eyes stung and his nose was hot. His tongue rolled fitfully in his dry mouth. Once, when the first light of day was peeking through the crack under the shed door, he had jerked awake and stumbled in circles until he vomited a thick yellow stream. Then he collapsed in a fetal position and fell moodily back to sleep.

Now the daylight shining under the door was brighter and the ache in his head had sharpened to a pulsing knife-cut between his eyes. He was half-dozing when he heard the sound. He raised his head and panted gobs of drool. He listened. He could make it out plainly now—footsteps crunching softly in the dead grass, drawing near.

Dimly he remembered the Girl. He had wanted to kill her last night. He had come very close to doing so. But the slow stroking of her hand on his head had been oddly soothing, and so he had let her go on petting him as his bloodlust subsided and he grew sleepy. He did not chase her when she left, and he did not attack when she returned with food. He ate, though he was not hungry. And then, all resistance gone, he allowed her to lead him by the collar into this cold, shadowed place and shut him in.

These memories returned to him now—because he knew, without question, that the footsteps were those of the Girl.

He got up carefully. He felt the blood sloshing from side to side in his head, the insistent throbbing at the backs of his eyes. His vision was blurred. The hairline crack of sun seemed painfully bright against the darkness.

Somewhere inside him, there flashed the wordless equivalent of a thought. It was a longing to go back where he was warm, safe, and taken care of, now that he was hurt and sick and feverish. He had spent enough time prowling the woods. He wanted to go home.

The idea was with him for only an instant. Then it was replaced by a new thought, a harder, cruder, and much more obvious thought.

The Girl had done this. The Girl had locked him away in the cold and damp and made him sick.

The Girl was Bad.

The footsteps stopped outside the shed, a hand fumbled with the latch, and the door swung wide, letting daylight stream in.

Bigfoot took a step back, into the shadows at the rear of the shed, and growled.

The Girl stood in the doorway, a big plastic bowl in her hands, her small, shivering body caught in an aureole of sun.

"Hey, doggie. Are you hungry? Want something good to eat?"

Bigfoot tensed. This time there would be no hesitation, no weakness.

This time he would kill.

# 28

"PAUL."

"Uh?"

"Have you seen Wylie?"

"Uh-uh."

"She's not in her room."

"I'm sure she's around someplace."

"I've looked everywhere."

"How about the bathroom?"

"I was just in the bathroom!"

Paul Gaines reluctantly abandoned the Larson briefs and glanced at his wife, standing at the door of the study. Barbara returned his gaze anxiously.

"You don't suppose"—he spoke carefully, chewing on his pen—"she could have run away or something?"

"Her coat's in the closet."

"She doesn't always wear her coat."

"It's freezing out!"

He rose, tossing the folder aside. "Maybe I'd better—"

Paul Gaines never finished his thought, because at that moment, from the backyard, came a single high-pitched scream. It rose in the morning stillness like the escalating wail of an alarm siren, struggled briefly at its peak, and was abruptly cut off.

Wylie's scream.

Then Paul was brushing past Barbara, who stood frozen, uncomprehending at first, and he was racing for the back door while his heart pounded a frenetic drumbeat in time with the pounding of his shoes.

- — -

She was on her back on the concrete floor of the shed with the dog all over her and he was trying to eat her, *trying to eat her,* and she wanted to scream again, but this time only choking sounds came out. The dog had leaped at her out of the dark and knocked her sprawling to the floor. Instinctively she had thrown the big plastic bowl in front of her face, spilling dog food down her shirt, and the dog's jaws had swung wide and slammed together, biting down hard on the bowl, seeking to wrench it out of her grip, and she would have been happy to let the doggie have the bowl if he wanted it, except she knew he didn't want the bowl at all. What he wanted was to bite her head off, and only the bowl was stopping him, so she held on tightly with both hands as the dog shook his head savagely from side to side and spattered her face with drool.

Then she felt the frantic slashing of his paws as they shredded her shirtsleeves and sliced the skin of her arms, and she was crying as blood ran down her arms in bright cherry streaks. She was blubbering, "Please don't eat me, you're a good doggie, good doggie, *good doggie,*" and the dog tugged harder at the bowl, and her fingers, slick with sweat, were losing their grip and she knew she couldn't hold on much longer. She was sobbing as another swipe of a giant paw caught her mouth and there was blood everywhere, bubbling out of ruptured lips, then a sting on her cheek, like a bee sting, and more blood, he was ripping her open like that Raggedy Ann she had torn apart once in a temper tantrum, and finally the bowl was jerked out of her grasp and thrown aside with a toss of the dog's head. Now she had only her small hands to protect her face from the deadly snapping jaws, her hands clutching the dog's muzzle, trying to hold him back, while he forced his head forward, closer, closer, till she was looking up into his open mouth and breathing in the stink of blood and vomit, sickeningly close, and there was nothing she could do, the dog was going to eat her, he was chewing on her fingers and *he was going to chew off her face*—

Then the dog was off her with a howl of agony, the steel scoop of a snow shovel lodged in its back.

- — -

The shovel, propped against one wall of the shed, was the first weapon Paul Gaines had laid his hands on when he burst inside and saw a wild animal—*Jesus Christ, what is it, a wolf, a goddamn wolf*—mauling his daughter to death.

His first swing had planted the scoop in the monster's spine. He held on to the shovel as the thing was sent reeling back, away from Wylie, and then he saw it was a dog, a German shepherd. He had time to glance at Wylie. Her eyes were open and she was going into shock. Rivers of blood crisscrossed her face, her arms. Every detail was clear but it was all unreal, some kind of Halloween prank, like the dog itself, the dog which had recovered its wits and was now advancing on him, its eyes glinting red and murderous.

He backed out of the shed, into the crisp reality of daylight, and the dog followed, like a stubborn nightmare that refused to vanish with the dawn.

- — -

Bigfoot blinked in the blinding sun. The Bad Man who had hurt him stood a few feet away, still wielding the shovel. The scoop, bent a little on one side, caught sparks of sun that burned Bigfoot's eyes. He growled.

"Barbara! Get away!"

The Man was yelling. Bigfoot turned his head slowly and saw a Woman nearby, staring, eyes wide.

"Get back!"

She shook her head and stood her ground.

Bigfoot ignored the Woman. It was the Man he wanted first. The Bad Man who had lit a fire in his spine, a fire that scorched his hind legs with each slow, unsteady step.

With a spasm of pain Bigfoot sprang at the Man. The Man swung out blindly with the shovel and missed, and Bigfoot, snarling, took him down.

- — -

There was a moment, just one moment, when Barbara Gaines did not react at all.

That was the moment when the dog sent her husband to the ground in soundless slow motion and the snow shovel skidded out of his hands. He might have been screaming, and the dog surely was barking, but she didn't hear it. She watched as if in a dream.

Then the cold, wooden handle of the shovel was biting into her palms as she swung it high over her head. There must have been some period of transition, of movement from there to here, a crucial moment of decision, but if so, she had not been aware of it.

She lowered the shovel in a deadly arc and the scoop thudded solidly into the German shepherd's skull.

The dog jerked its head up to glare at her. Its eyes were twin pinpoints of red in a blood-smeared mask, a mask misted over suddenly by a frozen cloud of Paul Gaines's breath. Paul was gasping, fighting for air, his jaw slack, his face pale and drained and looking ten years older than it had two minutes ago. Streaks of red bearded his chin.

The dog growled at Barbara.

She hefted the shovel again, feeling the strain in her arms and shoulders, the sudden small pops of unused muscles. She leaned forward with the downward swing of the shovel, throwing the whole weight of her upper body into the blow, and brought the flat of the scoop down hard on the dog's head.

The shepherd stumbled backward, and she followed, keeping the distance between herself and the dog unchanged. She watched the dog with an intense, almost impersonal fascination. She saw layers of dried blood around its mouth, flaking off in spots like chips of paint, and the fresh blood from Paul and Wylie flowing like spittle down its neck.

The dog snarled, baring its bloody fangs. It drew down on its hindquarters, and Barbara knew that it was going to leap, going to try to bring her down sprawling and helpless on her back, so that even if she held on to the shovel she would have no leverage and the dog could finish her easily. In the instant of the leap she swung out savagely, knowing her life depended on this one motion of her arms, and the shovel slammed into the shepherd's chin, ripping open the soft skin there, and the dog was flung back.

It got to its feet slowly, with effort, and Barbara took another step forward to close the gap between them again.

Then there was an unmeasurable stretch of time when the dog watched her and she watched it and neither moved. The scoop dripped blood onto the grass and the shepherd wagged its tail weakly. She heard the dull thudding of her heart against her eardrums and felt the rise and fall of her breasts under her cotton shirt, a summer shirt, too thin for autumn, and vaguely she was aware of the explosion of frost from her lips with each ragged, shivering breath.

On the road out front, a car rattled by and was gone.

There was silence again. She waited, holding the shovel tight in both hands like a knight's lance.

The shepherd made a low, ominous, rumbling sound, a sound that began somewhere deep in its throat and rose, trembling, to a thunderclap.

Trying to scare her. Trying to get her to back down.

"Go to hell," she said out loud. The sound of her own voice startled her. "Get out of here. You don't belong here.

Bastard!"

The dog was growling.

"You hear me? Back off, fucker. Don't make me kill you."

The dog hesitated, its bleary eyes fixed stupidly on hers, then took a step back, and for a dizzying moment she was sure it was retreating, acknowledging defeat. Then in the next instant it lunged at her and she hopped to one side, dodging it by less than a foot. The dog landed where she had stood and spun to face her again. Its upper lip curled over a scarlet fang.

The dog refused to surrender. It wanted a fight to the death. So be it.

Barbara Gaines moved forward, wielding the shovel like a club, and the scoop connected with the dog's muzzle and she heard the satisfying crunch of bone. The shepherd howled. She swung again and missed and was nearly pulled off her feet by the momentum of the swing, but with a supreme effort she kept her balance. The dog took a step toward her, expecting her to retreat, but instead she advanced, taking it by surprise, and before the shepherd could react, she brought the scoop down sidewise, its edge hammering into the dog's neck at the base of its skull. The shepherd collapsed in a heap, dazed. It struggled to rise. She slammed the shovel into its side, cracking ribs, and the shepherd yelped, a high-pitched, pitiful sound, but still it fought to get up as blood from some internal hemorrhage foamed out of its leering mouth. She batted it again, in the hind leg, and the dog barked in time with the wet snap of bone, but somehow it got to its feet. It refused to die. Like some creature out of a horror movie, it kept absorbing punishment and demanding more. It advanced on Barbara, dragging its crippled leg behind it, leaving a thick red trail in the grass. Barbara noted with a kind of sickened wonder that its tail was still wagging and its tongue was lolling out of its mouth, and absurdly she was reminded of Buster wanting to play.

Then the shepherd's growl, amazingly loud and powerful, blasted away any thoughts of Buster, and as the dog took its next step, she rotated the shovel's handle ninety degrees so the flat of the scoop was parallel to the ground, and she flailed the dog with the shovel, bludgeoning its back, its shoulders, its head, till finally the dog lay spread-eagled, its head half-buried in the dirt. The steel scoop was dented hopelessly out of shape, splotched with red, streaming blood onto the lawn.

She drew back, thinking the dog was dead, *must* be dead. She stared down at it and saw what looked like a shapeless, tattered mound of fur, a carcass half-eaten by scavengers, but as she watched, it stirred, it mewled piteously and pawed fitfully at air, its motions sluggish, but gaining strength. Slowly the shepherd rolled its eyes to look up at her out of the black rings of their sockets. One eye was half-obscured under a swelling lid, the other was veiled by a paste of blood, but despite all that, she could read the expression in those eyes clearly, and what she saw was a look so full of hate it made the pit of her stomach drop away down some endless, ice-cold elevator shaft.

Incredibly, the shepherd was struggling to its feet once more. She looked on, paralyzed, sick at the thought of inflicting more pain. Now the dog was up again, swaying drunkenly from side to side, its battered mouth leaking blood and drool and bits of broken teeth. And it was growling.

It took an unsteady step toward her, then another, and another, and all the while those hating, heavy-lidded eyes and the low, monotonous growl seemed to speak to her: *I'm going, yes, but I'll take you with me.*

The dog was a foot away, closing in, and she had no choice. She shut her eyes, gritted her teeth, and swung the shovel for the last time. It swept down at an angle and the scoop drove deep into the shepherd's skull, splitting it wide, and stayed there, embedded in the red mush of brains. The dog shuddered all over, stiffened, and went down in a heap.

Its tail swished once, tracing a crazy S-curve in the air, and a leg muscle jerked. A last sound, like a grunt, escaped the dog's mouth, and then it lay silent and motionless and finally, yes, finally dead.

The hating eyes still stared, and the trickle of blood from its splintered fangs went on, like the slow dripping of a faucet.

Barbara turned and saw Paul on his side, leaning on one elbow, looking at her. His face was utterly blank. His mouth moved but no words came. He had been cut and bitten, more than once, but he was alive and conscious and he would be all right.

But Wylie ...

In the shed Barbara found her daughter, knelt by her, and cradled the child in her arms. She put her ear close to Wylie's mouth. She heard breathing, soft and regular, but slow, frighteningly slow.

"Wylie? Baby?"

There was no answer.

# 29

THE RINGING of the telephone in the lobby of the Ocean-view Inn was a sound so unexpected in the offseason that it made Jessie jump.

She'd been jumpy all day, anyhow. Ever since break-fast and that news story. She couldn't help but think that Alex would be covering that story. She hoped he would be all right.

Now she put down her dustcloth, crossed the lobby to the desk, and picked up the phone on the third ring.

"Oceanview Inn."

"Howdy, stranger."

Jessie leaned against the desk as if it were the porch rail, and smiled.

"Top o' the mornin' to ye, Mr. Driscoll."

- — -

Alex had put off making this call for hours and had finally talked himself into it for one reason only: to prove that his estimation of himself was correct—he was a los-er and he couldn't help it and so what if Karl Masterson had started out with all the odds against him?

"Hey, Alex. Yoo-hoo."

"Whoops. Sorry. Just ... thinking. Incidentally, it's a tad late for the top-o'-the-mornin' routine. At the sound of the tone the time will be precisely—beep—12:04."

"Better reset my watch. So what's up?" Her voice lowered a notch. "Have they caught any of ... of *them* yet?"

"Uh-uh. Been pretty quiet, to tell you the truth. I couldn't get much cooperation from Masterson. You know, he's the guy—"

"I know. I heard on the radio."

*The guy who inspired this phone call,* Alex finished silently. *Did you hear that on the radio?*

"Actually, the reason I'm calling is to ask if you'd like to, I know this is crazy, but would you want to have dinner with me ... sometime?"

He wondered what excuse she would give him. He hoped it would be a bad one, transparently obvious. He hoped ...

"Alex, I'd love to."

He stared at the phone as if it were a rattlesnake and he had stepped on it barefoot.

"Alex?"

"Right. Uh. Okay. Great. I guess you can't do it tonight, though, what with a guest at the hotel—"

"He checked out," she said happily.

"Oh. Well, thing is, I'm not sure I'm free tonight. I've got to cover this story—"

"You got the night off, Alex," said Ed Clancy from across the room. His voice was unnaturally loud, booming in fact, so as to ensure it would be picked up over the phone. Alex glared at him and Ed grinned like a cat.

"I'll cover the story," Ed Clancy added more quietly. "You're only young once."

- — -

Jessie Blair picked up her dustcloth and polished the arms of the sofa, the two end tables, the porcelain lamps, and the windowsills. She did it without thought, without perception. Her mind was on the phone call, not the hotel, and right now she had to admit she loved the Oceanview less than usual, because the Oceanview meant living in the past, and finally, for today and tonight at least, she was living in the present and that felt fine.

She finished the last of the windowsills and went on to do the framed photographs on the lobby wall, without so much as a glance outside. Had she looked out the window, she would have seen the weed-strewn lot behind the apartment building across the street, and had she peered very carefully into a patch of weeds swallowed by the building's shadow, she might, just might, have been able to make out the crouching figure of the kid who called himself Mike Tuttle.

# 30

BEN HARPER and Karl Masterson sat in the rear storage section of the upside-down Van-dura. Masterson held one of his customized Walthers lightly in one hand. The Uzi 9mm pistol and the Thompson semiautomatic rifle, both fully loaded, rested nearby. Harper's .38, which seemed embarrassingly puny by comparison, was tucked in its holster. Harper touched the butt of the gun from time to time. The .38 might not be heavy artillery, but it felt snug and comfortable against his hip, as reassuring as an old friend.

The two men had been holding their lonely, frozen, silent vigil for more than four hours. Outside, the gored remains of the truck driver lay pasted to the frozen ground. Masterson had insisted that the body not be removed or even decently covered. Nothing must be done to disturb the area. His dogs would sense any tampering and back off.

The driver's name, Masterson had told him as they stared down at the mess of caked blood and blue entrails, was Mike Tuttle. Harper had grunted, not quite listening, because his attention was focused on the knife still embedded in the corpse's gut.

He had been considering that knife ever since, turning the slim, shining blade over and over in his mind. Masterson's dogs hadn't used it, that was for damn sure. Tuttle might have tried to fend off the dogs and accidentally stabbed himself. Or ... there might have been another party involved. Why had the Van-dura crashed, anyway? Why had it traveled miles off the Turnpike? Had Tuttle been forced to make a detour? Forced—at knife-point? By someone who had survived the crash and escaped on foot?

Harper had contemplated radioing in a report, but his squad car was parked on the shoulder of Pine Shadow Road, forty feet up. And anyway, Sullivan had more than enough to contend with as it was, without adding a hypothetical suspicious person to his worries.

Beside him, Karl Masterson tensed, listening.

Harper wet his lips and listened also. The Van-dura had landed with the rear door facing away from the woods. The automatic lift, still secured by its chain, hung down over the doorway, leaving the three-foot-high opening through which Masterson and Harper had crawled to hide inside the truck. Looking out, they could see nothing but the wall of rock slanting down from the road. They could not see Mike Tuttle's body or the woods beyond or anything that might come out of those woods. Harper had objected on this point and suggested that they wait in the truck cab instead.

Masterson had overruled him. "We cannot see them, true," he said evenly, "but they cannot see us, either. That will give us the advantage."

Harper's hand tightened on the butt of his gun, and he wondered now if he and Masterson did have the advantage, as they listened to the sound of something approaching the truck.

Slow, cautious footsteps crunching on the icy ground.

Harper could not tell if it was one animal or two. He could not judge how near it was. He unholstered the .38. He gripped it tight. He waited, wishing his mouth hadn't suddenly dried up, wishing he could see.

- — -

Cleo's leg hurt. The bullet was lodged deep in her thigh. Had it impacted a millimeter to the right it would have struck bone, her hind leg would have been broken, and she could not have walked at all. As it was, the flattened nose of the bullet rubbed agonizingly against the bone with her every step. The leg had bled for much of the night, but finally the bleeding had stopped. In the misty chill of dawn the leg had stiffened up, and now she was limping badly, hobbling on three legs while the fourth clumped uselessly behind her.

She had not been able to keep up with the others as they raced away from the farmhouse. She had spent the night and the morning wandering the woods, lying down occasionally to rest the leg and chew her paws. She had slept briefly at random intervals, and always her sleep was crowded with the same visions. There were Bad Men pointing sticks at her, and the sticks exploded and shot a lance of pain through her leg, and then she was stumbling into the safety of forest shadows and craning her neck to lick the wound, but her tongue could not reach it, and the pain went on and on. As she slept she whimpered and gave out low yelps of fear and her injured leg jerked with muscle spasms. After a short time she would awaken and move on, walking slowly, haltingly, aimlessly. By dawn she was exhausted and dehydrated and hungry. Her stomach bubbled. Daylight had brought no relief from the cold. The white sky glared down between the treetops like a sheet of ice. Each breath of freezing air stabbed her lungs. And the leg was worse.

Sometime during the morning, Cleo thought of going home.

Cleo could not have known Karl Masterson's prediction, but Karl Masterson knew Cleo, as he knew all his dogs. His prediction was accurate. She had searched the woods till she caught the blended scents of Razor, Bigfoot, Mr. Dobbs, and herself, the scents the four of them had left when they were a roving pack. The scents were faint, much time had passed, but there had been no rain to wash them away entirely, and to Cleo's sensitive, questing nose they were clear and unmistakable. She followed them, retracing the pack's twisting trail through the woods, all the way back to the edge of the trees, and there she saw the truck.

She limped forward into the clearing, sniffing the cold air. She thought she detected the scent of Men, a fresh scent, but she was not sure, and as she moved cautiously forward the strong, rancid odor of the Bad Man lying dead on the ground overwhelmed all other smells. The odor fascinated her. She had smelled death before, but only the clean smell of a new kill, not this dry-rot stink. She lowered her head to the corpse and sniffed deeply, her nose brushing against the dead Man's face while his wide eyes gazed sightlessly at the open sky.

Then, for some reason she could not grasp, Cleo slowly licked the Bad Man's cheek. Perhaps it was a gesture of atonement to the Man she and her companions had killed. Or perhaps it was only a desire to taste the salt of the frozen sweat sparkling there.

She lifted her head and limped on, toward the rear of the truck from which she had escaped, impelled by the dim, wordless certainty that the truck would take her home.

- — -

His mother had told him to hide in the closet, crouch down low in a corner, and make no sound. He had obeyed. He did not make a sound, not even when he heard jackboots tramping in the foyer, when he heard his mother's voice raised in trembling protest, and when he heard the slap that silenced her. He sat very still as the men ransacked the apartment, overturning furniture and throwing doors wide, until at last he heard one pair of boots march up to the closet door and he squeezed himself into a tight fetal ball. The doorknob rattled. The man on the other side swore. The door was locked. His mother must have locked him in and hidden the key. He smiled briefly in triumph, but his victory was short-lived. In the next instant the man slammed his boot against the flimsy door—again—again—each kick reverberating in the closet like the boom of a cannon, until finally the door was knocked off its hinges. And Karl Meyers, age seven, stared up at a looming figure in a Gestapo uniform silhouetted by the light from the hall.

The Gestapo had taken him away with his mother, whose lip was swollen and bleeding, and not long after that his mother had been sent away somewhere and Karl had been sent somewhere else, and that was the last he saw of her, ever.

Karl Masterson remembered that day now, as he crouched, hidden, in the rear of the Van-dura and listened to the dog's slow advance. He had traveled many years through many kinds of hell to get from that closet to this truck, and yet here he was again, huddled and waiting, with the black shape of death sniffling out his hiding place, just as before. But there was one difference. This time, he was not a child. This time he was a man, and that fact gave him the edge.

The dog was closer, only a few feet away. A lone dog. Masterson was sure of that. It would not be Razor, of course. That left Cleo and Bigfoot. He concentrated on the animal's slow, cautious footfalls but could not quite tell. The rhythm of the steps sounded awkward, and the German shepherd was clumsy, but the weight of the steps seemed light, and Cleo was the smallest of the Dobermans.

It did not really matter. Either dog was a killer. As he, of all people, ought to know.

Masterson pursed his lips ruefully, then pushed that thought out of his mind. He had a matter of more immediate importance to consider. Resting in his palm was a tranquilizer gun; at his side lay two deadly automatic weapons. He did not want to kill any of his animals unnecessarily. But the drug-tipped darts were less reliable than the Uzi's 9mm shells. Had he been alone he would not have thought twice about the risk. But the police chief, Harper, was with him. Too many innocent lives had been lost as it was. Still, they were his dogs—his children, Harper had said—and he hated the thought of watching one of them die at his hand.

He hesitated a moment longer, then lifted the Walther decisively.

Outside, the dog was closing in.

- — -

For Ben Harper, it all happened very quickly. One moment Masterson was still seated next to him, waiting tensely as the dog continued its slow, menacing approach; in the next moment Masterson had flung himself to a horizontal position and rolled under the overhanging plate of the automatic lift, onto the grass, to lie flat on his stomach, facing the dog that Harper still could not see, and with lightning speed he was aiming the gun— the *tranquilizer* gun.

What about the Thompson? The Uzi? Harper glanced to one side and saw both weapons, left behind.

*Son of a bitch. The guy must be crazy.*

Harper had no time to dwell on Masterson's psychological profile. He was too busy scrambling out the rear door, his .38 in hand.

He leaned out just as Masterson shouted, "Cleo! *Stop!*"

For one moment, the Doberman hesitated, hearing its master's voice.

Then it snarled and advanced on Masterson, lying prone and helpless less than five feet away.

Harper aimed his .38 and prepared to shoot.

Masterson swatted the gun away. "No!" he said savagely.

The Doberman was now less than one yard from Masterson.

Harper looked at the dog's eyes. In daylight, at close range, they did not look red; they looked pale, colorless, empty, the rheumy eyes of a drunk, but they did sparkle faintly, with a drunk's humorless malevolence, and they were fixed on Karl Masterson.

Masterson fired the tranquilizer gun. The Doberman jerked its head sideways, but not quickly enough. The dart caught it in the side of the neck and hung there, jutting out crazily like a needle poked in a stuffed animal. The Doberman pawed furiously at the dart and ripped it free in a red shout of blood. It took another step forward.

Harper did not know whether the drug was in the animal's system or had been washed out in the flow of blood from the wound. He was taking no chances. He aimed the .38, grimly determined to shoot if the dog took one more step.

The Doberman was now one foot from Karl Masterson. They watched each other, their faces so close as to nearly touch, like two men engaged in a staring match. The dog blinked first. It shook its head, fighting the sudden heaviness of its eyelids, the mounting sluggishness of its body. With a final effort the dog lifted its front paw to close the gap with its prey. Harper's finger tensed on the trigger.

Then the Doberman pitched forward and slumped unconscious on the grass, its snout brushing Masterson's face, its body limp and boneless. Its rib cage rose and fell in deep, shuddering breaths.

Harper slowly lowered his gun.

Neither man said anything. Harper crawled back inside the Van-dura and gathered up the Uzi and the Thompson. When he emerged he found Masterson standing with the Doberman cradled in his arms. His head was down as he studied the dog, and the pale sun glistened on his hairless scalp, throwing his face into shadow. Harper thought he looked like a man carrying his wounded son off the battlefield.

It was very touching, except for the fact that this dog and three others like it had been trained by this man to kill and had proved themselves to be more than capable of the job.

The thought spurred Harper to cruelty. "I don't know why you didn't let me shoot the goddamn thing," he said coldly. "Would have saved us the expense of having it destroyed."

Masterson lifted his head. His mouth was set in a hard line. "Destroyed? Absolutely not."

"That dog is a killer."

"I'll keep her muzzled, under sedation, locked up." He stroked the dog with one hand. "She wouldn't respond to my command. She's forgotten that part of her training, gone feral. She can never be sold, Chief. She'll be caged and harmless for the rest of her life."

Harper looked at the dog and saw rusty streaks of blood matting its fur.

"I don't believe that animal will ever be harmless," he said grimly.

# 31

THE PIER at Sea Cove's South End had been shut down after Labor Day, as always. The snack bars and concession stands were closed now, the video arcade was dark, and the merry-go-round stood silent. But this weekend, as an annual tradition in honor of Halloween, the funhouse would open its doors and stay open till November 1.

Billy Turnbul and T.W. Brolin braked their bicycles at the foot of the pier. A chain had been strung across the entrance, and a rusty sign swung in the wind: NO TRESPASSING.

The kids stashed their bikes behind a grove of holly trees. They didn't want any cops noticing the bikes and stopping to investigate. The two twelve-year-olds had broken some pretty strict rules already—they were cutting school, for one thing, and they were out on the streets on a day when people were supposed to keep indoors. And they were about to break another rule. Hell, they were about to break the goddamn law.

It had been Billy Turnbul's idea. He went to the funhouse every year, but this year he just didn't feel like paying for the privilege. T.W. Brolin had gone along because he was new in town and had never seen the funhouse, and besides, Billy was his best friend and T.W. always went along.

They ducked under the chain and ran up the pier. The breeze off the inlet stung their faces. Their coats flapped and the zippers jangled noisily.

They reached the funhouse. They stood still for a

moment, catching their breath and looking around furtively. No one had seen them, except perhaps the witch that hovered over their heads. She was cackling soundlessly, her toothless grin flaking away in bits of paint eaten by the salt air.

Billy turned his attention to the padlock on the front door.

"Rusty old piece of shit," he said with satisfaction. "No sweat."

T.W., still breathing hard, hugged himself against the cold. "You sure we ought to do this, Billy?"

Billy didn't bother to reply. He withdrew a nine-inch hacksaw from inside his coat and set to work raking its serrated blade across the padlock's steel ring. The saw made a harsh, grating sound. Rust fell like powder, followed by fine crumbs of steel.

T.W. Brolin shivered and thought about how his parents would kill him if he got caught doing this. He stamped his feet to keep warm and dug his hands deep into his coat pockets, while Billy kept on sawing for what seemed like an hour but was probably only a few minutes.

Finally the ring had been weakened to the point where Billy could crack the padlock in two with his bare hands. He dropped its remains and checked out the hacksaw.

"Think I fucked up the blade pretty bad," he admitted. "My dad won't be too crazy about that. Better hope he don't notice for a while." He shrugged and slipped the hacksaw inside his coat again.

The door opened easily. They went inside and came face-to-face with a plastic skeleton, Day-Glo green, dangling lifelessly from a wire.

"Real scary shit, huh?" said Billy, smiling. "They had this thing hanging here last year too." He pushed the skeleton lightly and it swung, its limbs clicking like chattering teeth.

"Hey, look at this." T.W. had found a jack-o'-lantern.

It sat on a pedestal draped in black cloth. "I bet they stick a flashlight or something in this, so it glows."

"Yeah. Big deal. Let's check out the rest of the place."

T.W. hesitated. He felt safe in the light from the open door, but up ahead ...

"Billy, it's pretty damn dark in there."

"'Course it's dark. What'd you expect? Power's off. It's more fun if you can't see, anyway."

"Suppose we get lost?"

"You're a wimp, Brolin. You eat wieners."

"Fuck you."

"We won't get lost. I told you, I've been in this place lots of times. I know the layout." He grinned. "So, you coming or what?"

"I'm coming, I'm coming!"

They started down the hall. Billy glanced back.

"Hey, dork. You left the door open."

"To let in some light. In case we—"

"Get lost?"

T.W. nodded sheepishly.

"Wiener-eater."

"Aw, fuck you."

Billy laughed. They disappeared into the dark.

- — -

Razor had stayed under the boardwalk all day, trotting restlessly from one end to the other, waiting for another victim. No victims came.

He was huddled at the South End when he heard distant footsteps and voices and low scraping sounds he could not identify.

He waited warily until the scraping sounds had stopped, then came out into the open and padded toward the pier. He caught a fresh scent. Two Men.

He slipped under the chain and followed the scent to an open door.

The scent was strong now. And Razor was hungry.

He crept inside, determined to claim his kill this time.

- — -

They were in a maze. There was no light anywhere. The corridors were narrow and twisting, and walls shot up without warning out of the dark. Billy Turnbul and T.W. Brolin felt their way along.

"I like this part," said Billy. T.W. could not see him, even though he was only a few feet ahead. "It's pretty damn spooky."

"Yeah. Except ... What if we get lost in here and—"

"Cut it, Brolin."

T.W. cut it. He bumped into another wall and stumbled on.

Then he paused, listening.

"Billy. You ... hear something?"

"Like what?"

"Like ... footsteps. Like there's something ... behind us ..."

"That's a good one, Brolin. You're practically making me pee in my pants."

"I'm serious."

"Give me a break."

They kept going. T.W. listened anxiously.

"Shit, man, I know I heard something."

"Probably the ghost of Lizzie Borden. She haunts this place, you know. Chops up wiener-eaters with her ax—"

"Will you shut up and listen, for Christ's sake?"

Reluctantly Billy listened. In the sudden quiet, the sound was unmistakable. A low scrabbling noise. Clawed feet moving on the wooden floor. And ... something else. Something worse.

"I hear it," whispered Billy. There was no humor in his voice now. "Am I fucked, or does it sound like it's ... sniffing?"

T.W. swallowed. "Like an animal. Like a ..."

"Shit." Billy's voice was barely audible. "You don't think it's ... one of those dogs?"

"I don't know. Let's get out of here, Billy. It's behind us. *It's in the goddamn maze with us.*"

"Okay, okay. No sweat. We're getting out. Just follow me, man."

They tried to make their way faster through the maze, but it was slow going. Unexpected walls and corners rose everywhere, there was no light, no way to see even a foot in front of your face, and behind them the sounds were growing louder, closer.

T.W. looked back and saw twin fireflies in the darkness. Red eyes, drifting forward.

"Oh, fuck," he breathed. "Fuck."

He turned a corner and the eyes were gone. For the moment.

"The thing's gaining on us," he said breathlessly. "I saw it."

"We're almost out."

"I think it's a dog, Billy. One of *them.* "

"Shut up. We're almost out, I said."

"Out of the funhouse?" There was pleading in T.W.'s voice.

"No. Just out of the maze. Funhouse goes on for a while."

"Great."

T.W. looked back and saw the red eyes again, closer. How could they glow like that, when there was no light? *Unless they're lit from inside, like a jack-'o-lantern,* he thought wildly. *Happy Halloween.*

"Told you," said Billy, and T.W. realized with a rush of relief that they had left the maze.

They were in a large room glowing softly with eerie light from cracks in the ceiling. T.W. couldn't see just what kind of room it was. He crept forward, trailing Billy, who had said he knew the layout. That's what he had *said.* T.W. glanced back, expecting to see the red eyes again, but there was nothing behind him, and he turned and stumbled into a large furry mass looming out of the darkness and felt its claws on him and looked up into red eyes—red eyes in a canine face—*oh, Jesus, it's got me, it's got me ...*

He almost screamed and then he realized it was only a wax figure of the Wolf Man. He pulled away, heart pounding.

"Hey, Brolin," Billy whispered. "We're in the Chamber of Horrors."

"Tell me about it."

He caught up with Billy and glanced around nervously. His eyes had nearly adjusted to the semidarkness. He saw a witch posed over a cauldron—Frankenstein's monster, arms outstretched—Dracula frozen in the act of rising from his coffin—a guillotine straddling a headless body—the Mummy—the Doberman ...

*The Doberman.*

"Oh, fuck."

Billy heard T.W.'s gasp, looked back, and saw T.W. staring, rigid with terror, at the dog. It stood very still, watching him, its red eyes luminous.

Billy backed away. The Doberman ignored him. Its gaze was fixed on T.W. Billy found a doorway and ran, blindly.

T.W. looked back and saw that the room was empty and he was alone.

"Billy," he croaked. "Don't leave me ..."

The dog barked, shattering his thoughts. The sound reverberated through the room with the power of an avalanche.

T.W. retreated, and the Doberman advanced. He could see a glitter of drool on its bared fangs. The dog barked again and coiled down on its hind legs, and T.W. knew it was going to strike.

He turned and crashed headlong into Mr. Hyde and shoved the wax figure out of his way. It toppled with a thud. The dog pounced on it, snarling, and bit deep into the mannequin's throat, then jerked back, shaking its head and growling. It looked up, but by then T.W. Brolin had found the doorway and—for the moment—escaped.

"Billy! Where are you?"

"Up ahead!"

"Where? Goddammit, I can't ..."

T.W. stopped abruptly, dazzled. A hundred T.W. Brolins stared back at him from fifty sheets of glass in the Hall of Mirrors.

In the faint light the reflections shimmered, ghost-like. They surrounded him. He was instantly lost. He stumbled forward and came up flat against his own face, gazing at him in terror. He spun, tried a different direction, and ran into himself again. His fists hammered the glass. He felt dizzy. He turned, trying to think straight, to come up with some sort of plan of action, and saw a hundred Dobermans watching him coldly.

He froze. One dog was real. The others were illusions. But he didn't know which was which. The dog could be a foot away or across the room. He didn't *know.*

The Dobermans, all of them, swung their heads quizzically, then let out a series of barks as if in challenge.

*It's confused. It thinks the mirror images are other dogs.*

He had to get out now, while the Doberman was distracted. He turned slowly, trying not to draw its attention, and slipped along the wall, hugging the cold glass at his back, seeking an opening, a way out.

The Doberman's barking died away. It seemed to have lost interest in the other dogs. It sniffed audibly, the same damp, snuffling sound T.W. had heard in the maze.

*To track me down,* he thought in terror. *It can follow its nose right to me.*

The hundred Dobermans crept forward. T.W. still did not know which one was real. Suddenly one shape out of a hundred resolved itself into three dimensions and he saw the dog, the real dog, slinking toward him, nostrils twitching.

He was going to die.

He took another sideways step, and behind him the wall of mirrors disappeared and there was only empty space.

A doorway.

The exit.

He ran.

The Doberman hesitated, startled, then loped in pursuit.

T.W. sprinted down a short hallway, turned the corner, and saw the shadowy figure of Billy Turnbul just ahead.

Billy was in some kind of tunnel and he was slipping and sliding and cursing.

"It's right behind me!" T.W. yelled as he entered the tunnel, and suddenly he lost his footing and fell on his hands and knees.

"I can't stop the damn thing from turning!" Billy shouted, his voice high with panic.

The tunnel had been built to revolve like the drum of a cement mixer. Normally it turned slowly, under mechanical power, and kids would struggle to keep their balance as they staggered through. Today the power was off, but the friction of Billy's shoes had started the tunnel turning, not at a constant rate, but unpredictably, so that the slick, rounded surface pitched and rolled under his feet like the deck of a distressed ship. Billy had lost whatever remained of his cool. He could feel the dog's hot breath on his neck. He kept trying to run with increasing desperation, as the tunnel mocked his efforts and knocked him down on all fours again and again.

T.W. half-grasped what was happening. "You gotta crawl!" he shouted. *"Crawl!"*

He started crawling himself. Billy made a final effort

to stand, fell instantly, then did the same.

The tunnel rocked with a sudden tremor. T.W. looked back. The Doberman had climbed in after them. It was slipping and sliding as Billy had done, fighting for traction, finding none, but advancing relentlessly anyway.

"Faster!" screamed T.W., at Billy's heels.

"I'm trying, goddammit!"

The Doberman took a swipe at T.W. and caught him in the butt, tearing open his pants.

"Motherfuck!"

T.W. flung himself forward like a swimmer executing a butterfly stroke. He and Billy slid out of the tunnel onto the floor in a tangled heap.

"Exit's just ahead," Billy gasped.

They ran for it. The Doberman, snarling, wriggled the rest of the way through the tunnel and tumbled out.

They reached the rear door. If it was padlocked from the outside, they were dead. The Doberman got up and raced toward them. It was a yard away when Billy's fumbling hands found the latch and the door swung open with a burst of sun. Billy and T.W. ran out and slammed the door behind them.

From inside rose a long, angry howl like the wail of a werewolf.

"No sweat," said Billy Turnbul weakly.

"Let's get the fuck out of here," said T.W. Brolin.

- — -

Razor made his way back through the twisting darkness, guided by his own scent, and emerged into daylight. He moved without haste. He knew his prey was long gone.

But his gnawing hunger remained.

Three times today he had been cheated. Three times he had stalked a kill, and still he had not fed.

He would not fail again.

# 32

IT WAS strange, she thought, how her hands were trembling.

They had not trembled when she squared off against the dog—an attack dog, she had since learned, one of four dogs trained by a man named Masterson, trained to kill. Even though she had seen the dull glint of murder in the dog's eyes, even though she had known her life was at stake, she had felt no fear. Yet now, in the quiet of a hospital waiting room in late afternoon, with the white sky turning gray through wide sheets of windows, she did feel fear—more than fear—cold, throbbing terror.

Somewhere down one of the hospital corridors was an operating room, and inside it her baby lay anesthetized on a table, her body open to a surgeon's tools, and nobody could say what the outcome of the operation might be. Wylie Gaines's condition was critical. That was what they had said. Critical. People in critical condition could die. Her baby could ...die.

Barbara Gaines glanced down at the unopened *Newsweek* in her lap and saw that the trembling of her hands was worse.

Another hand closed over her own. She looked up at Paul, who sat beside her, no doubt thinking the same thoughts. The lower portions of his face had been cut badly enough to require stitches; bandages wrapped his cheeks and jaw.

"You okay?" he asked gently.

She forced a smile. "Never better."

"You know, if you hadn't been there this morning ... You saved us, Barbara."

"You were the one who got to her first. Who got ... the shovel."

"Let's just say we both did pretty well."

She rested her head on his shoulder and he stroked her hair and she tried to remember the last time she had felt so close to him.

After a long time she said quietly, without moving her head, "If she recovers ..."

"Not if. When."

"I won't yell at her again. Ever."

"Sure you will."

She chuckled. "Not as much."

"Okay."

"I promise."

"I believe you."

They had been alone in the room for so long that at first they were not even aware that their privacy had been interrupted. Then Paul looked up and coughed.

Barbara raised her head to see Chief Harper standing awkwardly at the door, another man at his side.

"Sorry to barge in," said Harper slowly. "We just ..."

She understood. She straightened up in her chair and brought her emotions under control.

"Thank you for coming," she said.

The other man moved away from Harper to approach her and her husband. He stopped before Barbara's chair, looming over her, his bald head haloed by a rectangle of fluorescent light.

"Mr. and Mrs. Gaines. I'm Karl Masterson."

- — -

Harper had not wanted Masterson to come, but the man had insisted, and argument was useless.

Their vigil at the Van-dura had ended once the female Doberman was muzzled and left unconscious in the rear of the squad car. Harper, checking in with Sullivan over the radio, had heard the report on Wylie Gaines and the dead German shepherd.

"If Bigfoot is gone," said Masterson, "then we'd be wasting our time to stay here any longer." He was certain that Razor would not return to the truck. "Razor would die rather than surrender."

"Then he'll die," Harper snapped.

Masterson nodded. "He will."

They had not spoken again until Harper pulled into the driveway of his home. He had given Nikki Grant a spare set of keys and let her use the house for the day. He'd figured she must be tired, and there was no place for her to lie down and rest at the station.

As Harper braked the car, Masterson said very quietly, "Chief, as soon as we can ... I want to see that child."

"Wylie Gaines?" Masterson nodded. "Doubt she'll be in any condition to receive visitors."

"Her parents, then."

"I've got to check in at the station."

"After that."

"I'm not so sure it's a good idea—"

"I must."

Harper and Masterson had left the sleeping Doberman in Nikki's care. Before leaving, Masterson had given her detailed instructions, which she did not need, on removing the bullet from the leg, disinfecting and bandaging the wound, and maintaining a regular schedule of injections to keep the animal sedated.

The police station was in chaos. Telephones rang at every desk. Reports were coming in from all over Sea Cove. A Doberman had been seen on the beach near the inlet. A Doberman was definitely sighted on Potters Road. A stray dog, almost certainly a Doberman, was wandering on the shoulder of Route 71. A pair of Dobermans was in Mrs. Lillith's backyard. Three Dobermans were prowling the woods behind the Bristons' farm. All of these calls had been taken within the last half hour. More than a hundred similar reports had been logged in throughout the day by the officers on duty. None had been verified.

Harper left Sullivan to maintain whatever semblance of order was possible and chauffeured Masterson to the hospital in Manasecon, fifteen minutes away. "What are you going to say to them?" Harper asked once, as they sped over the bridge spanning Crab River.

"I'm sorry," said Masterson with quiet dignity. "That's all."

Now Ben Harper watched Masterson worriedly as he nodded to Mr. and Mrs. Gaines in turn. His first words, introducing himself, still hung thickly in the air of the room like the odor of Lysol.

"Why are you here?" It was Paul Gaines. He spoke slowly, carefully, with unnatural precision, as if each word were a step through a field of land mines. "What do you want?"

"I want ... to offer my sympathies." Masterson's back was to Harper. Harper could not see his face. He wondered if it showed the strain clearly audible in his voice. "And to say ... I take full responsibility. Full blame. For everything."

"That's damn big of you," said Paul Gaines.

*But it is,* Harper thought. It did take a big man to come here and say what Karl Masterson was saying. Only, Harper could hardly fault Paul Gaines for failing to appreciate the gesture, under the circumstances.

"Will your daughter be all right?"

"We don't know," said Paul. "Are you going to offer us your prayers too?"

"If I were a religious man, I would pray. As it is, I can only ... hope." He looked down at Barbara Gaines. Her face was raised to him, looking rigid and bloodlessly pale. "Mrs. Gaines, I wish—"

"Shut ... *up!*"

The first word was the hiss of a burning fuse, the second an explosion. The explosion jolted Barbara Gaines to her feet. Her fists shook at her sides. "Shut up, you fucking murderer!"

The flat of her hand struck Masterson's jaw with the crack of a rifle shot. Masterson's head barely moved. Barbara lowered her hand, staring at it wide-eyed, as if it had acted of its own will. Then Paul was standing beside her, taking her in his arms, drawing her away. He glanced at Masterson, standing immobile by the empty chair.

"It would be best, Mr. Masterson, if you left."

Barbara was sobbing. Her shoulders jerked. She buried her face in her husband's chest.

Masterson inclined his head gravely to them both and turned away. He crossed the room to the door, and Harper could see the red welt blooming on his jaw and the hairline trickle of blood from his mouth. But that wasn't the worst of it. The worst was Karl Masterson's face.

His head was level, but his eyes were cast down and unfocused, as if staring inward, and his lips were drawn tight, as if in this moment he did not like what he saw.

# 33

THE KID took a final look around to make sure the trees screened him from the road, then hoisted himself onto the windowsill. His heavy boots kicked out three times and shattered the glass.

He paused, listening intently. No burglar alarm. No shouts. No racing footsteps.

*Real good security you got here, Jessica-call-me-Jessie,* he thought as he slipped inside the Oceanview Inn.

Back again, the same day.

He hadn't intended to come back. But he'd had no choice.

He had been a quarter mile from the hotel when he saw the first police car. It was cruising down First Avenue, still a few blocks away. He barely had time to get to cover before the car rolled past. Five minutes later he spotted two more green-and-whites patrolling Second Avenue. He licked his lips. They were all over, for Christ's sake. Prowling everywhere. Looking for him, maybe, or for the dogs—or just keeping an eye out for pedestrians. The radio had warned people to stay off the streets.

The reason didn't matter. What mattered was that he couldn't get out of town with all those cops around. No way.

He remembered the vacant lot across the street from the Oceanview and decided to hide out there till nightfall, then sneak away in the dark. He didn't relax till he was safely out of sight in the tall, shadowed weeds. He waited, thinking of nothing. He dozed off a few times. Evening came, but the cops were still cruising, so he figured he'd better stay put a little longer.

Sometime after six, a Pinto parked outside the hotel and a guy picked up Jessie Blair. They drove off together. And he had an idea.

The hotel was empty. He could break in and rob the place, rifle the cash register the way he'd planned. And he could steal a new knife. He could ... he could ...

The short hairs of his groin prickled.

*I could wait for pretty little Jessie to come home, then carve her up, like I should've this morning.*

It was a risk. But what the hell. He lived for risks like this. And he couldn't shake the thought of Jessie Blair twisting under his blade, squirming as Mary Ann Foster had squirmed on the floor of the girls' restroom while he battered her again and again.

Now he moved away from the broken window, searched the hotel's ground floor, ransacked the kitchen, and found a knife. No, more than a knife. This mother made his old knife, the one he had used to kill Tuttle, look like a toenail clipper.

It was a meat cleaver. Huge. He hefted it in one hand, savoring its weight, studying his reflection in its wide polished blade.

He could chop off her fucking hands with a thing like this. He could take her apart inch by inch. Oh, yeah.

Mary Ann had gotten off easy.

He was going to have himself some real fun tonight.

# 34

Two wineglasses clinked together. It was the only noise made by the only couple in the only restaurant open in Sea Cove tonight.

They'd had their choice of tables. Alex had selected one by a corner window. The bough of a pine tree was framed in the glass, its needles whitening with snow against the opaque night beyond. The snowfall had started at dusk, a few spiraling flakes at first, then a torrent of glittering white caught in the Pinto's headlights like the plunging brilliance of a waterfall. Jessie had sat beside him as the car chugged west on Denham Avenue to Callaway's. She had told him she liked snow, and he had said he liked it too.

He did like it, and he liked having her beside him in the car, and he liked watching her now from across the spread of the ice-blue tablecloth. The flicker of the candle in the floral centerpiece danced on her face, bringing out highlights in her lips, her cheeks flushed red from cold, her green eyes. Had he ever really noticed her eyes before? They were the color of the ocean on a bright winter day. Sea green, he supposed they should be called, and like the sea they beckoned you to explore their depths.

She sipped the wine, and he realized he was doing the same. He settled back contentedly in his chair, letting the wine spread through his body, warming him, while he became aware, very gradually and naturally, of the rest of her. She wore a pale yellow dress cut low to leave her shoulders bare, the simplicity of its lines stressing her trim waist and small, perfect breasts. The dress looked expensive; Alex guessed it must be her best one. He had changed into his best clothes too, feeling a little foolish but doing it anyway. He had been a few minutes late picking her up, as a result. She hadn't seemed to mind.

He noticed that she was looking around at the empty tables and smiling.

"Kind of eerie, isn't it?" he said. "Like something out of a ghost town."

"Or like the restaurant in the Oceanview." Her smile was sad now. "It's been closed for years." Alex was about to say something when she added more brightly, "I guess we're the only ones brave enough to go out tonight, huh? Or crazy enough."

"Don't worry. There's just one dog left. And he's probably not even in town. He's probably out in the woods somewhere. Maybe miles away by now."

"Maybe. Or he could be outside in the parking lot." She laughed. A nervous laugh.

"Yeah, I thought of that. But, look." He hesitated, then drew back the lapel of his jacket to reveal the vest pocket. Something bulged inside. He pulled the object halfway out, holding it by two fingers.

Jessie gasped. "A gun?"

"Shhh. It's against the law to carry a concealed weapon, you know."

She lowered her voice. "But ... I didn't think you knew anything about ..."

"I don't. And it's not my gun, either. Ed Clancy gave it to me, just before I left. Insisted I take it. Showed me how to load it and everything."

"Let me see."

He glanced around to make sure the waiter was out of sight, then held the gun up in the candlelight.

"God, it's ... it's ancient!"

He balanced the small revolver in his palm.

"It's a Remington," he said. "Thirty-one caliber. Ed said they started making them in the nineteenth century. He doesn't know exactly how old this one is, but he bought it, used, when he was fifteen—and it was old, then."

"Does it work?"

"He claims it does. Holds five bullets. He gave me four. It's a single-action job. That means you've got to cock the gun before every shot. Really primitive. But he wanted me to have some protection."

"He's sweet."

Alex thought it over. "You know, I guess he is. Hides it pretty well, though, most of the time."

He slipped the revolver back in his vest pocket and buttoned his jacket again, while debating whether to tell her the rest of the story—how, as soon as he'd gotten home, he had unloaded the gun and stuck the four bullets in the side pocket of his jacket. Because a loaded gun, especially a rusty old museum piece like this baby, scared Alex Driscoll more than any antisocial canine. Besides, he could load the gun in a second, if he had to.

"I don't think Ed Clancy is the only one who's good at hiding things."

He looked at her, startled. She was watching him closely, the suggestion of a smile dimpling one cheek.

"What does that mean?" he asked cautiously.

"You know what it means."

He hesitated. "Yeah. I know what you mean. I'm not sure if I'm hiding something from you, Jessie. I think ... if I am ...I'm hiding it from myself too."

"I know you are."

"What is it?"

"You tell me."

"How can I, if I don't know, myself?"

She twirled her wineglass by the stem, her eyes lowered to the droplets sparkling at the bottom of the glass like beads of mercury. After a moment she asked, "What's important to you, Alex? What matters to you?"

"I'm not sure anything matters."

She raised her eyes questioningly to meet his. He thought again how beautiful her eyes were, and then he realized that something *was* important to him and had been for a long time, and maybe he had even known it, too, known it somehow without knowing.

"You're important, Jessie." He blurted it out, afraid to say it and afraid not to. "You matter."

He let a moment pass, then tentatively reached out to her. Midway across the table her hand joined his. He held on tightly, wonderingly, as if afraid to let go. They looked at each other for a long time without speaking, and he lost himself in the bottomless green depths of her eyes, and it was so good being lost there, he felt he never wanted to come out.

# 35

THE HONDA Civic had been parked at the beach since at least 11:00 in the morning. That was when Officer Danny Garrick had seen it for the first time. He had stepped out of his squad car to investigate, stood on the boardwalk, and scanned the beach, but he had seen no sign of people. He had not known that the Doberman named Razor lay almost directly under his feet, or that if he had lingered a minute longer, Razor would have attacked him and torn him apart.

As it was, Garrick had given the matter no further thought until he noticed, in late afternoon, that the car was still there. By that time, though Danny Garrick didn't know it, Razor was long gone, and so he was in no danger as he searched the beach on foot. He still found no one there, but glittering in the surf was a metallic object that caught the sinking sun's rays and reflected them with blinding stabs of flame. He retrieved it from the ocean. It was an RCA video camera trailing a power cord.

Ben Harper had dried the camera thoroughly after Garrick brought it to the station. Then he opened the camera and found a videocassette inside. The tape was three-quarter-inch, the stuff used by low-budget pros and semipros. The cassette was damp; but from what Harper could tell, the tape itself was undamaged and could be played.

Harper dispatched a man to the local high school to pick up the three-quarter-inch VCR stored with the rest of the audiovisual equipment. The VCR was delivered to

Harper's office and hooked up to the small color TV the men watched when their job got boring, as it did much of the time in the off-season.

Shortly after 6:00, as Alex and Jessie were sitting down to dinner, Ben Harper and Karl Masterson sat alone in the office with the door closed and the lights off and played the tape.

Harper used a remote control to rewind the cassette, then scanned through it once he discovered that the early material consisted of man-in-the-street interviews.

"News story," he grunted. "Local TV people. They ... Wait a second."

He stopped searching. On the television, a young woman was framed in close-up against the ocean. Her words were clipped, her expression grimly serious.

" ... threat of wild animals on the loose. Animals ... No, hold it." There was a burst of static as the camera switched off and on, and the woman began speaking again, delivering a terse summary of the situation in Sea Cove.

"She hasn't mentioned Wylie Gaines," said Harper. "This must've been filmed before that. In the morning."

Masterson nodded.

" ... reporting from Sea Cove, this is Deborah Bradbury for ... for ..."

Her eyes were not looking into the camera anymore, but past it, and her mouth moved, making inarticulate sounds, and then Deborah Bradbury let out a scream that crackled into static.

Harper leaned forward tensely. Masterson's position had not changed, but his giant hands were knotted into fists, the knuckles squeezed white with pressure.

The woman's face blurred out of frame as the camera swung around, bobbed wildly, then steadied.

"Freeze it," snapped Masterson.

Harper pressed the remote.

They stared in sudden silence at the frozen image.

The image of a Doberman caught and held in the rectangle of the TV screen like a fly in a cube of amber.

The dog had been running very fast. Its front legs were flung out, claws extended to rip space, and its head was raised as if to face the camera and stare it down. Its eyes shone red over saliva-streaked fangs.

"Razor," breathed Harper.

Karl Masterson nodded. "Yes, Chief. You saw him once before."

"Just barely. Never got a good look at him ... at *it*. Until now."

Masterson's voice was a whisper.

"Then take a good look now. That's our enemy, Chief. The only one left. The most dangerous one of all."

Harper studied the image a moment longer, then gritted his teeth, afraid of what he might see, and let the tape play on. He heard a man—the cameraman, he assumed—say, "Christ Almighty," and then as the dog loped closer the TV picture spun crazily and wiped to a sheet of static. Harper waited, but no new picture appeared.

"He dropped the camera," he said finally.

"Yes."

"He dropped it, and the two of them ran, and that thing killed them. Killed them both."

"He must have."

Harper rose, turned off the TV, and leaned against the window blinds, his head lowered, his face sagging with exhaustion. "Then where are the bodies?"

"I don't know."

"Could your dog have dragged them off and ... buried them someplace, like a dog burying a bone?"

Masterson shook his head.

"Well, then?"

"I told you. I don't know."

Harper slammed his fist against the wall. "Goddammit, two people can't just disappear into thin air."

"Chief." Masterson rose and crossed the room to touch Ben Harper's shoulder. "You're tired. I doubt you've had any more sleep than I have in the past twenty-four hours. Which is to say none."

"How in God's name can you think about sleep when that thing is running loose out there?"

"That's why I'm thinking of it."

"What do you suggest? A catnap?"

"Exactly." Masterson returned to his chair, stretched out his legs, and folded his hands in his lap. "We need to conserve our strength for the battle to come. I intend to do so, and I advise you to do the same."

"I don't need your advice," said Harper sullenly.

"You have it, anyway. Good night, Chief."

He shut his eyes. Harper watched, fascinated despite himself, as within seconds Masterson's breathing slowed, his head inclined gently, and his hands relaxed, fingers spread, until his massive frame went limp, as eerily bone-less as a cat. It was as if he had given a silent command to his muscles and they had obeyed instantly, with no hesitation between the mind's will and the body's response.

When, a minute later, Harper whispered Masterson's name, he got no reply.

Harper turned away and stared at the blank TV screen. He honestly did not know if he admired Karl Masterson or hated his guts. Either way, the feeling was intense. And the worst of it, he thought bitterly, was that Masterson had been right. He was jittery and on edge and he did need to sleep, but he couldn't. Just couldn't. Later, maybe. Not now.

He rewound the tape, shut off the VCR, and sat at his desk, remembering one image—the Doberman, Razor, frozen in the instant before a kill—and six words.

*The most dangerous one of all.*

# 36

RAZOR PADDED down darkened streets through drifts of swiftly falling snow. After leaving the pier, he had spent the rest of the day hiding in Sea Cove's commercial district, obeying some dim instinct to stay out of sight. He had shivered in back alleys, pawing through garbage cans to find scraps of food and assuage the hunger twisting in his belly like a knife. Past nightfall he had emerged to prowl the streets, seeking blood. But the streets were empty. The town was afraid.

He heard a car approaching and loped into a thicket of dead weeds half-buried in snow. A green-and-white squad car pulled leisurely past. Razor bared his teeth and growled softly. He did not like cars. He remembered, vaguely, that a car like this one had spirited away one of this morning's prey. Had he killed then, he would not have been hungry now. So very hungry.

The car rolled on. Its red taillights shrank to a single point, then winked out, obscured by a mist of snow.

Razor crossed the street, his lithe, angular body slipping like a shadow over the bleached ground. Shops lined the far side of the street. All were closed and dark.

He turned into an alley and foraged among the tilted garbage cans, their lids hanging askew like open mouths, drooling litter into the snow. He found a can of Franco-American Spaghetti-O's, with a few miserable frozen morsels clinging to the bottom. He licked the can clean and trotted on.

It did not help. He needed food, real food, hot and steaming, to flood his belly with warmth and drown the merciless beast clawing at his ribs.

He reached the back of a one-story building, indistinguishable from the others except for the broadcasting tower spiking its roof and the light that was on somewhere inside. It was the light that Razor saw. It glowed through a back window that had been broken and repaired with heavy masking tape. The tape made an irregular X, black against the glare.

Razor approached the building and gazed up at the window. He pricked his ears and could just barely make out the low drone of a Man's voice.

A memory came to him, the swimming, ghostly memory of glass shards singing around his head as he launched himself through a window like this one. He had heard voices that time too. He had found easy prey inside. But something Bad had happened, he could no longer recall quite what, but a Bad Thing that ended with a small explosion, another dog's twisting fall, and Razor's escape.

He hesitated, studying the window, wondering if the same Bad Thing lay in wait for him behind this pane of glass. His hindquarters were tensing for a leap, as if his hungry body were bypassing his mind and making the decision on its own, when a new sound broke through the drone of the Man's voice.

A car. Drawing near.

Razor hid behind a stack of moldering cardboard boxes a few yards from the rear of the building. He watched as a car sputtered down the alley, reached the building, and came to a stop with a squeal of brakes. A red-and-white plastic sign, internally lit, threw splashes of color across the alley, making watercolor streaks in the snow. ANTONIO'S PIZZA PALACE, said the sign.

A boy, nineteen, jumped out with a large, flat, square box carried level with the ground. He hurried toward the building's rear door.

Razor sniffed the air and caught the scent of the thing in the box, rich with the smells of hamburger and cheese and other fine things which reminded him of the Spaghetti-O's he had scraped off the bottom of the can. But this food was hot.

He crept forward, salivating.

- — -

The time was precisely 10:00 as Tommy Gertz fumbled to open the rear door of the radio station with a hot pizza scorching his hands. The door was unlocked, as usual. That fat fart Stevens had the routine of these nightly deliveries down pat.

Tommy got the door open and stepped inside. He would dump the pizza in the DJ's lap—if he could find it, he smirked—and be out of here in three seconds flat. He was going nuts tonight, two more pizzas sitting in the car getting cold, half a dozen pizzas and spaghetti dinners waiting back at the restaurant. Antonio's phone had been ringing all day, and the other delivery boy, Gary, had called in sick, which Tommy believed like he believed his old man was the Antichrist. Gary was "sick" for the same reason the phone kept ringing: everybody was scared to go outdoors, and all because some pack of dogs had wasted some Geritol junkie and a Farmer Brown and bitten a chunk out of some little girl's ass. *Big deal,* thought Tommy Gertz as he let the door swing shut—almost shut—behind him. He wasn't afraid of Fido. Let those mutts try something on him and he'd teach 'em how it felt to get neutered the old-fashioned way.

He chuckled, thinking that was a pretty good one, and headed for the broadcast booth a few doors down the short, narrow, unlighted hall.

He did not look back. And so he did not see the door inch open, hinges creaking softly in a warning that went unheard.

Razor nosed the door open a crack, then a crack farther, till finally there was room enough for him to squeeze inside, out of the cold.

His red eyes glinted in the dark.

He padded down the hall, trailing Tommy Gertz like a shadow, leaving bright droplets of saliva on the floor.

# 37

Nikki Grant paused at the top of the stairs to take one last look at Cleopatra.

The Doberman was curled up on the floor of the basement. Her hind leg was heavily bandaged. Nikki had gingerly removed the .38 slug and sterilized the wound. She had kept the muzzle in place, of course, and moments ago had given the dog her latest injection of pentobarbital.

She looked so peaceful, fast asleep. It was hard to believe she was a killer.

Nikki sighed, feeling suddenly tired, and flicked off the basement lights, leaving Cleo in darkness. She shut the door and locked it.

The radio filled Ben Harper's living room with the monotonous patter of Stevie Stevens' voice. Harper's tomcat, Hank, lounged in a corner. Nikki sat on the couch, resting her head on a pillow. Hank strolled over to rub against her legs. The radio babbled on. The DJ was talking to a scared Sea Cove resident about the dogs, the killer dogs, always the dogs. The interplay of voices provided her with at least the illusion of companionship, and the feel of the cat tickling her ankles was warm and comforting. She wondered how many nights Ben Harper had spent sitting here on the couch with his cat and the radio and the musty emptiness of this house. She wondered if he ever had friends over for dinner, or if he had friends, period, or if he had ever been in love.

On the radio Stevie Stevens had switched to the

more cheerful topic of a newly arrived pizza.

"Right on schedule, folks. Hot and delicious. Proof once again that Antonio's Pizza Palace on Route 71 delivers—just like it says on the box. I'm now opening the box, and what do my eyes behold but a delectable concoction of mushrooms, anchovies, pepperoni, spicy meatballs, onions, green peppers, black olives, double cheese, extra-thick crust—in short, the works. Yes, gentle listeners, it is yet another culinary triumph from the kitchen of ... hey ..."

Nikki glanced automatically at the radio, her reflexes conditioned by a lifetime spent in the television age, her attention caught by the break in the DJ's monologue.

"Hey, what the hell ...?"

From somewhere in the background came a scream, muffled by distance, and a snarl and the crash of something falling.

Nikki jumped up.

"Oh, Christ," mumbled Stevie Stevens in the voice of a dead man. "Oh, Mother of Christ."

Nikki listened, numb.

"Get away." The voice was pleading now. She could hear the tears welling in the man's eyes. "Get away, you ... you fucker." Then, apparently remembering the microphone, he shouted, "Help me! Send somebody quick! I need cops here! It's one of them! It's ... Oh, shit—"

His scream echoed through the house, as it did through houses and apartments scattered around Sea Cove and adjoining towns. It was a death cry, long, warbling, and sickeningly close, because his mouth must still have been inches from the microphone that picked up every detail. But worse than the scream, almost drowning it out, so loud it might have been the magnified sound effect of a horror movie, was the noise of the dog's brutal slashing and growling and slobbering and chewing—the wet, smacking sounds and the frantic gasping as its tongue lapped blood.

Nikki's hand was on the phone, dialing the direct line to Ben Harper's office.

- — -

Harper was nodding off when the phone rang. The sound jerked him up in his chair, instantly alert.

He had not intended to sleep. But as Karl Masterson dozed and the phones outside began to fall silent, Harper had felt himself slipping—slipping toward some dark, silent, restful place. His head had lowered, inch by inch, until his chin was nearly touching his chest, and he had slumped forward slowly across his desk ...

And the phone rang, yanking him back to reality— the reality where sleep was not permitted—where an animal more cunning and vicious than a wolf was stalking his town and leaving corpses in its wake.

As he picked up the phone on the third ring, he noted that Masterson was still asleep, and envied him.

"Harper."

Nikki's voice on the line triggered a split-second thought about the Doberman in her care—if it had hurt her, or escaped, Karl Masterson would have hell to pay— but that fear was swept away by her words. In three clipped sentences, spoken rapidly but with no trace of panic, she summarized the situation.

"Right," said Harper, feeling his heartbeat accelerate with a burst of adrenaline. "We're on our way."

He hung up, rose, shrugged on his coat, then turned to Masterson, intending to rouse him, only to see that Masterson was awake already and buttoning his coat with a swift economy of movement.

"At the radio station," said Harper. "The damn thing has killed again."

# 38

AT THE moment when Nikki Grant was sitting peacefully on the sofa with the cat rubbing her legs, Razor was crouched in a darkened doorway directly across from the broadcast booth, watching Tommy Gertz deliver the pizza.

Razor had forgotten all about Tommy Gertz. That Man was scrawny, his arms loose and gangling, his movements as skittish and awkward as a pup's. He would be easy prey—too easy.

The Doberman's eyes were fixed on Stevie Stevens.

Stevens sat behind a desk, speaking into a microphone, his voice droning on. He was a huge man. His chest sagged over the balloon of his belly. His buttocks overflowed his creaking chair and shimmered liquidly, like gelatin, as he swiveled slowly back and forth.

Razor wanted that Man.

The other one could go. He was unimportant. Razor had only one kill in mind.

Tommy Gertz walked out of the booth, leaving the door open, and made a mistake. It was a small mistake, the sort that could easily be forgiven in a more forgiving world.

He glanced at the opposite doorway and saw a pair of gleaming red eyes, gazing up at him silently.

This, however, was not Tommy Gertz's fatal mistake. At this point Tommy had three options, any of which might well have saved his life. He could have pretended to have seen nothing and strolled casually out the back door, whistling. Razor would have let him go. Or he could have bolted for the back door. Razor might have hesitated long enough to permit Tommy's escape. Or he could have taken a step back, into the booth, and slammed the door. Razor would have been locked out, and two lives would have been spared.

Tommy Gertz did none of these things. He stood motionless, staring, for what seemed to him like many minutes but was in fact less than a second. Then he opened his mouth and said out loud, "Holy shit."

In the booth, Stevie Stevens uttered the one word—"hey"—that had caught Nikki Grant's attention. He uttered it as he saw the peculiar way Tommy was standing in the doorway with his body swaying from side to side.

Razor had not planned to kill this Man, but now it was necessary to do so, and he did. The act took only a split second. Razor sprang—Tommy screamed—the Doberman buried his fangs in Tommy's throat and ripped it open like a paper bag. Then Tommy was on the floor, writhing on his back, gargling blood, while jets of scarlet spattered the hall like the twisting spray of a water sprinkler.

Razor ignored the Man's death throes. He slunk through the open doorway into the booth, where a deluxe extra-large pizza lay steaming, forgotten, on a desk and a very fat man named Stevie Stevens, aka Morton Thomas Tillinger, was about to die.

"Oh, Christ," said the DJ. "Oh, Mother of Christ." He was looking into the Doberman's eyes and seeing what Ben Harper had seen. Only Ben Harper had had a Smith & Wesson .38 and a steady hand. Stevie Stevens had neither.

The dog advanced, and Stevens sat rigid in his chair, unable to get up, his legs paralyzed. There was no place to run anyway. The booth was narrow, windowless, and the only exit was the doorway blocked by the dog.

Razor growled softly. His dripping fangs shone like ice picks.

That was when Stevie Stevens had started to beg. "Get away, you ... you fucker." Tears blurred his vision and thickened his voice.

Razor padded nearer.

At the last moment the DJ remembered the microphone. He clutched it with both hands, feeling the cold metal on his sweat-slick palms, and pressed his mouth close and shouted for help, for cops, for somebody, quick, because it was one of ... *them*!

Razor did not bother to pounce. There was no need. Not when he could simply close in on the helpless, quivering Man who exuded the sweet aroma of fear, then spring erect on his hind legs and thud his front paws down hard on the Man's chest and sink his teeth into the bulging stomach as the Man screamed in agony.

Razor tore out a chunk of meat and burrowed his snout deeper into Stevie Stevens' gut while the DJ shrieked and flailed his heavy arms. The dog's questing teeth gnawed through layers of fat and his slashing claws reduced his victim's shirt and skin to flapping tatters. Razor pawed furiously at the widening gap in the Man's gut, till the stomach ruptured and its contents spilled out like the insides of a dissected shark, the half-digested remnants of breakfast, lunch, dinner, second helpings of each and snacks in between. And still the Man was screaming, but weakly now, his eyes glazed over, his arms jerking involuntarily, all consciousness gone. Hazily Razor recalled another Man who had screamed like this as his body was torn to shreds, a Man lying on his back on the frozen ground under an open sky. But the memory passed fleetingly and vanished with the last of Stevie Stevens' screams.

Razor clambered over the mountain of flesh and fed as greedily as a hyena on a fresh carcass. His scrabbling paws sent the pizza sliding out of its box to sprinkle the Man with mushrooms, anchovies, pepperoni, spicy meatballs, onions, green peppers, black olives—in short, the works.

As Razor finished his attack, there was no longer any way to tell which parts of the thing slumped in the swivel chair had once been Stevie Stevens and which parts had been merely the latest culinary triumph from the kitchen of Antonio's Pizza Palace on Route 71.

Razor pricked up his ears at the sound of a car skidding to a halt out front.

Cars meant danger.

He bounded off the chair, out of the booth, down the hall. He lost his footing momentarily on the slick blood sprayed from Tommy Gertz's neck. Then he was up on all fours again and loping for the back door. With one push the door swung wide and he was free and the door slammed behind him.

The front door surrendered to Ben Harper's master key a second later, and Harper and Masterson were inside, racing for the booth, too late.

# 39

KARL MASTERSON barely glanced at the body of Tommy Gertz outside the doorway of the broadcast booth. He stepped inside and swept his Uzi over the room as his eyes took in the gutted corpse that still swiveled in its chair. Razor was gone. But the chair was still turning ...

The Doberman must have left only seconds before.

He stepped back into the hall, next to Harper, who stood gazing down at Tommy Gertz's remains, his stolid face drawn tight in lines of anger, his .38 unholstered and useless. Masterson looked past the police chief, down the hall, and saw the trail of paw prints traced in wet blood, leading out the back door.

"He escaped that way," Masterson snapped. He broke into a run. "I'll take the alley. You take the front!"

He was out the door before Ben Harper had the chance to reply.

Tommy Gertz's car sat where he had left it, parked at the rear of the building, its lighted sign still painting the alley in bright brushstrokes of red. The Doberman's tracks dotted the snow. Masterson followed them by eye till the glow of the sign was behind him, then switched on the Micro-Lite clipped to his belt. He had given Harper one of the miniature high-intensity flashlights also, and offered him the Thompson. The second offer had been declined. Harper still trusted his .38, it seemed. Masterson wondered how much longer that trust would hold.

The flashlight's pinpoint beam easily picked up the trail. Masterson followed it, jogging, breathing in, out, in, out, just as he did every morning back home. His body was a machine, finely tuned, obedient to his will. It would serve him well tonight. He only wished Harper had allowed himself some rest. A man could not run on adrenaline and black coffee indefinitely—not if he wanted to be sharp. And tonight, of all nights, they would both need to be sharp. Because their adversary was sharp.

Razor was the best dog Karl Masterson had ever trained. He knew that Razor could beat him in this game they were now playing, a game played to the death.

The Doberman's trail continued out of the alley into the street. Masterson shone his flashlight up the street and saw a line of paw prints vanishing into darkness, but no sign of the dog. Razor had escaped at a run, and he could run very fast. But he could not be far ahead.

The snow was still falling, hard enough to obliterate the trail in minutes. Masterson was about to run back for Harper when the squad car pulled around the corner and the side door swung open.

"Get in," said Harper. "We won't catch the bastard on foot."

"Exactly what I was thinking." Masterson slid into the passenger seat. The car pulled away, rear tires spitting snow. The high beams spotlighted the tracks, which charted a straight line down the middle of the street for two blocks, then veered into a side street and down another alley. Harper spun the wheel, first left, then right, always keeping the tracks framed squarely in the windshield, while the wipers beat steadily, brushing away clots of snow.

"Think he'll make it hard for us?" asked Harper without intonation.

"As hard as possible."

"We'll get him anyway." Harper did not take his eyes from the road. "He's going to die tonight."

# 40

ALEX HAD insisted on walking Jessie from his car to the front door of the hotel. He had no thoughts of trying to invite himself in. The major question in his mind, as he guided her through the whirl of snowflakes, was whether or not he should try to kiss Jessica Blair.

He wanted to. But, he admitted to himself with a touch of irritation, he wasn't quite sure how to go about doing it.

As they reached the shelter of the porch and left the snow behind, he decided the kiss could wait. He really didn't mind waiting. He could return to his apartment now, look out his window, and see the Oceanview rising in silhouette against the gray backdrop of the Atlantic, and he could think of Jessie sleeping there and know that he would see her again, soon, and maybe kiss her next time, and that would be enough.

"Well, we made it." Jessie's voice was low, nearly a whisper, all but lost in the crash of the breakers on the beach. "No dogs. But I'm glad I had you to protect me, anyhow." She smiled. "Alex Driscoll. Have gun, will travel."

Alex flushed. He leaned close to her, catching the sweet scent of perfume on her neck. "I hate to tell you this but ... uh ..."He tapped his coat over the spot where the Remington was concealed in his vest pocket. "This thing's not even loaded. Ed gave me bullets, but I ... I don't like loaded guns, so ..."

Jessie laughed softly, half-burying her face in his coat. He had an urge, such a powerful urge, to take her in his arms and kiss her. He hesitated, and the opportunity was lost. She was still smiling, but she had stepped back, fumbling with her keys.

"I'll call you tomorrow," he said quickly.

"You'd better."

Then, briskly and affectionately and without any fuss, she kissed him on the cheek.

"'Night, Alex."

She unlocked the door and stepped in, then turned just inside the doorway and gave Alex a parting smile.

Alex smiled back, shyly, still savoring the momentary brush of her lips against his skin.

His smile had not yet faded when—oddly—Jessie jerked back and gave a sharp cry, like a person slipping in a bathtub, her arms pinwheeling crazily, until another arm crooked around her waist, holding her tight, and metal flashed at her throat.

It took Alex a second to understand that the metal was the cold steel of a meat cleaver held close to Jessie's skin, a cleaver held by a shadow figure that had waited in ambush behind the door.

The shadow raised its eyes to Alex. It was a kid. A goddamn kid.

"Get inside," the kid said to Alex.

Jessie moaned and tried to shake her head. The knife quivered at her throat.

"Get inside, asshole, or I'll cut her fucking head off."

Alex stood motionless, thinking of the gun in his pocket, which he could not hope to pull out fast enough to use, even as a bluff, before the knife sawed through Jessie's neck.

"Count of three, fucker. Then she's meat. One ..."

Jessie's eyes locked with Alex's. Her lips moved soundlessly, forming one word: *Run.*

"Two ..."

Alex hesitated a moment longer, while Jessie silently

implored him to escape. He weighed his options. He made his choice.

"Three."

"Keep cool, friend." Alex's voice was firm and steady. "I'm coming."

Jessie bit her lip, trembling.

Alex Driscoll stepped through the doorway, into the lobby of the Oceanview Inn, and shut the door behind him.

# THIRD DAY

# 41

IT WAS shortly past midnight when Harper and Masterson trapped Razor in the alley.

They had been in close pursuit of the Doberman for an hour and a half, following a trail that wound through the streets and alleys of Sea Cove's commercial district. Twice they had lost the trail. The first time, the dog's tracks led up to the edge of a frozen pond in the middle of Memorial Park. The pond was sheltered on all sides by trees, and little snow had fallen there; its glassy surface left no tracks; there was no way to guess which direction the Doberman had taken when he crossed the ice, or where his trail might be picked up. For twenty minutes, as a light snow continued to fall, threatening to wipe out whatever tracks might remain, the two men had searched the perimeter of the pond on foot, traveling separately, guns drawn, flashlights shining on the snowy ground.

Halfway around the pond, Harper had stumbled on tracks. They led through the trees and out into the maze of streets. The paw prints were faint, nearly filled in with new snow, doomed to vanish into oblivion before long. Harper ran back to the squad car while yelling hoarsely for Masterson, who met him there. Together they took off, Harper at the wheel, speeding recklessly through the park, dodging trees and benches, until the car thudded over the curb onto the street again. The headlights caught the dwindling remnants of Razor's trail. The motor hummed in a desperate race with the falling snow.

Then—just when the tracks were clean and fresh again, and Harper knew they were gaining on the dog—the footprints disappeared.

It was as simple as that. One moment the trail was drawing the headlights onward as surely as a magnet, and the next moment there was no trail, only blank drifts of snow piled high in the center on the street.

"Goddammit," muttered Harper, slowing the car. "Gust of wind must have blown snow down off the roofs and trees. Covered everything."

"Keep driving," said Masterson evenly. "Maybe we can pick it up again."

The squad car crawled forward, plowing through the deep snow, its headlights finding nothing. Even when the drifts were behind them, the trail did not reappear.

"He must have changed direction," said Masterson.

"Yeah."

Harper turned the car around and probed the edge of the street with his high beams, looking for tracks. There were none. He executed another U-turn and searched the street on the opposite side.

"There," said Masterson suddenly.

Harper squinted but saw nothing.

"That vacant lot. Next to the bicycle shop. He cut through there."

"I don't see any tracks."

"Neither do I."

Harper started to object, but Masterson merely added, "I know this dog, Chief."

Harper did not argue. He drove around to the other side of the lot, and his headlights zeroed in on a line of tracks veering out of the bushes, down the street. The tracks were faint, not too recent, but he could follow them.

The trail led past the Exxon station at Main and Brighton, down an alley back of Gilbert's Hardware, over the railroad crossing, then back again a half mile down the line, through the parking lot of Bertram's Grocery—twisting, turning, circling, but always growing fresher, the prints more distinct, more recent.

"We're gaining on him," said Harper. Masterson nodded.

Then they rounded a corner and the high beams caught the distant black shape of a Doberman loping down the middle of the street.

Harper drew in a sharp breath and gunned the engine. The car picked up speed. Masterson rolled down his window and leaned out with the Uzi in hand. He fired three times.

"Get him?"

"No."

Masterson steadied the gun with both hands, preparing to shoot again. Razor was close now, only fifteen yards away, but the car was bouncing on the snow and the dog was not running in a straight line anymore. He was weaving back and forth, refusing to give his pursuers any chance at a clean shot. *Who taught him that?* Masterson wondered briefly. Then he reminded himself that this was Razor, and Razor possessed an instinct for survival that had made Karl Masterson's training almost irrelevant.

Masterson fired off four more shots and missed. The pistol was fully loaded, thirty-two rounds, and he had nine more magazines available. He was not worried. He needed to connect with only a single shot. Perhaps his next shot ...

Razor bolted sideways, down an alley, with the car less than five yards behind.

Harper spun the wheel and made a sound that was almost a triumphant laugh. "He outsmarted himself this time. That alley's a dead end. We've got the bastard now."

The car skidded into the alley. Its headlights burned

like white fire on the spread of snow that extended to a high brick wall at the alley's far end. Razor's tracks made a beeline through the snow, then veered sharply into a pile of trashcans and green plastic garbage bags near the alley wall.

"He's taken cover. He knows he's trapped." Masterson's voice was low and cautious.

"Damn right he is."

"Chief. A cornered animal—"

"I know, dammit." Harper unholstered the .38. "Let him fight. Let him try."

Harper pulled the car to a stop ten feet from the end of the alley. The headlights lit the scene starkly as the two men got out.

They approached slowly, their shoes crunching on the snow, the headlights' beams throwing their long, distorted shadows across the length of the alley. They reached the Doberman's hiding place, and now their shadows loomed on the far wall, gigantic and menacing. Masterson held the Uzi in both hands. Harper gripped his .38. Neither man could see the Doberman. But Razor was there. They could sense his presence, as surely as he sensed theirs.

- — -

Razor had known all along that he was being chased. Several times since his escape from the scene of his last kills, he had paused in his running and listened, ears pricked, and heard the distant rumble of a car behind him. Sometimes the car sounded close and sometimes it sounded far away, but always it was there, tracking him remorselessly. So he had kept going, running aimlessly, never tiring, but never able to shake off his pursuer.

Now the car idled nearby and the two Men who had emerged from it were inching toward him. He waited, muscles taut, concealed behind a stack of garbage cans. He could not yet see the Men, but he watched their grotesque shadow show playing on the wall, heard their footsteps, smelled their fear. Ordinarily he would have liked that smell, but not tonight. Tonight he sensed something more, something ominous. Fear made Men run or stand paralyzed; fear was for the prey, not the hunter; and tonight these Men were hunting him.

Razor did not like being hunted. He did not like having to hide himself in shadows. He did not like standing rigidly, waiting out danger's slow approach. He did not like it, any of it, and his spine stiffened, arching almost like a cat's, as some dark recess of his mind decided to put an end to it—now.

The Men took a step closer, and Razor struck.

- — -

The garbage cans swayed, as if impacted by a sudden blow, then toppled with an echoing crash and rolled crazily, drawing the fire of Masterson's Uzi and Harper's .38. The Uzi stabbed flame in a series of rapid-fire shots, strobe-lighting the trash, turning the shadows on the brick wall into flickering pantomimes. Harper's Police Special coughed three times, puncturing three of the cans. Then both guns fell silent simultaneously as the men realized Razor was not in their sights.

"It's a trick," snapped Masterson. He whirled, and Harper did the same, in time to see the Doberman dart out from the stack of Hefty bags behind them and streak along the side of the squad car, racing in the direction of the street. The car's headlights, blinding against the darkness beyond, swallowed up the dog in their glare.

Harper rushed around the car on the opposite side, hoping to get a clean shot at the dog before it escaped again.

Behind him, Masterson shouted, "Wait!" Harper ignored the warning. He reached the rear of the squad car and stopped, peering down the alley, the .38 gripped squarely in both hands, target-practice style.

The alley was empty.

But that wasn't possible.

It couldn't run that fast, couldn't cover the fifty feet of the alley in the time it had taken him to cover a single car length.

Which meant ...

Ben Harper looked down. Razor was there. Hunched behind the car, his red eyes gazing up at Harper, his hindquarters tensing.

Harper swung the .38 around while knowing with utter certainty that he did not have time to fire, because the Doberman was already launched in flight, springing for his throat, and his finger could not pump the trigger fast enough to ward off the fangs sweeping toward him.

In the split second before he knew those dagger teeth would open his neck in a sluice of blood, Ben Harper had time to feel a pang of regret for all the things life had not given him—the wife, the children, and most of all the friends he had not known outside the comforting rectangle of the Rivoli's movie screen.

Only a pang—that was all he had time for—but that was enough.

He never felt the hand on his shoulder. His whole consciousness was fixed on the dog, and so at first he did not understand why he was plunging sideways to the pavement, landing in a tangled heap with Karl Masterson, while the Doberman sailed past, inches away, its claws shredding one sleeve of his coat—it had been that close—and then the dog hit the ground in a puff of snow and rolled to its feet, its fur bleached white. Masterson groped for the Uzi he had dropped in the fall. He couldn't reach it in time. Razor gave Ben Harper a parting glance, then spun as artfully as an ice skater and streaked down the alley, into the street, out of sight.

Harper did not move for a long moment. He lay on his side, fighting to catch his breath, feeling the sudden fever between his temples, and tasting dry vomit at the back of his mouth. And remembering. Most of all, re-membering. Remembering that last look the dog had giv-en him, the merciless intelligence that burned in its coal-ember eyes. Those eyes had gazed straight at him, into him, and they had made a promise, and the promise was:

*Next time.*

Harper shook his head and concentrated on filling his lungs with cold, pure air.

"Chief?"

He looked up. Masterson had untangled himself from Harper's legs and retrieved the Uzi. He was kneeling by Harper, his face composed.

"I'm all right," said Harper softly. "Just a little shook up, that's all."

"That makes two of us."

"You told me to wait."

"He pulled one trick. I expected another."

"An ambush ..." Harper shook his head, as if part of him were still refusing to accept it.

"He's smart, Chief. I said he'd make it as hard as pos-sible."

"Yeah."

Harper got up slowly and leaned against the car until his legs seemed willing to support him again. "So the chase continues," he said finally.

Masterson nodded. "I thought it would. This"—he waved a hand at the alley—"was too easy."

Harper considered saying something in retort, then thought better of it. Wordlessly he climbed back into the car, behind the wheel. Masterson slid in on the passenger side. Harper put his hand on the gearshift, then hesitated. He looked at Masterson.

"Where's that Thompson, anyway?"

"Back seat."

"Get it for me, will you?"

Masterson got it. Harper hefted the automatic rifle in one hand, feeling its weight, liking that feel. He laid the gun across his knees and shifted into reverse. The car backed out of the alley. Its lights picked up the Doberman's trail, zigzagging up the street into darkness.

They drove for a few minutes, following the trail in silence.

Then, as he turned down a side street, Harper said quietly, "Thanks."

Masterson grunted, shrugging.

"You know," said Harper slowly, "I've been acting like this whole thing is your fault. It's not. And I'm sorry."

"No need for apologies, Chief."

"Call me Ben."

Masterson took a moment to reply.

"All right ... Ben."

The two men looked at each other, their faces lit from below by the dashboard glow, their eyes veiled by shadow, their mouths set in ruler-straight lines. The glance was like a handshake between them.

They drove on, saying nothing, feeling no need to speak. The quiet was broken only by the hum of the engine and the slow, regular scraping of the windshield wipers on the glass.

# 42

SOMETIME DURING the night they had both drifted off to sleep, huddled together on the waiting room's couch. Behind them the wide snow-flecked windows framed a dark void. Down some side corridor a vacuum cleaner, the big industrial kind, was burring fitfully, a low snoring sound that rose and fell. Paul and Barbara Gaines were too deeply asleep to hear it with their conscious minds, but in Paul's dreams the sound became the faraway voice of a child calling for her daddy, but fading, always fading before he could find her, and in Barbara's dreams it was the sound of a surgeon's tool, an electric scalpel perhaps, peeling away flesh with a dull metallic whine that went on and on.

It was shortly before 1:00 AM. The fourth floor of the hospital was nearly deserted. When they had checked the last time, forty-five minutes ago, their daughter was still in surgery. Nobody was saying anything. Nobody had to. Close to twelve hours of surgery on an eight-year-old girl. There was really nothing anyone could say.

Dr. Lewis paused at the threshold of the waiting room. His kind middle-aged face was haggard. Deep circles bruised the hollows under his eyes. He had pulled off his rubber gloves but still wore the green surgical gown, hanging off him in rumpled folds. The sterile mask, tugged loose, flapped around his neck like a bib. He took a breath to clear his head, approached Mr. and Mrs. Gaines, and roused them gently.

They saw his face and snapped alert. They said nothing. He stood looking down at them, feeling the odd, almost impersonal sense of discomfort that came to him at these times, when he saw eyes gazing up at him in helplessness and dread, eyes pleading for a message of salvation. He wondered if God felt this way when he handed down his judgments on the souls of the dead, and if those souls looked up at him with eyes like these. He wondered if God enjoyed his work. Perhaps it depended on whatever particular judgment he had to make.

Dr. Lewis took another breath, then told Wylie Gaines's parents the news.

# 43

HE WISHED it could have been any way but this.

Jessie stood trembling before him. The yellow dress—*her best dress,* he thought dimly—looked paler now, as pale as her skin and her bloodless lips. He hesitated and felt the knife blade tickle the back of his neck like a barber's electric razor.

"Do it," breathed the kid.

Alex looked at Jessie. Jessie swallowed, nodded, and turned.

With one swift motion Alex unzipped the dress and let it fall to the carpet, where it lay in yellow folds like the petals of a flower. Jessie kicked the dress free of her high heels and stood without turning. Alex saw the skin of her back and the white strap of her bra and the translucent V of her underpants. He felt sick to his stomach, because he had wanted this so much, but not this way.

"Pick it up."

Alex picked up the dress. It sagged limply in his hand, just a scrap of fabric now, all magic gone.

"Now tear it up. Into strips. Long strips. Go on, tear it."

Alex shredded the dress to yellow ribbons, which was appropriate, wasn't it, because yellow ribbons were what people put out to remember hostages and prisoners. He and Jessie had been prisoners for the past two hours, while the kid brandished the meat cleaver and seemed to debate what to do next. At last he had reached a decision.

"Now," said the kid, "you take one strip and you tie her pretty wrists with it. You tie 'em behind her fucking back."

Alex tied Jessie's wrists. Her hands were small, and the bones of her wrists were as delicate as wishbones. He didn't make the knot very tight, because he didn't want to harm those fragile wrists, but the kid whispered, "Tighter," and the knife was shaving the short hairs at the back of his head again, so he gritted his teeth and jerked the knot tight. Jessie moaned, and silently Alex apologized.

"Good. Real good. You're doing a bang-up job, scum. What was your name again?"

"Alex."

"Yeah. Okay, now. Miss Jessica-call-me-Jessie Blair, you turn around."

Jessie turned, gazing down, avoiding Alex's eyes.

"This is a hell of a room," said the kid mockingly. "I found it after I broke in. And when I did, I said Jessie is going to die here. It's a good place to die, isn't it? Come on. Say it. Say it's a good place to die."

Jessie's eyes bulged. She said nothing. She did not seem able to speak.

Abruptly Alex felt the flat of the knife blade pressing hard against his cheek, cold and stinging like ice.

"Say it. Or I cut him. Bad."

Jessie struggled for words. "It's a ... good place ... to ... die."

"You did that real good. What is this fucking place, anyway?"

"It's ... the game room. There used to be parties here. Long ago."

"Yeah. That's what I figured. Now"—he shoved Alex forward—"pick up your girlfriend and put her on the table."

It was a billiard table, one of several in the large musty room lit with green-shaded lamps. Alex lifted Jessie in his arms and set her down gingerly.

"Stretch her out. Face up. Tie her down with the dress."

Alex turned slowly to look at the kid.

"What are you going to do?"

"Tie her down."

*"What are you going to do?"*

The knife flashed once. The pain hit Alex an instant later, simultaneously with Jessie's gasp. He raised his hand to his cheek and felt the wet gash above his jaw. His hand came away gloved in red. He looked down, feeling dizzy, and saw droplets of blood splattering the carpet like a light rain.

It was not too bad a wound. Only a warning. And a promise of things to come.

The kid watched him. His Adam's apple jerked. His eyes were filmy and dead. The meat cleaver dripped.

"Tie her down."

Alex turned to Jessie. She winced, seeing the cut. He ignored her, just as he ignored the hot spot of pain searing one side of his face. He had a job to do.

He did it slowly, carefully, correctly, winding the long yellow ribbons around her waist and under the table and knotting them in place. "Her feet too," said the kid. Alex bound her ankles. "Gag her." He wadded a strip of fabric into a ball and wedged it between her teeth, not too tight. She could spit it out if she had to.

He did it all without thinking. His thoughts were fixed on the Remington revolver in his vest pocket and the .31-caliber bullets in his side pocket. Together they were the only hope. Somehow he had to distract the kid, at least for a few seconds, long enough to load the gun—why had he ever unloaded it, anyway? How could he have been so stupid? But that didn't matter now. The gun had to be loaded. He didn't think he could bluff his way out with an empty gun. Some criminals could be bluffed, but this kid with the dead eyes … No. It would be suicide to try. Worse than suicide, because it would condemn Jessie to death too.

The kid looked Jessie over, inspecting Alex's work. She glared up at him, her eyes as darkly green as a stormy ocean, wide and unblinking above the rag stuffed in her mouth. Strands of hair spilled over her face, making tangled red-blond streaks against the billiard table's green baize.

He nodded, satisfied, then turned to hold Alex's glance.

"First you," said the kid evenly. "I'll save her for last."

# 44

ED CLANCY peered over the steering wheel of his ancient Chrysler and wished he were a younger man.

Because if he were younger, his night vision would be better and his chances of spotting the Doberman in the deserted streets of downtown Sea Cove would be that much improved.

He knew the dog was running loose around here someplace. He had heard Ben Harper's most recent report over the police-band radio he kept in the *Citizen*'s editorial offices. And even though it was late and Ed was tired, he could not pass up the opportunity to see the dog, perhaps even to obtain a firsthand account of its demise.

He'd been covering the news in Sea Cove for nearly forty years, and this was the biggest story ever to hit this town. The biggest story of Ed Clancy's career. Bigger than the Suffolk Hotel scandal, which had been Ed's previous favorite. Back in 1975, that was. He had broken the story himself, the story of the town council's secret plan to turn the Suffolk into townhouses by granting an exemption to the local ordinance against condominium developments. The fellow to get the exemption was Garret W. Drake, prominent local citizen, real-estate developer, and close personal friend of many council members. The story had embarrassed a lot of people and killed the plan. A year later, the Suffolk had gone under the bulldozers anyway, but the land was sold off as private plots. Houses, not condos, stood there now. It had been a major victory for the Sea Cove *Citizen.*

But this story was bigger. When the fuss about the plane crash in Newark died down, this story would make the New York papers and even the TV news.

Now if only he could find the dog, the goddamn dog.

He had just turned a corner when the Doberman streaked out of a side street, its lithe body impaled on his headlight beams, directly in the path of his car.

Instinctively Ed hit the brakes.

The Chrysler went into a skid. The dog vanished under the hood and Ed heard a heavy, sickening thud of impact, and the next moment the car sat motionless, its front end brushing the curb, its rear jutting into the street.

Ed waited, gripping the steering wheel, breathing hard.

The dog did not reappear.

He had killed it. Jesus God, he had run the bastard down.

And the irony was, he hadn't even meant to. His habit of braking for animals was so deeply ingrained that he'd forgotten, in that instant, that this particular animal deserved no mercy.

He wondered where Ben Harper was, then remembered that the police chief had reported only that he was following the Doberman's trail. He might be a mile away, crawling along, losing the trail and picking it up again, not even knowing that the chase was over and the dog was dead.

Ed reached for the door handle, then hesitated.

Of course, just because the dog had been hit did not necessarily mean it was dead. It might merely be injured. Might be waiting outside, leaking blood and plotting revenge.

Ed thought about his Remington. *Shouldn't have let Alex have it,* he thought. *Foolish sentimentality on my part.* By now Alex and Jessie were no doubt safe and warm somewhere, never having so much as laid eyes on an attack dog. And meanwhile he was stuck in his car, afraid to go out and see if he had finished the job.

He turned off his motor, leaving his headlights on, and listened in the sudden silence.

If the dog were hurt but not dead, it would be making some sort of sound. Whimpering or licking its wounds or growling. An animal in pain, struck head-on by an automobile, could not stay completely still.

Ed heard nothing.

He cranked down his window a few inches to let in the night air. No sound drifted in.

The dog was either unconscious or dead. One way or the other, it was no threat to him.

And he wanted to get the first photos. He wanted to be standing by the dog when Harper's squad car pulled up. The great white hunter posing by his kill.

Ed chuckled at the thought as he screwed the flash-bar onto his camera and looped the camera strap around his neck. He depressed the door handle and climbed out.

The headlight beams caught flakes of falling snow. The dead brown grass at the curb crackled under his feet. He crept around to the front of the Chrysler, looking for the dog. He stopped.

"Oh," he said very simply.

The thud he had heard was not the Doberman. It was a fire hydrant. The car had slammed into the hydrant at the end of its skid. The bumper had caved in.

There was no sign of the dog anywhere.

Ed had not seen it escape. And now he did not believe he had hit it, after all. Which meant it must still be near. Unhurt. Hiding. Waiting.

*All right now, Clancy. No need to panic. The car door is only two, three steps away. Just get back to it and get inside. Once you're in the car, you're safe. Come on, now. Nice and easy.*

He took his first step toward the door, and the Doberman leaped up from the opposite side of the car, onto the hood, and lunged for his throat.

Its fangs sliced through the camera strap. The camera whirled into space. Ed flung himself at the open door, missed, and fell, sprawling half on the curb, half on the street. He tried to get up, and the dog landed on his back and bit deep into the flesh between his shoulder blades.

The shock killed Ed Clancy instantly. He had no time for last thoughts, for regrets or epitaphs. He did not even know he had been bitten. He felt no pain. One moment he was on his belly in the snowy grass, struggling to rise, and the next moment his heart had stopped and he was gone.

Razor did not know the Man was dead. He tore ruthlessly at the corpse, his jaws snapping wildly, slitting Ed Clancy's throat in a dozen places. Blood streamed into the gutter and spiraled down a storm drain. Razor nosed the body over onto its back and slashed at the Man's face till Ed Clancy's mane of white hair was soaked scarlet.

The sound of a car approaching reached the Doberman's ears. He abandoned his prey and raced away into the night.

Ben Harper and Karl Masterson leaped out of the squad car seconds later and probed the scene with their flashlights.

"That's Ed Clancy's car," said Harper softly. He moved cautiously to the driver's side, saw the body and crouched down beside it. "Ed. Oh, for Christ's sake, Ed."

Masterson watched, saying nothing.

After a moment Harper got to his feet.

"A friend of yours?" asked Masterson, his voice strained.

"I ... I guess so. I knew him. Everybody knew him." Harper's face was pale and his eyes were too wide and too dry.

He brushed past Masterson and slid behind the wheel of the squad car and called for an ambulance to pick up a body at the intersection of Third and Wilkins.

The police-band radio, which Ed Clancy had forgotten to turn off, broadcast the report to the empty offices of the Sea Cove *Citizen.*

# 45

ALEX'S HEART pulsed hard in his throat. The rest of his body was numb. He was seated in a chair, hands spread palms down on the smooth mahogany surface of a table that must have been used for all-night poker games once, but had now been requisitioned for different sort of game—one played for higher stakes.

Jessie watched helplessly from across the room. Alex kept his eyes on her as best he could, which wasn't easy, because the kid stood between them, weaving back and forth, his Adam's apple bobbing like a yo-yo. His mouth hung open, gaping stupidly, and his shoulders twitched. He shifted the meat cleaver restlessly from hand to hand. Alex pleaded silently with some impersonal Fate, begging for the knife to slip out of his grasp. If it fell, Alex could scramble for it or kick it aside or maybe hurl the table over on top of the kid as he stooped to retrieve it, and any of those maneuvers would give him the few seconds he needed to draw and load the gun.

The knife glinted hypnotically, switching from right hand to left, left to right, right to left, like the flashing signal lights at a railroad crossing, but never leaving the kid's grasp.

"So, scum. What'll it be?"

Alex tried to moisten his mouth, but his tongue was a dry cotton swab. He cleared his throat. His heartbeat was maddeningly loud.

"I don't know what you mean," he said, his words evenly spaced and unnaturally distinct.

"It's carving time, is what I mean, fucker. I'm going to kill you—in case you hadn't guessed. You and your girlfriend too."

"Why?" asked Alex slowly. "What's in it for you?"

He slid his left hand an inch toward the edge of the table, then another inch. If he could get the bullets in his hand, he could load the gun before the knife struck. Maybe. His hand slid back another inch.

"Because I like it." The kid focused his eyes on Alex. Alex kept his hand still. "And I don't like you."

"What have we ever done to you?"

The kid made a snorting sound that might have been laughter. He looked away. Alex moved his hand another inch.

"You didn't do shit to me. You couldn't. Know why? Because you're weak. Both of you. All of you. You're all sheep. You follow rules and do what you're told and never talk back. You don't have the goddamn guts to know what you want and take it."

"And you do?" Two inches more.

"Damn right I do."

"So what's so great about that? You break the law and that makes you special? Why?" Alex's hand was at the very edge of the table. "Why are you superior?"

"Well, for one thing, asshole, I'm smarter than you."

"Are you?"

"Yeah."

Alex's hand was halfway off the table, poised to plunge into his side pocket, when the meat cleaver swung around suddenly like the whirling blade of a helicopter and came to rest jammed tight against the underside of his jaw.

"Both hands flat on the table," said the kid calmly.

Alex moved his hand back. He felt nothing but a crushing sense of defeat.

"See?" The kid smiled. "Like I said, I'm smarter. So

don't try to outsmart me again."

The kid drew the knife back and lowered his head to face Alex from across the table.

"Now. Which part do you want to lose first?"

Alex took a long, shuddering breath. There was no way out. No escape. He couldn't even reach for the gun as a bluff now. The slightest move would get him killed.

But the kid didn't want to kill him. Not right away. He wanted to ... mutilate. And in that fact there might lie one last chance.

Alex met the kid's eyes levelly.

"Take your pick," he said with all the calm he could muster.

Past the tangle of dirty blond hair framing the kid's face, Alex saw Jessie turn her head away.

"You got it, man." The kid's yellow teeth blossomed in an unhealthy grin. "Oh, yeah. You *got* it."

The meat clever swung up in a glittering arc, then swept down, striking the table hard, embedding itself in the wood, severing the upper joints of the index and middle fingers of Alex Driscoll's left hand.

Alex screamed.

The pain was so intense that for a moment he thought the whole hand had been lopped off at the wrist. He had an image of the hand crawling feebly across the table, inching toward the edge as it had done before, but of its own will this time, like a thing out of a horror movie.

Then he raised his hand to his face and saw that it was only those two joints that were gone, lying somewhere on the table, on the other side of the knife—the knife half-buried in the wood, resisting the kid's efforts to wrench it loose—stuck.

Stuck.

*The knife was stuck.*

Past the pain and shock of the red ribbons winding like lava flows down his arm, Alex realized this was it, this was his chance.

The kid was disarmed.

And he had four bullets and a gun.

He jumped up, kicking the chair away, and pistoned both arms out, slamming the kid in the chest, knocking him back. The kid's legs tangled and he crashed to the floor.

*I've got you now,* Alex exulted. *I've got you.*

Fighting pain, he thrust his wounded hand into his side pocket and closed his fist over the bullets. The hand came out shaking, while with his right hand he groped for the Remington, yanked it free, and snapped open the five-chambered cylinder.

The kid was on his feet, his mouth twisted.

Alex fumbled with the bullets, trying to load them, but the bullets were slick with blood and he had only two good fingers on that hand. He dropped one bullet, losing it under the table. Three left. He had nearly slid one into its chamber when the kid lunged for the gun and Alex leaped back and the bullet slipped loose and vanished into the carpet. Two left. The kid seized the handle of the meat cleaver and with a final effort pulled it free. Alex got one bullet loaded and was struggling with the last one as the kid advanced, swinging the cleaver. Alex dodged, the bullet he had been trying to load squirted out of his hand, and he snapped the cylinder shut—*one shot, that's all you've got, don't miss*—he cocked the gun and aimed it with two unsteady hands, targeting the kid's chest. He fired.

Click.

Alex blinked, not understanding at first, thinking the gun must be defective, then realizing there were five chambers and only one bullet. So. It was like Russian roulette. A new game for the game room.

He aimed again and tried to squeeze the trigger. This time nothing happened, not even a hollow click, and he remembered that the revolver was a single-action job and he had to pull down the hammer for every shot. Before he could, the kid was on top of him and the knife swung and Alex jumped clear and the knife whistled past like the descending blade of a guillotine.

"You scum!" shrieked the kid. Spit bubbled on his lips and lathered his chin. "Think you can scare me?"

Alex cocked the gun and fired.

Click.

He cocked again. The kid picked up a lamp and threw it, jerking the plug out of the socket. The bulb winked out. The electric cord whipped, eel-like. Alex ducked, but not fast enough. The lamp's ceramic base struck him in the forehead and swept his glasses off his face. He was sent reeling to the floor. He landed on his side. He looked up. The world was a blur. Out of the haze stepped a swirling, ghostly figure. The kid. Alex fired.

Click.

The kid towered over him. The cleaver, a foggy streak, was raised high above his head.

Alex rolled to one side and the knife shredded the carpet where he had lain a split second before.

He scrambled to his feet and found himself backed into a corner, trapped. The kid was closing in. Alex cocked and fired.

Click.

The kid was three feet away, close enough for Alex to see him clearly, every detail coming into focus—the long hair dangling in sweaty ropes, the spittled fuzz of beard, and the yellow teeth leering beneath those dead eyes.

He stood with the knife handle wrapped in both fists like a baseball bat. Alex, jammed tight into the corner, knew with sick certainty that the meat cleaver's next descent would split his skull.

He had one more shot and then it was the end—one way or the other.

He jerked back the hammer and aimed the Remington at the kid's face.

The knife arced up.

Alex fired.

The recoil and the blast struck him at the same instant. He was thrown back, flattened against the wall, while his ears rang like anvils and part of his mind assured him that it was all right, no problem, this was how you were supposed to feel when your forehead was cleaved in two by a butcher knife.

The geyser of blood doused him a moment later. His own blood. He was sure of it. Blood spouting from the crack in his brain. He dropped the gun and pawed wildly at his face, groping for the knife, seeking to pry it loose.

After an interminable length of time, half a second at least, he understood.

He swept the mask of blood from his eyes. He stared, fascinated.

The kid still stood before him. He had not moved or fallen. His hands still gripped the meat cleaver with ferocious intensity, but, funny thing, he had no face. There was only a huge gaping hole dead center where his nose used to be. Above it were two eyes rolled up all the way in their sockets so that only the whites were showing, like eggshells, and below it was a mouthful of yellow teeth that still grinned, like the Cheshire cat, even after the face was gone.

The kid swayed drunkenly, his fingers surrendering their hold on the knife. It fell, and then, very simply, the kid's legs folded and he crumpled to his knees at Alex's feet, remained there for a moment as if in supplication, and collapsed in a twisted heap.

Alex looked down at the head of blond hair matted with blood. He saw a muscle spasm shudder through the kid's right arm like the slow ripple of a wave. That was all.

"Fuck you," said Alex thickly.

He heard somebody crying. He didn't know who or why. He stepped over the dead body and stooped to pick up his glasses. Both lenses were shattered. He dropped the glasses and felt his way to a sofa, tugged loose a pillowcase, and wrapped his left hand in it. He watched with an impersonal sort of interest as the fabric was instantly measled with ugly red blotches. He continued to watch until the pillowcase was soaked through with blood.

"Alex," said a low, whimpering voice. "Alex ... oh, God, Alex ..."

He turned to the billiard table. Jessie was there, all tied up. Of course. He had tied her up, hadn't he? Now, why would he do that?

Then the shock passed, his mind cleared, and he remembered.

He ran to her. She had spit out the gag and was sobbing and hiccupping and saying his name over and over. He untied her with his good hand, fumbling with the knots but managing to undo them. He tried to lift her off the table but his hand hurt too much and he gave up, exhausted. She sat on the table with her face buried in his chest, mumbling that she had been scared, so scared, and he stroked her hair, saying nothing.

After a long time she lifted her head. The green ocean depths of her eyes were misted over with tears. "Your hand," she whispered. "I saw what he did to your ... I didn't want to look, but when you screamed ... Oh, God." She was looking at the rust-colored pillowcase covering his hand like an oven mitt. "Oh, God, Alex."

"I know. Looks like I can't type ten-fingered anymore. Fortunately, I never could."

She made a sound halfway between a chuckle and a moan and shook her head slowly. He touched her chin and raised her face to his.

"Howdy, stranger," he said softly.

She sniffed back a tear and swallowed and ran a hand through her hair, brushing it back.

"Top o' the mornin' to ye, Mr. Driscoll."

He smiled, and she smiled back uncertainly. He leaned close and, very gently, he kissed her mouth. It felt good. It felt like life.

*Alex Driscoll,* he thought. *The born loser.*

*Sure.*

He kissed Jessie again, deeply.

# 46

BEN HARPER killed the engine and let the squad car coast into the parking lot. They were close. Both he and Masterson knew it. The tracks illuminated by the headlights were only minutes old. They dotted the snow in a straight line through the empty lot to an enormous rectangular bulk.

It was the shell of an A&P, still under construction. The workers had broken ground last summer, and in record time the behemoth had taken shape in sheets of glass spanning the length of a football field and red brick walls towering thirty feet high.

The building was dark and empty. Harper let the car coast the final few feet and come to rest directly before a metal frame laced with glass shards. It was one half of what had been a sliding door. Someone—or something— had smashed the glass to glittering dust. But a dog couldn't do that. Could it? Harper recalled the broken window at the Andersons' farm. But that window hadn't been made of heavy plate glass. Even if the Doberman could have launched itself through the door, the glass would have scissored its body to ribbons.

And yet ...

Razor's tracks led up to the shattered door and were gone.

Harper switched off the headlights. He and Masterson sat in the car.

"It's inside," said Harper finally.

Masterson nodded.

"Waiting for us. Right?"

"Yes."

"It got tired of running. Now it wants to make some sort of last stand. Is that it?" Masterson did not answer. "Come on," Harper snapped. "You know this animal. Is that what it's got planned?"

"Razor," said Masterson slowly, "would never think of a last stand, Ben. Not for him. Only ... for us."

"Your dog figures it's got the edge on us?"

"That's right."

"Does it?"

"In there, we'll have no tracks to follow. It's a large building. Dark. He could be hiding anywhere."

"We've got these." Harper raised the Thompson rifle and nodded at the Uzi handgun.

"True." Masterson considered it. "It's an even match."

Harper picked up the radio mike. "Want me to call for reinforcements?"

"No. Do you remember the story I told you about the Rottweiler that escaped from my ranch? I went after him alone—because half a dozen men make more noise than one ... or two." He looked straight at Harper. His eyes were calm and certain. "Anyway, we both know he's ours. He wants us. That's why he's led us here. And we want him. Don't we, Ben?"

Harper's voice was a whisper. "Yeah ..."

A moment passed. The wind howled shrilly, kicking up swirls of snow. Harper switched on the radio mike.

"Sullivan? Harper."

Frank Sullivan was hoarse from sleepless hours spent on the phone and the radio. "Chief. What's up?"

"I think we've got the son of a bitch. It's holed up in the new A&P on 35."

"I'll send backup."

"Negative."

"Ben—"

"We're going in now. I don't want a lot of sirens or engine noise or anything else that might scare off the dog. This may be our best shot. You got that?"

A pause. "I got it."

Harper hesitated. "Listen, if I don't report back in a half hour, send cars. Send everybody. Till then, nobody crashes this party."

"Okay, Chief. Hey, you in the mood for some good news?"

"Try me."

"The Gaines kid is all right. Off the critical list. She's gonna make it."

Harper felt himself smiling for the first time in … How long? He didn't know.

"Thanks, Frank. Like they used to say in the TV commercials, I needed that. Out."

Harper switched off, then glanced at Karl Masterson. Masterson was not smiling, but his eyes were closed and his expression was almost tranquil. After a minute he raised his head and looked at Harper.

"One less worry, at least," he said softly.

"Yeah," said Ben Harper. "Who knows? Maybe our luck has changed."

# 47

A FEW steps inside the doorway, the mystery of the shattered glass was solved.

Both men had switched on their flashlights. The wavering beams prowled over the litter of glass fragments and paused on a large, heavy rock.

Harper picked it up and studied it, his face grim.

"Vandals?" Masterson whispered.

"I hope so," Harper said. "But I've got a feeling ..."

He didn't always trust his hunches, but he did this time and, goddammit, he was right. Well, it made sense, didn't it? The night was cold, the coldest so far this fall, with the season's first snowstorm to boot. The sort of night when even people who had learned to live without a roof over their heads found themselves seeking shelter. And one of them had sought it here.

Huddled in a corner, draped in a plastic tarpaulin, lay a middle-aged tramp. He must have smashed the door with the rock, then slipped inside and pulled the tarp off a crate and bundled himself up, feeling warm and safe, reveling in the protection the solid brick walls provided from the gusts of wind and the lashing snow, and fallen peacefully asleep. Harper hoped his sleep had been a good one and his moment of awakening had been mercifully brief. He *had* awakened, that was certain, because his eyes still bulged wide with shock and horrified dismay. On the slick surface of the tarp, directly over his chest, were stamped two snowy paw prints. The dog had thumped its front paws down hard—that would have jolted the tramp awake—and then there must have been an unknown length of time while the man's eyes focused in the darkness and saw the blood-smeared canine face leering down. Had he screamed then? Or had that come later, a heartbeat and a lifetime later, when the Doberman's teeth sank into the man's unshaved neck and punctured it like a balloon?

Harper reached out to touch the corpse's forehead.

"Still warm." He looked at Masterson. "This just happened."

Masterson frowned. "If we had been quicker—"

"We weren't," Harper snapped. "And that's not the point. The point is, the bastard is in here. And close."

Harper swiveled around and searched the concrete floor with his flashlight. He found a few red-wine splotches evenly spaced in a straight line, heading toward the rear of the building. Harper and Masterson followed the trail for a few yards, until the spots became more infrequent and finally vanished.

"Now what?" Harper's whisper echoed in the empty structure. The wind swirled fitfully outside.

"We split up," said Masterson, his voice low. "Keep looking. At the first sign of anything unusual—"

"Don't worry. You'll hear me loud and clear. Me"—Harper tapped the Thompson—"or this."

- — -

In the darkness Razor waited. His pricked ears had caught the low scraping of footsteps on the concrete floor and the distant murmur of voices. The two Men had followed him here, as he had known they would.

His paws tingled with the electric anticipation of a kill, of two kills. The sensation triggered a stream of associations in his mind. He had claimed so many victims he could no longer remember any one of them clearly; his memories were jumbled, feverish, a whirlpool of scents and sounds and images, blending together. Even the Man he had killed mere moments ago, here in this building, was already losing his separate identity and merging with the others to form one composite victim, nameless, faceless, formless, merely a blur of arms and legs beating a frenzied counterpoint to the primary melody of the scream. The scream was always the same. It was high and long and warbling like a banshee's wail. It was the sound of death, and Razor liked it.

He lay coiled and hidden, listening to the two Men's cautious footfalls and waiting, with infinite patience and pitiless certainty, for the moment when he would hear that scream again.

- — -

Harper was alone. Karl Masterson's footsteps had long since faded into the distance. He walked on, gripping the Thompson tightly.

He paused, swung the flashlight in a wide curve, and saw nothing. For the first time he looked around, studying the building's cavernous interior. It was a single vast room, like a warehouse. He had the dim impression of machines, construction vehicles of some kind, hulked together in the deeper darkness beyond. He looked up. The ceiling, dizzyingly high, was invisible, but closer to ground level he could make out the crosshatched tracings of catwalks.

He kept going. Up ahead a shape resolved itself out of the murk. He played the Micro-Lite's beam over it. The words LOED HANDLER slipped past under the light. He moved closer, and the flashlight revealed massive tires, three and a half feet in diameter, supporting the squat metal mass of a forklift truck.

There was no door on the operator's cab. Harper squinted and made out an irregular black shape on the driver's seat.

The Doberman?

He wasn't sure.

He switched off the flashlight and crept toward the truck. Near the forklift lay a stack of plywood planks. He stepped carefully over them, making no sound. He reached the truck and hugged the side of the vehicle immediately to the left of the open doorway.

Then with one quick motion he switched on the flashlight and spun to face the cab, shining the light inside.

Empty.

The dark mass on the seat was the crumpled sports section of yesterday's *Press*.

Harper let out a sigh of relief. He backed away from the cab, shaking his head, tripped over the plywood, and fell on his butt. The Thompson flew out of his hand and slid under the truck.

"Shit."

He rubbed his stinging buttocks. *Nice one, Chief.*

Spreading out flat on his stomach, he crawled under the truck to retrieve the rifle. The Micro-Lite's beam revealed the Thompson, lying just beyond his reach. He wriggled toward it, then looked past the gun and froze.

Two red eyes gazed back at him.

*Oh, holy Christ.*

Not in the cab. Under the truck. It was hiding under the truck.

Harper lunged for the rifle but the dog was too quick. With one swipe of its paw it slit open the back of his hand. Harper jerked his arm back. The dog squirmed toward him, its nails clicking madly, its breath hot and close. Harper tried to retreat but in the cramped space he had no room to maneuver. He shoved himself back, inch by inch, grunting in terror. The dog was faster. It was closing in.

"Jesus," Ben Harper gasped.

The Doberman was less than a foot away.

His heart was beating a syncopated rhythm. White

sparks burst like fireworks before his eyes. His hands slapped down hard on the concrete and thrust him back another foot, almost clear of the truck, and then the dog propelled itself forward and locked its mouth on his left arm. Its teeth drove like nails through his coat sleeve, into his flesh. He shook his arm frantically, fighting to tear himself loose, but the dog hung on while its eyes, hypnotic as a cobra's, remained fixed on his, telling him this was the end, no escape this time.

Harper's free hand made a fist and pounded the Doberman's snout. The dog slashed his face with its fore-claws, turning his cheek into a bloody sieve. Now the teeth were traveling up his arm, chewing it to pieces, as the Doberman crawled forward, worming its way toward Harper's throat.

He was finished. He knew it. The dog had him.

If only he hadn't dropped the gun, the goddamn gun ...

But he had another gun.

Harper's right hand whipped back, fumbling at his hip, and closed over the butt of his holstered .38.

He yanked it free and aimed point-blank at the Doberman's skull. Somehow the dog must have sensed sudden danger, because just as Harper squeezed the trigger, Razor let go of his arm and jerked back. The bullet hit the Doberman in the shoulder. Razor howled. Harper did not hear it. His ears were ringing with the gunshot blast. He was certain he had punctured an eardrum. He tried to fire again but already the Doberman was slipping and sliding back, and then it was gone, rolling out from under the truck on the opposite side, melting instantly into the dark.

Harper dragged himself out and got to his feet. He holstered the gun. He leaned against the truck, eyes shut. The ringing in his ears was quieter now. He did not think the eardrum had been broken, after all. He held his wounded arm and tried to gauge the extent of the injuries. Multiple bites and cuts, blood loss, but the fingers flexed, painfully, and the elbow bent, and from what he could tell, no bones were broken.

Karl Masterson burst out of the shadows.

*"Ben!"*

"I'm all right," said Harper evenly, fighting not to let his voice betray the effort it took to speak. "Son of a bitch bit me. Then I shot it."

"Dead?"

"Only wounded. That's something, anyhow."

Masterson looked at him with an expression that said a wounded animal could be even more dangerous. Then he shrugged, accepting the situation, and looked more closely at Harper.

"Can you keep going?"

"Hell, yes."

Masterson shone his flashlight on Harper's face, where blood still leaked from jagged claw marks, then lowered the beam to the pockmarked coat sleeve and bleeding hand.

"Ben. You're hurt. You need—"

*"I'm all right, dammit!"*

From somewhere in the building rose a low, echoing growl. The two men looked up, listening. The sound went on for an endless moment, rumbling ominously through the darkness like distant thunder, then faded out.

Harper said softly, "We don't have time to argue. The dog is hurt. It can't have gotten far. Somebody has to track it down. You can't do it alone and we can't wait for help. So ... I'm all right. Understood?"

Masterson held Harper's glance. "Understood, Ben," he said, his voice low and respectful.

Harper turned, unclipped his flashlight, and scanned the floor until he found the Thompson. It had been knocked clear of the truck by Razor's scrabbling paws. He picked it up with his left hand and felt the scream of protest in his arm. He ignored it. There was no time for that. Right now he had a job to do.

"That way," he said to Masterson, pointing.

They circled the truck to the far side and saw bright patches of blood from the bullet wound. Wordlessly they followed the path the Doberman had taken.

*Twice,* Ben Harper thought randomly as he struggled to keep his attention focused, like his flashlight beam, on the winding trail of blood. *Twice I've tangled with it. Twice I barely got out alive. Now here I go again.*

*Three strikes ... you're out?*

He shoved the thought angrily out of his mind and kept walking with Karl Masterson at his side.

Somewhere in the darkness ahead, Razor was growling again.

# 48

MASTERSON KNEW that Razor had not meant to do them any favors. Nevertheless, he had.

They were still following the Doberman's trail, five minutes after starting out, when it brought them almost face-to-face with the generator—a large industrial generator sprouting octopus tentacles, rubber-insulated cables an inch thick.

Masterson found the power switch and flicked it on. Instantly the generator came to life, vibrating noisily. The two men were blinded by banks of arc lights strung along the catwalks, flooding the building with light.

"Jesus," breathed Harper. "Wish we'd found this thing sooner."

"Just be glad we found it now. Ben … suddenly I believe the odds are in our favor."

Harper nodded.

They switched off their flashlights and followed the blood trail at a run. In less than a minute they reached the foot of an iron stairway ascending steeply to the catwalks. The grilled steps were damp with blood.

"He's up there," said Masterson, scanning the network of crisscrossing walkways fifteen feet above the floor. Harper followed his gaze.

"I don't see the bastard."

"He's hiding. Unless …" Masterson kept his eyes on the catwalks. "Is there another stairway?"

Harper looked carefully around. "I don't see one," he said finally. "I think this is the only way up."

"Or down. Then he is up there."

"So," said Ben Harper, "what are we waiting for?"

Together they climbed the stairs. Their footsteps rang on the grillwork. Masterson marveled that the Doberman, wounded, could have negotiated the stairway without a sound.

As they neared the top, Masterson glanced at Harper, beside him. The man was breathing hard. His face was unnaturally pale. He was blinking. Masterson was certain Harper was feeling light-headed.

"Take it easy, Ben."

"I'm okay." The words came with effort. Harper's grip tightened noticeably on the rail.

They made it to the top. Masterson looked down the walkway in both directions. Razor was nowhere in sight. Harper stood unmoving for a moment, head down, catching his breath. He was pushing himself hard, all right. Too goddamn hard. Masterson frowned, worried. They had to finish this business fast—before Harper's strength gave out entirely.

At least the pause in the action gave Masterson an opportunity to survey the field of battle. He studied the catwalks. Each walkway was a narrow beam, three feet wide, enclosed by wooden railings. The beams seemed solid enough but the railings looked flimsy. He would not have trusted one to support his weight.

He peered over the edge. The arc lights, linked by electric cables, were evenly spaced along the bottoms of the walkways, shining down; the concrete floor caught their brilliance and reflected it, lighting the catwalks from below. The arrangement turned the catwalks into semi-silhouettes, thin strips of gray against a white-hot glare, like precarious bridges spanning a spread of molten steel.

Somewhere in this network of intersecting beams was a Doberman named Razor. Masterson turned his body slowly, rotating a full three hundred sixty degrees, scanning every visible inch of the catwalks.

Harper was watching him tensely. "See it?" he asked. His voice was normal once more, and the color had returned to his face.

Masterson shook his head. "But we've still got a trail to follow." He gestured at the walkway. Harper looked down and saw the line of blood spots. The trail snaked down the beam and vanished at the distant point of an intersecting walkway.

"Damn thing doesn't believe in standing still, does it?"

"No," said Masterson. "And neither do we. Come on."

They raced along the catwalk, turned the corner, and pursued the splashes of blood to another intersecting beam. Masterson noted that the blood seemed to be flowing faster than before. It was a bad wound Harper had given the dog, possibly a mortal wound. But they couldn't count on that.

They rounded the corner and saw Razor at the far end of the walkway, a hundred feet away.

Harper opened fire. The Thompson spat .45-caliber shells like flashes of blue lightning. The building boomed with multiple explosions. Razor was hit in the leg, in the side. Then he was gone, scrambling down a side walkway, out of range.

Harper shook his head. "Damn thing won't die!"

"Oh, yes, he will," breathed Masterson.

They ran. Razor was just ahead, somewhere on the crosswise walkway, lost to sight. But with his wounds he could not have run far. He was trapped. Masterson knew it. Trapped—and doomed.

He ran with the Uzi outstretched before him, his left hand clasping his right wrist to steady his aim, ready to shoot as soon as he and Harper turned the corner.

They were a yard from the end of the walkway when a black shape flickered at the edge of Masterson's vision, and before he could react, the shape was hurtling toward them with the deadly velocity of an express train. Masterson had time to realize that the Doberman had not even tried to run, had crouched low, then sprung at his pursuers from over the rail, arrowing his body to intercept theirs.

Masterson fired, but his aim was wrong and the shots went wild. Then the Doberman's claws were digging into his forehead. Beside him, Harper screamed. The Thompson blasted uselessly, its bullets streaking into the air. The two men were hurled back. Harper hit the rail. It splintered. Masterson twisted free of the Doberman and thudded down on his back. The Uzi slid out of his hand and came to rest balanced on the edge of the beam. He grabbed for it, missed, and the gun dropped over the edge.

Razor tumbled down on all fours. He skidded around a corner, out of sight.

Masterson glanced back at Ben Harper and saw a three-foot gap in the split railing, and the catwalk—empty.

"Christ." He whipped around to a squatting position and peered over the rim, expecting to see Harper's broken body spread-eagled on the concrete fifteen feet below. But the floor had claimed only the Thompson rifle as its victim. The gun's shattered components were scattered across the concrete. Ben Harper had not fallen. Not yet.

He clung with both hands to a sagging loop of the electric cable strung underneath the catwalk. The cable strained under his weight. The arc lights mounted on both sides swayed dangerously. Harper's grip was weakening.

Masterson was not certain he could pull Harper up, not without something to give him leverage, but he had to try. He planted one foot firmly on the walkway and extended his hand.

"Ben."

Harper looked up. His face was chalk white. His lips, stretched tight with strain, were thin, colorless bands.

"Can't," he gasped.

"Yes, you can."

Harper shook his head.

The arc lights swung crazily, shooting sparks into Masterson's eyes. The cable sagged lower. It was pinned to the beam by a steel clamp. One bolt in the clamp popped loose like a champagne cork. The cable jerked down a foot. The clamp, secured by one remaining bolt, held.

Masterson took a long, controlled breath.

"Ben," he said softly. "If you trust me ... if I am your friend ... take my hand."

Harper looked up at him and his pale face was lit by a flicker of life.

Keeping his right hand on the cable, he reached up with his left. Masterson's hand closed tightly over his.

"I've got you," he said calmly. "Now, just hang on." He was pulling Harper up, inch by inch, ignoring the eruption of agony in his back. "Just hang on, and I'll ..."

The cable sagged lower.

" ... lift you ..."

The clamp trembled. The second bolt, groaning in protest, was dragged slowly out of the wood.

" ... up."

The bolt came free with a firecracker pop. The clamp fell away. The cable plunged down, carrying Ben Harper with it. Masterson, still gripping Harper's hand, was pulled off balance, over the edge, into space.

The cable snapped.

Then both men were falling and one of them was screaming as the concrete floor rushed up. Harper still gripped one half of the severed cable. As he fell, the cable was pulled taut, then ripped free of the catwalk, yanking the nearest arc light off its mounting to plummet down in a kamikaze dive.

The light exploded into fragments in the split second after two human bodies hit the floor.

Ben Harper hit first, with a sickening crack. Masterson landed on top of him, his impact cushioned by Harper's body. The torn cable, hissing and writhing like a high-voltage snake, whipped out of Harper's hand and coiled on the concrete a yard away, spitting sparks.

Masterson lay stunned for a moment. He came to slowly, conscious at first only of excruciating pain in both legs. He glanced up. Half the overhead lights had gone dark. The others still shone. The building was divided into pools of shadow and shafts of light. He swiveled his head toward the dark recesses of the building, drawn by a low sound. Ragged breathing. Claws clicking on metal.

Razor.

Padding down the iron stairway, fifty yards away.

Masterson looked to his other side and saw Ben Harper, lying flat on his back, motionless, his eyes open, his breath faint and failing.

"Ben ..."

Masterson raised himself on one elbow and peered down into Harper's face. Harper stared past him, unaware. Masterson remembered the rifle crack of impact and wondered if it had been the snap of the man's spine.

"Ben," he said more loudly. "Can you hear me?"

Harper blinked. His eyes focused on Masterson. His lower lip twitched with a hint of recognition.

"Did we get the bastard?" he croaked.

"Yes, Ben," said Karl Masterson. "We got him."

Harper's mouth relaxed into a smile. He tried to speak again. Masterson bent close, listening, but no words came, only the slow, labored, halting breath.

A moment later, even that did not come.

Masterson closed his eyes and lowered his head,

fighting for control.

After a long moment he looked up, his mouth set tight. He turned to face the Doberman slinking toward him through blurred columns of light and dark.

Razor was close. Less than twenty yards away. He had been shot in the shoulder, the side, the hind leg. Three bullets. He leaked blood. He was dying. He *must* be dying. But he had not been stopped.

Masterson had lost his Uzi. The Thompson was shattered. But there was still Harper's .38. He unholstered it from the dead man's hip, then rolled to face Razor as flares of agony shot through his knees. Vaguely he realized that both legs had been fractured in the fall. The thought, like the pain, was only a distraction, and he shoved it aside.

Razor limped closer, into a pillar of light.

Masterson fired.

He hit the Doberman in the front paw. Razor collapsed on three legs, snarled, then struggled to his feet and stumbled closer. His muzzle was lathered with bloody froth. His body trembled with exertion. But his eyes, unblinking red pinpoints, still glowed, luminously alive, fixed on his prey.

Masterson fired again.

The bullet shaved Razor's skull. One clipped ear drooped abruptly. A trickle of blood ran down the dog's jaw.

Razor kept coming.

Masterson fired again but the gun was empty.

Razor was ten feet away.

Masterson wrenched his body around and fumbled in Harper's pockets, searching for ammunition. He could not find any. He glanced back.

Razor was one yard away. The red eyes were spots of flame.

Masterson clubbed the dog's snout with the butt of the gun. Razor stopped, as if mildly surprised that this

Man should still wish to put up a fight. Masterson lashed out again with the gun, and Razor sank his teeth into Masterson's wrist. The gun clattered to the floor. Masterson swung his fist. He connected. The dog released his grip and pulled back. The red eyes narrowed. The fang-studded mouth widened in a grotesque grin.

Razor drew down on his haunches, poised for a final leap.

Masterson had to throw himself clear, but his legs were broken, useless, and he could not do it. The Doberman was about to slash his throat. He had to escape. But he could not *move.*

Razor sprang in the instant Karl Masterson found the strength to hurl his crippled body to one side.

The arc of the Doberman's leap carried the dog over his head by inches. Masterson slammed down on the floor. The hammerblow of pain in his legs nearly knocked him unconscious. The world grayed. He bit his tongue. The spurt of blood in his mouth shocked him alert.

Razor spun, a yard away, then took a step forward. He had been denied his kill, but only for a moment.

His next step would bring his mouth within reach of Karl Masterson's throat.

Masterson glanced helplessly around him and saw his chance.

The severed cable, still live, still throwing off white pinwheels of sparks.

Razor took his last step.

Masterson's hand closed over the cable.

Razor's jaws swung wide with a snarl of triumph, and Karl Masterson plunged the end of the cable into the Doberman's mouth.

Instinctively Razor bit down.

*Bit down.*

Razor's body rocked with the first wave of the high-voltage stream. He tried to open his mouth but his jaws, clamped shut by electric shock, refused to obey. He could not release the cable. Currents of electricity surged through him, sizzling.

Masterson pulled back, staring, as the Doberman thrashed in agony.

Then Razor twisted his head and the red eyes locked on Masterson's own.

The dog was dying—but not yet dead.

Razor lunged for Masterson, and his right foreclaws sank deep into Masterson's side, lodging between his ribs, stiffening, and now sheets of lightning were racing through both bodies as the Doberman fought savagely to drag his last victim with him to the grave.

Masterson's brain buzzed. His vision was blasted into shimmering television static. His body jerked with seizures. Every hair bristled. Every muscle contracted. Even his broken legs flapped fitfully.

Some part of him, detached from his paralyzed brain and wildly jackknifing body, spoke to him calmly, not in English, but in German, the language of his childhood, and told him that things were best this way. He had created Razor and it was proper that he should die with him, for both of them were guilty, but he most of all. *The Doberman has an excuse, Karl Meyers*, said the voice implacably, *the oldest excuse of all, the one your tormentors claimed as their own. He was only following orders.*

*Your orders.*

*Oh, yes, Karl. It is best this way ...*

The soothing voice had nearly lulled whatever was left of his conscious mind into unresisting acceptance, when suddenly a spark in him that had never died, the spark of that child who had survived Auschwitz, flamed up and reduced the voice to ashes with a single word: *No.*

With the greatest effort of his life, Karl Masterson closed one hand over the Doberman's paw and ripped it free.

He rolled away, his limbs still twitching with multiple aftershocks, and dragged himself mindlessly to Ben Harper's body and collapsed on top, hugging it, shaking, crying, as his consciousness flickered, then died out. His last moment of awareness, before he drifted into a dreamless neverland, was of Razor.

The Doberman was on his back now, kicking and writhing, the stub of his tail vibrating like a tuning fork, the red eyes rolled up in their sockets, the corners of his mouth bubbling with bloody foam. There was no way for Masterson to know, but somehow he did know that Razor's final thoughts were of him, and they were not pleasant thoughts.

Razor had been denied his last kill, and the pain of that defeat was worse than the eternity of electric shocks violating his body.

He had been cheated. He had lost. The Men had beaten him, after all.

The electrocution went on, endlessly, long after the Doberman's heart had slammed to a stop and his brain had been blanked of all its contents—animal cunning, bloodlust, instinct, memory—all wiped clean. And still the dead jaws did not loosen their hold on the cable, even as the smell of charred flesh began to rise from the floor, to the catwalks, to the ceiling, even as the dog's body smoked and shriveled and was reduced finally to a scorched pile of meat twitching lifelessly with an electric hum.

When six police officers burst into the building ten minutes later, they found Karl Masterson, comatose, near death, still hugging Ben Harper's body in an unbreakable embrace, while a few yards away the remains of the Doberman named Razor crackled and smoldered like the last embers of a dying fire.

# FOURTH DAY

# 49

LONG PAST midnight, nearly twenty-four hours after he had been taken to the hospital, Karl Masterson finally opened his eyes.

His first awareness was of Nikki, leaning over him, gripping his hand. He thought, *Now here's a switch. She got up before I did.* Then he realized it was not morning and they were not in their bedroom. And he remembered. Everything.

"Razor," he croaked. "He's dead. Isn't he?"

She nodded. "He's dead."

"Good."

He raised his head with effort and saw that both legs were in plaster casts.

"How bad?"

"Multiple fractures. You were on the operating table a long time. But the doctors said you'd regain full mobility, if ..."

"If what?"

She shut her eyes. "You suffered a severe electrical shock. You were ... in a coma. They told me you might never wake up."

"They were wrong."

She gripped his hand tighter. Her voice was a whisper.

"I knew they would be."

- — -

A few doors down the hall, Wylie Gaines was talking with her parents.

She had slept all day and now was wide-awake. Her face was bandaged and swollen, and her small body seemed lost in the hospital bed.

"I guess I was bad," she said softly, puffed lips slurring her words. "I shouldn't have hidden the dog in the toolshed. I got Daddy hurt. I'm sorry."

"It's all right," said Paul Gaines gently. He patted her hand. "No one's mad at you."

"I bet Mommy is. Aren't you?"

Barbara shook her head. "No, sweetheart. Mommy's not mad at you."

Wylie looked up at her in wide-eyed astonishment. She had been sure her mommy would be mad. But since she wasn't ...

Wylie took a breath, then asked the question she had wanted to ask since waking up from surgery.

"Mommy, when I get better ... can I get a *new* dog?"

"Yes, dear. You can have any dog you want."

Paul hugged Barbara tight, and Wylie wondered why her mommy was crying.

# 50

A PATROL car escorted Nikki Grant back to Ben Harper's house shortly after dawn. The doctor had ordered rest for Karl Masterson—and for her. She had been at Masterson's side through the night. She had not slept at all.

She let herself in and smelled the musty air of the home Ben Harper would never see again. Then she stopped, staring at the syringes of pentobarbital laid out on the coffee table.

Cleo's last injection had been given more than twenty-four hours ago.

It must have worn off by now.

She turned back to the door to call for the policeman who had driven her here, but the car had already pulled away.

Slowly she shrugged off her coat, then found one of the customized Walthers. She checked the gun and found it fully loaded with seven tranquilizer darts.

She was not certain the dog was awake. Cleo had been under extremely heavy sedation. Even if she had come to, she was still muzzled. A muzzled dog, even a Doberman, was not *too* dangerous.

Dangerous enough, though. Still an attack dog. Still a manstopper.

Nikki hesitated, then walked decisively to the basement door, unlocked it, and flung it wide.

She peered into the windowless darkness, and saw nothing. Her hand found the light switch at the top of the stairs. An unshaded ceiling bulb flashed on. It lit the room in faded yellow, the color of an old photograph.

The floor was empty. The Doberman was gone.

So Cleo was awake. And nowhere in sight.

But she could not have escaped. There were no exits except this door.

She was hiding.

And that was bad.

Nikki almost shut the door, locked it, and phoned the police. Almost. But ...

They wouldn't use tranquilizer guns. They would kill Cleo. Karl Masterson had risked his life to capture her alive. And Nikki did not want to see the dog die either. She had watched Cleopatra grow from a pup.

Besides, the Doberman was muzzled.

Nikki stepped through the doorway, onto the top step, and studied the basement.

It was a small, cluttered room. Cardboard boxes were piled untidily against one wall. Summer lawn chairs had been folded and stacked in a corner. The steel bulk of the furnace threw an oblong shadow across the floor.

Cleo could be concealed behind any of those things, or in half a dozen other places.

Nikki gripped the Walther tightly. She was hardly an expert shot, but Masterson had made her practice on the shooting range at the ranch. She could hit the dog on her first try. She hoped.

She crept down the stairs and moved forward slowly, looking for the subtlest flicker of movement, listening for the faintest sound.

She stopped in the middle of the room. She had heard something. Hadn't she?

No. Only her imagination. There was no sound but the hum of the furnace and her own soft breathing.

*Behind her.*

The click of a clawed foot on the concrete floor.

Her breath froze in her throat. She stood paralyzed. She heard it again. Closer.

But the dog couldn't be behind her. *Couldn't.* There had been no place for her to hide back there. No place—

The sound came again, still closer, and she whirled, aiming the Walther in two shaking hands, and saw Ben Harper's tomcat, Hank, looking up at her quizzically with his serious eyes.

"Oh, Jesus." She lowered the gun, brushed her hair back, and fought to catch her breath.

The cat meowed.

"Scat," whispered Nikki. "Go on, now. Scat!"

Reluctantly the cat turned and glided away, claws still clicking lightly on the concrete, then climbed the stairs and was gone.

Nikki surveyed the basement again from where she stood. Nothing had changed. Cleo still lay in wait.

The thought ran through her mind that she had taken a bullet out of this dog's leg and sterilized and bandaged the wound, and the damn thing was trying to kill her, for God's sake, and it just didn't seem right.

She pushed the thought away. Cleo knew nothing of right and wrong. For her there was only instinct and training, and both told her to kill.

Nikki stepped forward, and the heel of her shoe made a crunching sound.

She looked down. There was something on the floor, some tattered object lost in the shadow cast by the furnace. She almost ignored it. The basement was full of junk, scattered everywhere. But she sensed something oddly familiar about this particular object, as if she had seen it before.

She kept her head level, eyes glancing warily around, as she stooped to lift it off the floor.

She looked at it and felt a rush of liquid terror sweeping over her, leaving her dizzy and shaking, as she realized what she held in her hand.

The muzzle.

Shredded. Ripped to pieces.

But that wasn't possible. A dog could not—*could not*—tear a muzzle off its own face. No dog could.

But Cleo had.

She could picture the Doberman coming to, struggling to its feet, then stumbling in blind circles in the dark as it pawed furiously, uncomprehendingly, at the alien thing clamping its jaws shut, pawing and slashing and ignoring the knifecuts of its claws on its bleeding snout—until finally, minutes or hours later, the plastic straps had disintegrated and the muzzle had come loose with one last shake of the dog's head.

The Doberman was awake. It was hiding. And its fangs were bared.

Nikki took a step back.

She had to get out. She could not handle this job alone. She needed the police. She had to have Cleo shot. It was the only way. The only way.

The basement walls seemed closer. The ceiling was lower. The furnace hum was deafening. She felt trapped. She could not breathe. She took another step back.

Red eyes were watching her. She knew it. She could feel it. Watching her and preparing to strike. Now. Before she could escape.

But from where?

She retreated another step. The gun was slippery in her hands. Her blouse was glued to her back. How much farther till she reached the stairs? She didn't know. She didn't dare turn her head to look.

She backed up one more step, and from behind the furnace Cleo sprang.

The Doberman launched itself directly at her. It did not growl or bark. It was eerily silent. Its eyes were red and cold and hating.

Nikki fired, once.

The dart punctured the dog's belly.

A split second later Cleo hit Nikki Grant full-force in the chest and threw her backward onto the floor.

She slammed down hard on the concrete. Her spine shrieked at the impact. She didn't notice. Her whole attention was fixed on the dog—the dog that was pinning her down—its foreclaws digging into her wrists, nailing them to the floor—its hind legs straddling her hips—its mouth twisted in a soundless snarl.

She could not move her hand, the dog's grip was too strong, so she could not use the gun. She squirmed. The dog wriggled closer. Its stomach pressed down hard on her breasts. She kicked her legs wildly but it was no use, the dog was out of her reach. It leaned in close, so *close* to her face, only inches away, and she inhaled the stink of its breath. She shook her head, *no no no,* and the dog's eyes met hers and seemed to mock her weakness. The foam-flecked fangs gleamed in the overhead light. Then the Doberman lowered its head, and she screamed in helpless terror as it closed its jaws over her throat ...

The dog went limp.

Instantly. Totally.

The tranquilizer had taken effect.

The Doberman lay unconscious, draping Nikki's body like a blanket.

Nikki was crying. She let the tears run down her cheeks, making no effort to stop them, knowing she did not have the strength even to try.

After a long time she tried to move. She felt a stab of pain and realized that Cleo's teeth still gripped her neck, their needle-sharp points pinching the soft skin there, but not quite breaking through. Not quite. Just one more instant and ... She felt another trembling wave of terror pass over her at the thought of how narrowly she had escaped.

She fumbled at the dog's mouth and gently pried its jaws loose and pushed its head away. She struggled out from under it and got to her feet. She stared down. The Doberman's rib cage rose and fell, rose and fell, with slow breath.

"You just won't quit, will you," Nikki gasped. "Not *ever.*"

# EPILOGUE

ON CHRISTMAS morning, two months after the events that had rocked Sea Cove, Joey Cooper, age ten, climbed out of bed, pulled on his clothes, and tiptoed downstairs to see what Santa had brought.

The tree was encircled with brightly wrapped packages. Joey ran his hands over them, trying to guess their contents. After a few minutes he reluctantly gave up. He would know soon enough, just as soon as his parents and older brother were awake.

He went into the kitchen to fix a bowl of cereal, and there he found his very best Christmas present of all.

"Oh, wow," he breathed, staring at the corner of the kitchen where Lucy had slept ever since the family had learned of her condition.

The puppies had not been due for another couple of days. They had come early. They had come on Christmas.

Joey knelt by the corner, where six pups were competing for their mother's milk. Lucy looked tired and dreamily content. Her amber eyes gazed up placidly at Joey. He stroked her silver-gray fur.

"Wait'll Mom and Dad see," Joey whispered. "Jeez."

He left the dog and raced upstairs to wake the household, while the Weimaraner's litter went on wriggling and squirming and suckling. Their tails, which would soon be cropped, wagged playfully. Their fur was mottled with patches of silver-gray, standing out sharply against fields of midnight black. The mixed markings of two German breeds—the Weimaraner and the Doberman.

Razor was dead. But part of him lived on.

What that fact meant for the future—if it meant anything at all—was a matter only time would resolve.

# AUTHOR'S NOTE

AS ALWAYS, readers are invited to visit me at www.michaelprescott.net, where you'll find contact info, a list of all my books with links to sales pages, and other good stuff.

*Manstopper*, my first novel, was originally published in 1988. When I revised the book for digital publication, I was a little put off by all the blood and gore, and I considered toning it down, since I wouldn't write anything that graphic today. Eventually, however, I decided that the story's impact depends largely on the shock value of the dog attacks, so I left it mostly as it was.

Besides the usual line-editing, I made just two substantive changes. First, I found it implausible that such a horrific rampage would go unnoticed by the major media and state authorities, especially in a state as densely populated as New Jersey. There was no perfect way to fix this without rewriting the whole book, but I did insert the idea that a devastating plane crash at Newark Airport had distracted everybody's attention. It's better than nothing.

Second, the two kids who venture into the funhouse were originally named Jeff Norris and Marty Koch, and had no connection with the rest of the book. After *Manstopper* was published, a friend pointed out that it would have worked better if I'd used two of the bullies who abused Wylie Gaines on the school bus. Very true! In this edition, Jeff and Marty morph into Billy Turnbul and his sidekick T.W. Brolin, who, after all these years, finally get their comeuppance.

Thanks to editor Kevin Mulroy, who acquired the book for Penguin, and to my agent Jane Dystel, who sold the book for me. For the new edition, thanks go to Diana Cox of www.novelproofreading.com, who did her usual excellent job of catching my mistakes.

—Michael Prescott

# ABOUT THE AUTHOR

After twenty years in traditional publishing, Michael Prescott found himself unable to sell another book. On a whim, he began releasing his novels in digital form. Sales took off, and by 2011 he was one of the world's best-selling e-book writers.